The DREAMS *of* CHANG

AND OTHER STORIES

The DREAMS *of* CHANG
AND OTHER STORIES

Authorized translation from the Russian of

IVAN BUNIN

by Bernard Guilbert Guerney

Fredonia Books
Amsterdam, The Netherlands

The Dreams of Chang and Other Stories

by
Ivan Bunin

ISBN: 1-58963-959-6

Copyright © 2002 by Fredonia Books

Fredonia Books
Amsterdam, The Netherlands
http://www.fredoniabooks.com

CONTENTS

CONTENTS

The DREAMS *of* CHANG

AND OTHER STORIES

W HAT does it matter of whom we speak? Any that have lived and that live upon this earth deserve to be the subject of our discourse. Once upon a time Chang had come to know the universe and the captain, his master, to whom his earthly existence had become linked. And six entire years have run since then,—have run like the sands in a ship's hourglass.

It is again night,—dream or reality? And again comes morning,—reality or dream? Chang is old, Chang is a drunkard,—he is always dozing.

Outside, in the city of Odessa, it is winter. The weather is nasty, sullen,—far worse than that of China was when Chang and the captain met each other. Fine, stinging snow whirls through the air; it flies obliquely over the ice-covered, slippery asphalt of the desolate seaside boulevard, and painfully lashes the face of every running Jew who, with his hands shoved deep into his pockets, and with his shoulders hunched up, is zigzagging to the left and right,—awkwardly, Hebraically. Beyond the harbour, likewise deserted, beyond the bay, hazy from the snow, the barren shores, low and flat, are faintly visible. The jetty is hazy all the time with a thick, gray haze: the sea, in foamy, bellying waves, surges over it from morn till night. The wind whistles and reverberates among the telephone wires overhead. . . .

On such days life in the city does not start at an early

[9]

hour. Nor do Chang and the captain awake early. Six years,—is it a long time, or short? In six years Chang and the captain have grown old, although the captain is not yet forty; and their lot has harshly changed. They no longer sail the seas,—they live "on shore," as seamen say; nor are they living in the same place they lived in at one time, but in a narrow and rather dark street, in a garret; the house is redolent of anthracite, and is occupied by Jews,—of the sort that come to their families only toward evening and who sup with their hats shoved on the back of their heads. Chang and the captain have a low ceiling; their room is large and chill. Besides that, it is always gloomy and dark inside; the two windows placed in the sloping wall-roof are small and round, reminding one of port-holes. Something in the nature of a chest of drawers stands between the windows, and against the wall to the left is an old iron bed,—and there you have all the furnishings of this bleak dwelling,—unless the fireplace, out of which a fresh wind is always blowing, be included.

Chang sleeps in the nook behind the fireplace; the captain on the bed. What sort of a bed this is, sagging almost to the floor, and what kind of mattress it has, any one who has lived in garrets can easily imagine; as for the dirty pillow, it is so scanty that the captain is forced to put his jacket under it. However, the captain sleeps very peacefully even on this bed; he lies on his back, his eyes shut and his face ashen, as motionless as though he were dead. What a splendid bed had formerly been his! Well built, high, with chests underneath; the bedding was thick and snug, the sheets fine and smooth, and the snowy-white pillows were chilling! But even

[10]

then, even when lulled by the rolling of the waves, he had not slept as heavily as he sleeps now: now he gets very tired during the day, and besides that, what has he to worry about now,—what can he oversleep, and with what can the new day gladden him? At one time there had been two truths in this world, that had constantly stood sentry in turns: the first was, that life is unutterably beautiful; and the second, that life holds a meaning only for lunatics. Now the captain affirms that there is, has been, and will be for all eternity but one truth,—the ultimate truth, the truth of Job the Hebrew, the truth of Ecclesiastes, the sage of an unknown tribe. Often does the captain say now, as he sits in some beer shop: "Remember now thy Creator in the days of thy youth, while the evil days come not, nor the years draw nigh, when thou shalt *say*, I have no pleasure in them!" Still the days and nights go on as before, and now there has again been a night, and again morning is coming on. And the captain and Chang are awaking.

But, having waked, the captain does not change his position and does not open his eyes. His thoughts at that moment are not known even to Chang, who is lying on the floor beside the fireless hearth from which the freshness of the sea had come all night. Chang is aware of only one thing,—that the captain will lie thus for not less than an hour. Chang, after casting a look at the captain out of the corner of his eye, again closes his lids, and again dozes off. Chang, too, is a drunkard; in the morning he, too, is befuddled, weak, and beholds the universe with that languid queasiness which is so familiar to all those travelling on ships and suffering from seasickness. And because of that, as he dozes off, in this

[11]

morning hour, Chang sees a dream that is tormenting, wearisome. . . .

He sees:

An old, rheumy-eyed Chinaman has clambered up onto a steamer's deck, and has squatted down on his heels; whiningly, he importunes all those who pass by him to buy a wicker-basket of spoilt small fish which he has brought with him. It is a dusty and a chill day on a broad Chinese river. In the boat with a bamboo sail, swaying in the muddy water of the river, a puppy is sitting,—a little rusty dog, having about it something of the fox and something of the wolf, with thick, coarse fur at its neck; sternly and intelligently his black eyes look up and down the high iron side of the steamer, and his ears are cocked.

"Better sell your dog!" gaily and loudly, as though to a deaf man, the young captain of the ship, who was standing idling on his bridge, yelled to the Chinaman.

The Chinaman,—Chang's first master,—cast his eyes upward; confused, both by the yell and by joy, he began bowing and lisping: "Ve'y good dog, ve'y good." * And the puppy was purchased,—for only a single silver rouble,—was called Chang, and sailed off on that very day with his new master to Russia; and, in the beginning, for three whole weeks, he suffered so with seasickness, and was in such a daze, that he saw nothing: neither the ocean nor Singapore, nor Colombo. . . .

It had been the beginning of autumn in China; the weather was bad. And Chang felt qualmish when they had barely passed into the estuary. They were met by lashing rain and mist; white-caps glimmered over the

* In English in the original. *Trans.*

[12]

plain of waters; the gray-green swell swayed, rushed, plashed, many-pointed and senseless; meanwhile, the flat shores were spreading, losing themselves in the fog,—and there was more and more water all around. Chang, in his fur coat, silvery from the rain, and the captain, in a waterproof great-coat with the hood raised, were on the bridge, whose height could be felt now more than before. The captain issued commands, while Chang shivered and tossed his head in the wind. The water was widening, embracing all the inclement horizon, blending with the misty sky. The wind tore the spray from the great noisy swell, swooping down from any and every direction; it whistled through the sail-yards and boomingly slapped the canvas awnings below; the sailors, in the meanwhile, in iron-shod boots and wet capes, were untying, catching and furling them. The wind was seeking the best spot from which to strike its strongest blow, and just as soon as the steamer, slowly bowing before it, had taken a sharper turn to the right, the wind raised it up on such a huge, boiling roller, that it could not hold back; it plunged down from the ridge of the roller, burying itself in the foam,—and in the pilot's round-house a coffee cup, forgotten upon a little table by the waiter, shattered against the floor with a ring. . . . And then the fun began!

There were all sorts of days after that: now the sun would blaze down scorchingly out of the radiant azure; now clouds would pile up in mountains and burst with peals of terrifying thunder; or raging torrents of rain descended in floods upon the steamer and the sea; or else there was rocking,—yes, rocking, even when the ship was at anchor. Utterly worn out, Chang during all the three weeks did not once forsake his corner in the hot, half-dark corridor of the second-class cabins on the poop, where he lay near the high threshold of the door leading onto the deck. Only once a day was this door opened, when the captain's orderly brought food to Chang. And of the entire voyage to the Red Sea Chang's memory has retained only the creaking of the ship's partitions, his nausea, and the sinking of his heart, now flying downward into some abyss together with the quivering stern, now rising up to heaven with it; also did he remember his prickly, deathly terror whenever, with the sound of a cannon firing, a whole mountain of water would splash against this stern, after it had been raised high and had again careened to one side, with its propeller roaring in the air; the water would extinguish the daylight in the port holes, and then would run down in opaque torrents over their thick glass. The sick Chang heard the distant cries of commands, the thundering whistle of the boat-swain, the tramp of sailors' feet somewhere overhead; he heard the plash and the noise of the water; he could distinguish through his half-shut eyes the semi-dark corridor filled with jute bails of tea,—and Chang went daft, became tipsy, from nausea, heat, and the strong odour of tea. . . .

But here Chang's dream breaks off.

Chang starts and opens his eyes: that was no wave hitting against the stern with a sound of a cannon firing, —it was the jarring of a door somewhere below, flung back with force by somebody or other. And after this the captain coughingly clears his throat and slowly arises from his sagging couch. He puts on and laces his battered shoes, dons his black coat with the brass buttons,

[14]

taking it out from under the pillow; Chang, in the meanwhile, in his rusty, worn fur coat, yawns discontentedly, with a whine, having risen from the floor. Upon the chest of drawers is a bottle of vodka, some of which has already been drunk. The captain drinks straight out of the bottle, and, slightly out of breath, wiping his moustache, he goes toward the fireplace and pours out some vodka into a little bowl standing near Chang for him as well. Chang starts lapping it greedily. As for the captain, he begins smoking and lies down again, to await the hour when it will be full day. The distant rumble of the tramway can already be heard; already, far below in the street, flows the ceaseless clamping of horses' hoofs; but it is still too early to go out. And the captain lies and smokes. Having done with his lapping, Chang, too, lies down. He jumps up onto the bed, curls up in a ball at the feet of the captain, and slowly floats away into that blissful state which vodka always bestows. His half-shut eyes grow misty, he looks faintly at his master, and, feeling a constantly increasing tenderness toward him, thinks what in human speech may be expressed as follows: "Oh, you foolish, foolish fellow! There is but one truth in this world, and if you but knew what a wonderful truth it is!" And again, in something between thought and dream, Chang reverts to that distant morning, when the steamer, after carrying the captain and Chang from China over the tormented restless ocean, had entered the Red Sea. . . .

He dreams:

As they passed Perim, the steamer swayed less and less, as though it were lulling him asleep, and Chang fell into a sweet and sound sleep. And suddenly he started,

[15]

awake. And, when he had become awake, he was astonished beyond all measure: it was quiet everywhere; the stern was rhythmically vibrating, without any downward plunges; the noise of the water, rushing somewhere beyond the walls, was even; the warm odour from the kitchen, creeping out on deck from underneath a door, was enchanting. . . . Chang got up on his hind legs and looked into the deserted general cabin,—there, in the obscurity, was a softly radiant, aureately-lilac something; a something barely perceptible to the eye, but extraordinarily joyous; there the rear port holes were open to the sunlit blue void, open to the spaciousness, to the air, while over the low ceiling streamed sinuous rills of light reflected from mirrors,—they flowed on, without flowing away. . . . And the same thing happened to Chang that had also happened more than once in those days to his master, the captain: he suddenly comprehended that there existed in this universe not one truth, but two truths: one, that to be living in this world and to sail the seas was a dreadful thing, and the other. . . . But Chang did not have time to think of the other,—through the door, unexpectedly flung open, he saw the trap-ladder leading to the spar-deck, the black, glistening mass of the steamer's funnel, the clear sky of a summer morning, and, coming rapidly from under the ladder, out of the engine room, the captain. He had shaved and washed; there was the fragrance of fresh Eau-de-cologne about him; his fair moustache turned upward, after the German fashion; the glance of his light, keen eyes was sparkling, and everything upon him was tight-fitting and snowy white. And upon beholding all this Chang darted forward so joyously that the captain caught him in the air,

[16]

kissed him resoundingly on the head, and, turning him about, carrying him in his arms, with a hop, skip and a jump came out on the spar-deck, then the upper deck, and from there still higher, to that very bridge where it had been so terrible in the estuary of the great Chinese river.

On the bridge the captain entered the pilot's round-house, while Chang, who had been dropped to the floor, sat for a space, his fox-like brush unfurled to its full length over the smooth boards. It was very hot and radiant behind Chang, from the low-lying sun. It must also have been hot in Arabia, that was passing by so near on the right, with its shore of gold, with its black-brown mountains, its peaks, that resembled the mountains of some dead planet, also all deeply strewn with gold dust; Arabia, its entire sandy and mountainous waste visible with such extraordinary distinctness that it seemed as if one could jump over there. And above, on the bridge, the morning could still be felt, there was still the pull of a light, fresh coolness; the captain's mate,— the very same who later on used so often to make Chang furious by blowing into his nose,—a man in white clothes, with a white helmet and wearing fearful black spectacles, was sauntering briskly back and forth over the bridge, constantly looking up at the sharp tip of the front mast that reached up to the sky, and over which was curling the flimsiest wisp of a cloud. . . . Then the captain called out from the round-house: "Here, Chang! Come on and have coffee!" and Chang immediately jumped up, circled the round-house, and deftly dashed over its brass threshold. And beyond the threshold it proved to be even better than on the bridge: there was a broad

[17]

leather divan, fixed to the wall; over it hung certain things like wall-clocks, their glass and hands glistening; and on the floor was a slop-bowl with a mixture of sweet milk and bread. Chang began lapping it greedily, while the captain busied himself with his work. Upon the counter, placed under the window opposite the divan, he unrolled a large maritime chart, and, placing a ruler over it, firmly drew a long line upon it with scarlet ink. Chang, having finished his lapping, with milk on his muzzle, jumped up on the counter and sat down near the very window, out of which he could see the blue turned-over collar of a sailor in a roomy blouse, who, with his back to the window, was standing at the many-horned wheel. And at this point the captain, who, as it turned out afterward, was very fond of having a chat when he was all alone with Chang, said to him:

"You see, brother, this is the Red Sea itself. You and I have to pass through it as cleverly as we can,—just see how gaily coloured it is! I have to land you in Odessa in good order, because they already know there of your existence. I have already blabbed about you to a most capricious little girl; I have bragged to her about your lordship, over a sort of long cable, d'you understand, that has been laid down by clever people over the bottom of all the seas and oceans. . . . For after all, Chang, I am an awfully lucky fellow, so lucky that you can't even imagine it, and for that reason I am terribly averse to getting stuck on one of these reefs, to have no end of disgrace on my first distant cruise. . . ."

And, saying this, the captain suddenly gave Chang a stern look and slapped his muzzle:

"Paws off!" he cried commandingly. "Don't you dare climb on government property!"

And Chang, with a toss of his head, growled and puckered up his face. This was the first slap he had ever received, and he was offended; it again seemed to him that to be living in this world and to be sailing the seas was an atrocious thing. He turned away, his translucently yellow eyes dimming and contracting, and with a low growl he bared his wolfish fangs. But the captain did not consider Chang's offended feelings of any importance. He lit a cigarette and returned to the divan; having taken a gold watch out of a side pocket of his *piqué* jacket, he pried back its lids with a strong nail, and looking upon a glistening, unusually animated, bustling something which ran and resoundingly whispered within the watch, again began speaking in a comradely tone. He again told Chang that he was bringing him to Odessa, to Elissavetinskaya Street; that in Elissavetinskaya Street he, the captain, had apartments, first of all; secondly, a wife who was a beauty; and, thirdly, a wonderful little daughter; and that he, the captain, was a very lucky fellow after all.

"A lucky fellow, after all, Chang!" said the captain, and then added:

"This daughter of mine, Chang, is a lively little girl, full of curiosity and persistence,—it is going to be bad for you at times, especially for your tail! But if you only knew, Chang, what a beautiful creature she is! I love her so much, brother, that at times I am even afraid of my love: she is all the world to me,—well, almost all, let us say; but is that as it should be? And,

[19]

in general, should any one be loved so greatly?" he asked. "For, were all these Buddhas of yours more foolish than you and I? And yet, just you listen to what they say about this love of the universe and all things corporeal, beginning with sunlight, with a wave, with the air, and winding up with woman, with an infant, with the scent of white acacia! Or else,—do you know what sort of a thing this Tao is, that has been thought up by nobody else but you Chinamen? I know it but poorly myself, brother, but then, everybody knows it poorly; but, as far as it is possible to understand it, just what is it, after all? The Abyss, our First Mother; She gives birth to all things that exist in this universe, and She devours them as well, and, devouring them, gives birth to them anew; or, to put it in other words, It is the Path of all that exists, which nothing that exists may resist. But we resist It every minute; every minute we want to turn to our desire not only the soul of a beloved woman, let us say, but even the entire universe as well! It is an eerie thing to be living in this world, Chang," said the captain; "it's a most pleasant thing, but still an eerie one, and especially for such as I! For I am too avid of happiness, and all too often do I lose the way: dark and evil is this Path,—or is it entirely, entirely otherwise?"

And, after a silence, he added further:

"For after all, what is the main thing? When you love somebody, there is no power on earth that can make you believe that the one you love can possibly not love you. And that is just where the devil comes in, Chang. But how magnificent life is; my God, how magnificent!"

Made red hot by the now high risen sun, and quivering slightly as it ran, the steamer was tirelessly cleaving the

[20]

Red Sea, now stilled in the abyss of the sultry empyrean spaciousness. The radiant void of the tropical sky was peeping in through the door of the round-house. Noonday was approaching; the brass threshold simply blazed in the sun. The glassy swell rolled more and more slowly over the side, flaring up with a blinding glitter, and lighting up the round-house. Chang was sitting on the divan, listening to the captain. The captain, who had been patting Chang on the head, shoved him to the floor: "No, it's too hot, brother!" said he; but this time Chang was not offended,—it was too fine a thing to be living in this world on this joyous noonday. And then. . . .

But here again Chang's dream is interrupted.

"Come on, Chang!" says the captain, dropping his feet down from the bed. And again in astonishment Chang sees that he is not on a steamer on the Red Sea, but in a garret in Odessa, and that it really is noonday outside,—not a joyous noonday, however, but a dark, dreary, inimical one, and he growls softly at the captain who has disturbed him. But the captain, paying no attention to him, puts on his old uniform cap and his old uniform great coat, and, shoving his hands deep in his pockets and all hunched up, goes toward the door. Willy-nilly, Chang, too, has to jump down from the bed. It is a hard thing for the captain to descend the stairs and he has no heart for it, as though he were doing it under the compulsion of harsh necessity. Chang rolls along rather rapidly,—he is still enlivened by that yet unallayed irritation with which the blissful state induced by vodka always ends. . . .

Yes,—it is two years now since Chang and the captain

[21]

have been occupied, day in and day out, in visiting one restaurant after another. There they drink, have snacks, contemplate the other drunkards who drink and have snacks alongside of them, amid the noise, tobacco smoke, and all sorts of bad odours. Chang lies on the floor, at the captain's feet. As for the captain, he sits and smokes, his elbows firmly planted on the table,—a habit he has acquired at sea; he is awaiting that hour when it will be necessary, in accordance with some law which he had himself mentally formulated, to migrate to some other restaurant or coffee-house: Chang and the captain breakfast in one place, drink coffee in another, dine in a third, and sup in a fourth. Usually the captain is silent. But there are times when the captain meets some one of his erstwhile friends, and then he talks all day long without cease of the insignificance of life, and every minute regales with wine now himself, now his *vis à vis*, now Chang,—the last always has some bit of china on the floor before him. They would pass the present day also in precisely the same way: they had agreed to breakfast this day with a certain old friend of the captain's, an artist in a high silk hat. And that meant that at first they would sit in a certain malodorous beer-shop, among red-faced Germans, —stolid, business-like people, who worked from morn till night with, of course, the sole aim of drinking, eating, working all over again, and propagating others of their kind. Then they would go to a coffee-house filled to overflowing with Greeks and Jews, whose entire existence, likewise senseless but exceedingly perturbed, was swallowed up in ceaseless expectation of stock-exchange news; and from the coffee-house they would set out for a restaurant whither flocked all sorts of human rag-tag, and there they would sit far into the night. . . .

A winter day is short, but with a bottle of wine, sitting in conversation with a friend, it is still shorter. And now Chang, the captain, and the artist had already been both in the beer-shop and in the coffee-house, and it is the sixth hour that they have been sitting and drinking in the restaurant. And again the captain, having put his elbows on the table, is ardently assuring the artist that there is but one truth in this world,—a truth evil and base. "You just look about you," he is saying, "you just recall all those that you and I see every day in the beer-shop, in the coffee-house, and out on the street! My friend, I have seen the entire earthly globe—life is like that all over! Everything that these people pretend as constituting their life is all bosh and a lie: they have neither God, nor conscience, nor a sensible purpose in existing, nor love, nor friendship, nor honesty,—there is even no common pity. Life is a dreary, winter day in a filthy tavern, no more. . . ."

And Chang, lying under the table, hears all this in the fog of a tipsiness, in which there is no longer any exhilaration. Does he agree with the captain, or does he not? It is impossible to answer this definitely,—but since it is impossible, it means that things are in a bad way. Chang does not know, does not understand, whether the captain is right; but then, it is only when we experience sorrow that we all say: "I do not know, I do not understand,"—whereas when joy is its portion every living being is convinced that it knows all things, understands all things. . . . But suddenly a ray of sunlight seems to cut through this fog of tipsiness: there is a sudden tapping of a baton against a music stand on the band-stand of the restaurant—and a violin begins to sing, followed by a second, a third. . . . They sing more and more passionately, more and more sonorously,— and a minute later Chang's soul overflows with an entirely different yearning, with an entirely different sadness. His soul quivers from an incomprehensible rapture, from some sweet torment, from a longing for something indefinite,—and Chang no longer distinguishes whether he is in a dream or awake. He yields with all his being to the music, submissively follows it into some other world—and once more he sees himself on the threshold of that beautiful world; silly, with a faith in the universe, a puppy on board a steamer in the Red Sea. . . .

"Yes, but how was it?" he half-thinks, half-dreams. 'Yes, I remember: it was a good thing to be alive on that hot noonday on the Red Sea!" Chang and the captain were sitting in the round-house; later on they stood on the ship's bridge. . . . Oh, how much light there was; what a deep blue the sea was, and how azure the sky! How amazingly vivid against the background of the sky were all these white, red, and yellow sailors' blouses hung out to dry at the prow! Then, afterwards, Chang and the captain and the other men of the ship (whose faces were brick-red, with oily eyes, whereas their foreheads were white and perspiring), breakfasted in the hot general cabin of first-class, under an electric ventilator buzzing and blowing out of a corner. After breakfast Chang took a little nap; after tea he had dinner, and after dinner he was again sitting aloft, before the pilot's round-house, where a steward had placed a canvas chair for the captain, and gazing far out at the sea; at the sunset, tenderly green among the many-coloured and many-formed little clouds; at the sun, wine-red and shorn of its beams, that, as soon as it had touched the turbid horizon, lengthened out and took on the semblance of a dark-flamed mitre. . . . Rapidly did the steamer run in pursuit of it; over the side the smooth, watery humps simply flashed by, giving off a sheen of blueish-lilac shagreen. But the sun hastened on and on,—the sea seemed to be absorbing it,—and kept on decreasing and decreasing, and became an elongated, glowing ember. It began to quiver and went out; and, as soon as it had gone out, the shadow of some sadness immediately fell upon all the world, and the wind, constantly blowing harder as the night came on, became still more turbulent. The captain, gazing at the dark flame of the sunset, was sitting with his head bared, his hair a-flutter in the wind, and his face was pensive, proud, and sad. And one felt that he was happy none the less, and that not only this entire steamer, running on at his will, but all the universe as well was in his power; because at that moment all the universe was in his soul,—and also because even then there was the odour of wine on his breath. . . .

And when the night fell, it was awesome and magnificent. It was black, disquieting, with an unruly wind, and with such a vivid glow from the waves swirling up around the steamer that Chang, who was trotting behind the captain as the latter rapidly and ceaselessly paced the deck, would jump away with a yelp from the side of the ship. And the captain again picked Chang up in his arms, and putting his cheek against Chang's beating heart,—for it beat in precisely the same way as the captain's—walked with him to the very end of the deck, on

[25]

to the poop, and stood there for a long time in the darkness, bewitching Chang with a wondrous and horrible spectacle: from under the towering, enormous stern, from under the dully raging propeller, myriads of white-flamed needles were pouring forth with a crisp swishing; they extricated themselves and were instantly whirled away into the snowy, sparkling path that the steamer was laying down. Now, again, there would be enormous blue stars: now some sort of tightly-coiled blue globes that would explode vividly, and, fading out, smoulder mysteriously with pale-green phosphorescence within the boiling watery hummocks. The wind, coming from all directions, beat strongly and softly upon Chang's muzzle, ruffling and chilling the thick fur upon his chest; and, nestling closely to the captain, as though they were both of the same kin, Chang scented an odour that seemed to be that of cold sulphur, breathed in the air coming from the furrowed inmost depths of the sea. And the stern kept on quivering; it was lowered and lifted by some great and unutterably free force, and Chang swayed and swayed, excitedly contemplating this blind and dark, yet an hundredfold living, dully turbulent Bottomless Gulf. And at times some especially mischievous and ponderous wave, noisily flying past the stern, would illumine the hands and the silvery clothes of the captain with an eldritch glow. . . .

On this night the captain for the first time brought Chang into his large and cozy cabin, softly illuminated by a lamp under a red silk shade. Upon the writing table, that was squeezed in tightly near the captain's bed, in the light and shade thrown by the lamp, stood two narrow frames, holding two photographic portraits: one of

[26]

a pretty little petulant girl in curly locks, seated at her capricious ease in a deep arm-chair; and the other that of a young woman, taken almost at full length, with a white lace parasol over her shoulder, in a large lace hat, and wearing a smart spring dress,—she was stately, slender, beautiful and pensive, like some Georgian *tsarevna*. And the captain said, as he undressed to the noise of the black waves beyond the open window:

"This woman won't like you and me, Chang! There are some feminine souls, brother, which languish eternally in a certain pensive yearning for love, and who just for that very same reason never love anybody. There are such,—and how shall they be judged for all their heart-lessness, falsehood, their dreams of going on the stage, of owning an automobile, of yachting picnics, of some sportsman or other, who pretends to be an Englishman, and tortures his hair, all greasy with pomatum, into a straight parting? Who shall divine them? Everyone according to his or her lights, Chang; and are they not fulfilling the innermost secret behests of Tao Itself, even as they are being fulfilled by some sea-creature that is now freely going upon its way in these black, fiery-armoured waves?"

"Oo-oo!" said the captain, sitting down on a chair and unlacing his white shoe. "What didn't I go through, Chang, when I felt for the first time that she was not entirely mine,—on that night when for the first time she had gone alone to the Yacht Club ball and had returned toward morning, like a wilted rose, pale from fatigue and her still unabated excitement, with her eyes all dark, widened, and distant from me! If you only knew how inimitably she wanted to hoodwink me, with what artless wonder she asked: 'But aren't you asleep yet, poor dear?' Right then I could not have uttered even a word, and she understood me at once and became silent; she merely threw a quick glance at me,—and began undressing in silence. I wanted to kill her, but she dryly and calmly said: 'Help me unfasten my dress at the back,'—and I submissively approached her and began with trembling hands to unfasten all these hooks and snaps,—and just as soon as I saw her body through the open dress, saw her back between the shoulder blades, and her chemise, dropping off the shoulders and tucked into the corset; just as soon as I felt the scent of her black hair and caught a glimpse of her breasts, raised up by the corset, reflected in the bright pier glass. . . ."

And, without finishing, the captain waved his hand in a hopeless gesture.

He undressed, lay down, and extinguished the light, and Chang, turning and settling in the morocco chair near the writing table, saw how the black cerement of the sea was furrowed by rows of white flame, flaring up and fading out; saw how some lights flashed up ominously upon the black horizon; saw how an awesome living wave would run up from thence and with a menacing noise would grow higher than the side of the ship, and look into the cabin,—like some serpent of fairy tale shining through and through with eyes of the natural colours of precious stones, shining through and through with translucent emeralds and sapphires. And he saw how the steamer thrust it aside and evenly kept on in its course, amid the ponderous and vacillant masses of this primordial element, now foreign and inimical to us, that is called Ocean. . . .

In the night the captain emitted some sudden cry; and, frightened himself by this cry, which rang with some basely-plaintive passion, he instantly awoke. Having lain for a minute in silence, he sighed and said mockingly:

"Yes, there's a story for you! 'As a jewel of gold in a swine's snout, *so is* a fair woman! . . .' Thrice right art thou, Solomon, Sage of Sages!"

He found in the darkness his cigarette case and lit a cigarette, but, having taken two deep puffs at it, he let his hand drop,—and fell asleep so, with the little red glow of the cigarette in his hand. And again it grew quiet— only the waves glittered, swayed, and noisily rushed past the ship's side. The Southern Cross from behind the black clouds. . . .

But here Chang is deafened by an unexpected thunder peal. He jumps up in terror. What has happened? Has the steamer again struck against underwater rocks through the fault of the intoxicated captain, as was the case three years ago? Has the captain again fired a pistol at his beautiful and pensive wife? No; this is not night all about them now; neither are they at sea, nor in Elissavetinskaya Street on a wintry noonday,—but in a brightly-lit restaurant, filled with noise and smoke. It is the intoxicated captain, who had struck his fist against the table, and is now shouting to the artist:

"Bosh, bosh! As a jewel of gold in a swine's snout,— that's what your Woman is! 'I have decked my bed with coverings of tapestry, with carved *works*, with fine linen of Egypt. . . . Come, let us take our fill of love . . . for the goodman *is* not at home. . . .' Bah! Woman! 'For her house inclineth unto death, and her paths unto the dead. . . .' But that is enough, that is enough, my friend. It is time to go,—they are closing up this place; come on!"

And a minute later the captain, Chang, and the artist are already in the street, where the wind and the snow make the street-lamps flicker. The captain embraces and kisses the artist, and they go in different directions. Chang, sullen and half asleep, is running sidewise over the sidewalk after the captain, who walks rapidly and unsteadily. . . . Again a day has passed,—dream or reality?—and again darkness, cold, and fatigue reign over the universe. . . . No, the captain is right, most assuredly right: life is simply poisonous and malodorous alcohol, nothing more. . . .

Thus, monotonously, do the days and nights of Chang pass. But suddenly one morning the universe, like a steamer, runs at full speed against an underwater reef, hidden from heedless eyes. Awaking on a certain wintry morning, Chang is struck by the great silence reigning in the room. He quickly jumps up from his place, rushes toward the captain's bed,—and sees that the captain is lying with his head convulsively thrown back, with his face grown pallid and chill, with his eyelashes half-open and unmoving. And, upon seeing these eyelashes, Chang emits a howl as despairing as if he had been thrown off his feet and cut in two by a speeding automobile. . . . Then, when the door of the room has been taken off its hinges, when people enter, depart, and arrive again, speaking loudly,—the most diversified people: porters, policemen, the artist in the high silk hat, and all sorts of other gentlemen who used to sit in restaurants with the captain,—then Chang seems to turn to stone. . . . Oh, how fearfully the captain had said at one time: "On that day the keepers of the house shall tremble . . . and those that look out of the windows be darkened . . . also they shall be afraid of *that which is* high, and fears shall be in the way . . . because man goeth to his long home, and the mourners go about the streets. . . . For the pitcher is broken at the fountain, and the wheel broken at the cistern. . . ." But Chang does not feel even terror now. He lies on the floor, his muzzle toward the corner; he has shut his eyes tight that he might not behold the universe, might forget it. And the universe murmurs over him dully and distantly, like the sea over one who descends deeper and deeper into its abyss.

But when he does come to himself again, it is near the doors of a chapel, in the porch. He sits near them with drooping head; dull, half-dead,—only he is all shaking in a chill. And suddenly the chapel door is flung open,— and a wondrous scene, all mellifluously chanting, strikes the eyes and the heart of Chang. Before Chang is a semi-dark Gothic chamber, with the red stars of flames, a whole forest of tropical plants, a coffin of oak raised high upon a black scaffolding. There is a black throng of people; there are two women wondrous in their marble- like beauty and their deep mourning, who seem just like two sisters of different ages; and, over all this, reverbera- tions, thunder peals, a choir,—of men sonorously clam- orous of some sorrowful joy of the angels. Solemnity, confusion, pomp,—and chantings not of this earth, drown- ing all else in their strains. And Chang's every hair

[31]

stands up on end from anguish and rapture before this sonorous vision. And the artist, who, with reddened eyes, stepped out of the chapel at that moment, stops in amazement:

"Chang!" he says in alarm, stooping down to him, "Chang, what is the matter with you?"

And, laying a hand that has begun to tremble upon Chang's head, he stoops still lower,—and their eyes, filled with tears, meet with such love for each other, that Chang's entire being cries out inaudibly to all the universe: "Ah, no, no,—there is upon earth some third truth, that has not been made known to me!"

That day, having returned from the cemetery, Chang moves into the house of his third master,—again up aloft, to a garret; but a garret warm, redolent of cigars, with rugs upon the floor, with antique furniture placed about it, and hung with brocaded stuffs. . . . It is growing dark; the fireplace is filled with glowing, sombrely-scarlet lumps of heat; Chang's new master is seated in a chair. He had not even taken off his overcoat and his high silk hat upon returning home; he had sat down with his cigar in a deep chair, and is now smoking and gazing into the dusk of his *atelier*. As for the fatigued, tortured-out Chang,—he is lying on a rug near the fireplace, his eyes shut, his muzzle resting on his front paws. And he dreams, he sees as in a vision:

Some One is lying there, beyond the darkening city, beyond the enclosure of the cemetery, in that which is called a crypt, a grave. But this Some One is not the captain,—no. If Chang loves and feels the captain, if he sees him with the vision of memory,—that divine thing within him which he does not understand himself,—

[32]

it means that the captain is still with him: in that uni-verse, without beginning and without end, which is in-accessible to Death.   In this universe there must be but one truth,—the third; but what that truth is, is known only to that last Master to whom Chang must now soon return.

1916.

THE DREAMS OF CHANG

A COMPATRIOT

THIS *moujik* of Briansk had been brought from the village to Moscow when he was a little boy; he had run errands at a merchant's warehouse in Iliyinka; he used to fly like an arrow to taverns to get hot water for tea: seizing the tea kettle, he would dash through the galleries of the Stariya Riyady—the Old Shops—drawing, with a dark jet of water, the figure eight upon the gray floor. . . . On a brisk winter day, perhaps with a light snow falling, the Iliyinka thoroughfare would be black with people; the horses of the cabbies would be shufflingly trotting along,—but he, in just his shirt and without a cap (his head resembling a rusty hedgehog), would jump out of the house, dart off the sidewalk, and start sliding on his soles upon the ice in the gutter. . . .

Imagine, then, how strange it is to see this *moujik* in the tropics, at the equator! He is sitting in his office in an old-fashioned house of Dutch architecture. Beyond the window lies the white city in the blaze of the sun; there are naked black rickshaw-men, shops of Australian wares and of precious stones, hotels filled with tourists from all the ends of the world; in the warm green water of the harbour float American and Japanese steamers; beyond the harbour, along the lowlands of the shores, grow cocoanut groves. . . . Clad all in white, tall, knotty, with flaming red hair, with a blueish freckled skin, pale, energetically exhilarated (or, to put it more simply, just

[34]

daft) from the heat, from nervousness, from constant tipsiness and from business activity,—he is, to look at him, either a Swede or an Englishman. His desk is all cluttered with papers, with bills. The air is filled with the crisp rattling of typewriters. An old Hindu, bare-footed, in robe and turban, noiselessly and rapidly changes with his dark, exquisite, silver-ringed hands little bottles of cold soda water, and every minute, with a mysterious expression on his face, announces the visitors, adding "Sir" at every word. But the "Sir" is completely absorbed in conversation with his friend from Russia, before whom he is playing the rôle of the affable lord of this tropical island. Upon the table are several open boxes of the most expensive cigars; of Turkish, Egyptian, English and Havana cigarettes. He is a connoisseur of tobaccos,—as well as of everything else, by the way. He regales his guest now with this brand, now with the other, saying, as though in passing: "This, I think isn't at all bad. . . ." Throwing a casual glance at some paper submitted to him, he, in the midst of the conversation, firmly and abruptly dashes off his signature upon it. Upon seeing a visitor enter, he changes the expression on his face, disposes of the matter in hand in two or three phrases, and again renews the interrupted conversation. When receiving some dispatch, his manner of opening it is especially negligent; for a moment, as he runs through it, he frowns: "What idiots!" he will say vehemently, in vexation; and throwing the dispatch to one side, immediately forgets about it,—or pretends that he does so. . . . All are idiots to him. He has already succeeded in astonishing his guest with his self-assurance, his deci-sive and sceptical mind, his enormous worldly experience and his wide acquaintance with people of the most diverse classes and stations. No matter who among the celebrities of Moscow is named,—merchants, administrators, physicians, journalists,—he knows them all, and knows well, besides, the price of each and all. And what information does he not possess concerning back-stage mysteries, exceptional careers, and shady histories!

His guest had heard a great deal about him while still at Port Said from a certain friend of this man; which friend had said, with a cynical gaiety, that Zotov had gone through fire, water, and brazen pipes. "Ye-es," this friend had said, shaking his head with a derisive and enigmatic smile, "he's a fine lad!" On the spot the guest came to know still more, and chiefly through the fragmentary phrases of Zotov himself. Strangely and unexpectedly do talents manifest themselves in Russia, and they work miracles when lucky lots fall to their share! For he had drawn an unusually lucky lot when he had come as an urchin to Moscow. He had an uncle there; a well-fed, clever *moujik*, who had already attained to a competence and a consciousness of his own worth; who knew how, adroitly, without lowering himself, to do a good turn for any decent gentleman. This uncle worked in the Sandunovskiya baths, and many of those whom he enveloped in clouds of hot and fragrant soapy foam called him by name and liked to chat with him. And one of these was Nechaev, a liberal, educated Crœsus, a large-built, stout merchant in gold spectacles. Was it a hard thing, having thrown a fine, slippery sheet over the pink, steamed body, to put in a word about his urchin nephew? And this urchin did not get to twisting waxen thread, nor to blowing up the fire under sad-

irons, but got into a sombre, clean and quiet warehouse on
the Iliyinka. All the rest was a matter of his personal
liveliness and aptitude. Everyone knows how these
lucky fellows and born geniuses begin: during the day the
urchin runs errands; of evenings, by his own volition,
without any guidance, he pours by the dim light of a
candle-end, learning to read and write; in the morning,
before the clerks get in, he, without understanding, but
stubbornly, overcomes the newspaper, and, let the clerks
but open their mouths, he is right there on the spot, all
alert and obedient, catching every word, every
glance. . . . When he was about twelve this urchin, who
had aroused his employer's special interest, was taken into
the latter's home; while in his eighteenth year he was already in Germany, studying the paper industry, working
as hard as any German,—the foreigners, it would seem,
did not want to believe that he was a Russian. "They
often don't believe it even now, the blockheads!" said
Zotov, roughly and abruptly, as is his wont, throwing
away one cigarette and immediately lighting another. . . .
"But, after all, does he resemble a European so very
greatly?" the guest wonders as he looks at his host.

He is thirty-seven years of age, but seems older. Yes,
—in appearance he is altogether an Englishman; even his
hands are English, the red hair upon them so thick that
they seem to be covered with tow. "But then," the guest
reflects, "would an Englishman talk so amazingly much
and so animatedly?" Hands really English would not
be trembling at his age, and, moreover, if possessing such
strength as Zotov's, an Englishman's face would not be
so pale, so uneasy without any visible cause. Zotov is
wearing black spectacles for the second day now, be-

[37]

cause one of his eye-brows is injured,—he slipped, so he says, on a banana peel in a bar; which means that he was rather far gone! And yet here, on this island, he is a personage because of his position. His hold on his guest's curiosity and attention does not flag for a minute. This man, audacious to the verge of insolence, infects one with his audacity, his energy,—at times even enraptures. But, listening to him, wondering at him, one looks upon him and thinks: "But he is drunk,—he is drunk!" He is always tipsy,—from nervousness, from the heat, from whiskey; Englishmen drink a great deal, but, of course, not a single one of them in all this white city drinks as much as Zotov, nor swallows iced soda water as avidly, nor smokes such a quantity of cigars and cigarettes, nor speaks so much and so confusedly. . . .

After his training abroad he worked at home and enjoyed the unbounded trust of the man who had brought him up. But he no longer wanted to know any mean in his independence, as well as in his expenditures. Sent into Central Asia, he suddenly, on some trifling pretext, quarrelled with Nechaev, severing all connections with him,—and, from a man steadily and surely climbing upward, was transformed into something very like an adventurer. He had traversed all of Siberia; had been in Amur, in China, consumed with impatience to found some enterprise all his own,—let it be something new, let it be something he was not familiar with, let it even be of a predatory nature,—but an enterprise such as would quickly lead to riches. Having returned to Russia he had insinuated himself into a great tea firm, besides having arranged two other posts for himself,—and it is now the sixth year that he has been living here in the tropics, clad in no mean powers. . . . It is a rare European who would have so easily cancelled his fate, amazing in its successfulness,—or even his specialty, which had taken so many years of toil to acquire! No European would have yielded himself to the whims of chance, or have shouldered not only a governmental post, but also a steamship agency and a tea business; or have started, along with all these, certain affairs with pearl-bearing shells; or would have maintained a black mistress all his own,—a rare beauty, according to rumour,—to the wonder of the whole city. . . . He keeps his counsel very much to himself, but at times he is very tactless; reveals, with equal force, now great firmness of character, now unrestraint; now secretiveness, now loquacity. He flaunts his common origin and at the same time boasts of his acquaintance with people of rank; swears, for all he is worth, at the Russian Government,—and with evident pride keeps on his desk a photographic portrait of a Russian Grand Duke, handsome and rather young, who had personally bestowed this portrait upon him, with a short signature in autograph. When he is narrating something that, in his opinion, is humorous, he frequently does not comprehend that the point of this amusing matter may be interpreted not at all to his advantage,—for example, it was from no other source than his own stories that the guest found out that Zotov had appeared as far too omniscient, almost as a passer-by, to those men of affairs in Siberia and Manchuria with whom he so rapidly attained to terms of intimacy, whom he so quickly charmed at first with his obligingness and sociability, his mannerisms of a man used to living on a grand scale, a man conversant with what is what, in absolutely all things, beginning with cigars, wine, women, and culminating with some excavations on the Philippine Islands, rather lethal, it would seem, on account of an earthly microbe. . . .

In the evening the guest rides with him beyond the city.

Beyond the city, on the shore of the ocean, stands a small but a very fashionable restaurant, where the tourists and the residents rest from the sultriness of the city, drinking tea, brandy, and champagne, and admiring the sunset from the front piazza of the restaurant. They come there in tiny rickshaws, following one another, over an endless road amid age-old vegetation, past bungalows and past the huts of the savages. And for a whole hour the guest from Russia sees before him only the naked body of a brown man, carrying him at a run farther and farther under the green vault of the branches of spreading trees; and beyond him, beyond this body and black-haired head, the big white figure of Zotov, sitting high and erect in his little carriage. Halfway to their destination he suddenly turns around and, raising his stick, calls out to his guest:

"Would you care to drive in?"

For answer the guest assents,—Zotov had pointed out a small Buddhistic monastery,—and the savages, breathing heavily, bathed in perspiration, roll up along the passage way, lying between the cabins, that stand underneath the palms and all other species of trees.

"Well, isn't this like a bit of our own; isn't this Russian?" Zotov is saying, stepping out of his carriage. "Only in our country is there so unconscionably much of this verdure, of this forest, so many of these hovels, so many dirty urchins like these! Just look!" he is saying, pointing with his stick at the trees, at the huts and their roofs of leaves and of rushes, at the naked children, and at the natives, young and old, who have surrounded the little carriages in their curiosity. "And the evening, too, is like one of our own,—oppressive, and so wearisome, so wearisome!" he is saying in irritation, going in the direction of the old idol temple standing on a knoll underneath slender cocoanut palms, where a priest is already waiting, clad in a yellow mantle, with his right shoulder bared,—his shaven head is small and pressed in at the temples, and his eyes are black, almost insane, and have an intense gaze.

Having entered the dark little sanctuary, the compatriots take off their helmets, wet with perspiration and cool on the inner side. The priest points a finger at their heads and shakes his head: as much as to say that this is not required.

"A lot you know, you fool," says Zotov in Russian; and for a long while, with a certain strange gravity, gazes at the fourteen-foot wooden statue, gilded and painted in red and yellow, lying on its side beyond a sacrificial altar of black stone, upon which are heaped small coins and nickel rings, and with the slenderest of brown joss-sticks sending forth thin jets of aromatic smoke standing upon it.

"And how he is painted and lacquered all over, though!" says Zotov jerkily. "Every bit just like the wooden bowls and cups sold at our fairs!"

And he carelessly tosses a heavy gold coin upon the silver plate extended by the priest. . . .

When they arrive at the restaurant, his face is almost chalky, and it is a frightful thing to see the black spectacles upon it. "For two whole hours I have not been

[41]

poisoning myself with anything, have drunk nothing, nor have I smoked; and because of all that I have become dead tired," he is saying. And just as soon as he is seated at a small table on the little terrace before the restaurant, over the steep shore, cumbered below with blue bowlders that eternally bathe in the warm water of the ocean, hè immediately orders champagne.

The wine is very chill, and they both drink it avidly, rapidly growing tipsy, and contemplate the darkening lilac ocean, the infinitely distant sunset, turbidly and tenderly roseate. A faint, warm breeze is stirring; the cicadas are drowsily strumming in the brushwood. . . . And suddenly Zotov flings his cigarette far from him, quickly lights another, and again, with the pertinacity of a maniac, begins talking of the similarity of this island and Russia.

The guest smiles. Zotov, hurriedly and not at all clearly, argues with him. The matter does not lie, he urges, merely in an outward resemblance. . . . And it was not even the resemblance that he had in view, but rather his reactions. . . . Perhaps these reactions are not firm, are unwholesome,—but then, that is another matter. . . . The devil himself would go out of his mind in a climate like this,—it is not a climate to be trifled with. . . . But now, in a discussion of all the various dangers of the Far East, people somehow forget entirely about that fact; messieurs the Aryans, and especially we Russians, ought to carry out our conquering expeditions into the tropics with extreme cautiousness, recalling with a greater frequence our forefathers and their conquest of Hindustan, so significantly terminating in Buddhism,—when all is said and done, it is we, the Aryans, after Thibet intruding ourselves into the tropics, who have given birth to this teaching, with its appallingly inapplicable wisdom! And then he warmly begins to asseverate that "all the force of the thing" lies in that he had already seen, had already felt the tropics even before his arrival here, at some time very remote, perhaps a thousand years ago,—with the eyes and the soul of his most distant ancestor. . . .

He tells,—with a subtlety, passionateness and an eloquence never to be expected from him,—that he had experienced extraordinary sensations on the way over here, on those sultry, starry nights when he had first beheld the Southern Cross, Canopus, and those first-created starry mists that are called the Clouds of Magellan; when he had beheld the Coal Sacks, those funereal fissures into the infinitude of universal voids; and the awesome magnificence of the Alpha of the Centaur, glimmering upon the utterly empty horizon, where some immeasurable Nothingness, unattainable to our reason, seemed to be in its inception. "Yes, yes!" exclaims he insistently, fixing the guest with his spectacles: "The horizon was utterly empty about the Alpha! A spectacle of a new world, of new heavens, was opened before me, but it seemed to me,—and this sensation was vivid to the verge of terror within me, I assure you!—it seemed to me that I had seen them before, once upon a time. All the days and all the nights a smooth, dead swell rocked us wide on the ocean. We were sailing toward an Eastern monsoon; it blew sharp and strong, and its ceaseless current of air made the sailyards hum and blurred the vision, and made our speed seem rapid. . . . Awaking at night in the hot darkness of my cabin, I, in order to rest after the exhausting sleep, would go on the upper decks, out into the

[43]

wind, under the stars,—altogether different from those I had seen all my life, from my very birth, and with which I had already grown intimate; stars that were altogether, altogether different,—yet at the same not altogether new, seemingly, but as though they were *dimly recalled*. Under their dim light hovered the ceaseless noise of the sea, the steamer rolled slowly from one side to the other, and, like strangled suicides in gray shrouds, with arms outspread, the long canvas ventilators swayed and quivered near the funnel, avidly catching with their orifices the freshness of the monsoon, upon which was already borne toward us the hot breath of the dread Land of our First Parents. And at such times I would be seized by such melancholy,—a melancholy of some infinitely remote recollection,—that one can not express in human speech even a hundredth part of it!"

A faint, delightful breeze is stirring; there is a drowsy strumming in the brushwood. The twilight begins to swell as with sap with that faery orange-aureate colour which always arises in the tropics when some time had elapsed after the sunset. The surf boils up in orange-aureate foam; the faces and the white costumes are bathed in an orange-aureate light. . . .

"How connect that with which he amazed me to-day with what he is amazing me now?" the guest from Russia is reflecting, almost in fear, about his astonishing compatriot. But the latter, is looking at him through his black spectacles and is stubbornly reiterating:

"Yes, yes,—I have already been here. . . . And, in general, I am a doomed man. . . . If you but knew how dreadfully muddled my affairs are! Even more, it would seem, than my soul and my thoughts. . . . Oh, well, there is a way out of everything! Just jerk back the trigger of your revolver, having thrust its muzzle as far as possible into your mouth,—and all these affairs, thoughts, and emotions will fly into pieces to the devil and his dam!"

1916.

BRETHREN

Behold brethren, slaying one another!
I would discourse of grief.
SUTHA NIPPATHA.

THE road out of Colombo, lying along the ocean, runs through dense cocoanut groves. To the right, within their sun-dappled shady depths, under the high canopy of feathery broom-like tree-tops, are scattered the Senegalese cabins, half-hidden by the pale green laminæ of bananas, resembling gigantic ears of corn, so small and low are they in comparison with the tropical forest surrounding them. To the left, through the dark-ringed trunks, tall and slender, fantastically bent in all directions, one sees stretches of deep, silky sands, a gleam of a golden, blazing mirror of smooth water, and, anchored upon it, as though blending with the tree trunks, are the coarse sails of primitive pirogues,—frail, cigar-shaped hollowed-out small oaks. Upon the sand, in paradisaical nudity, are sprawling the coffee-coloured bodies of black-haired striplings. Many such bodies are also plashing, with laughter and yells, in the warm transparent water of the stony coast. . . . Of what need, one thinks, to these people of the forests, these direct heirs of the Land of our First Parents, as Ceylon is styled even now,—of what need to them are cities, cents, rupees? Do not the forest, ocean, sun give them everything? And yet, upon attain-

[46]

ing the years of maturity, some of them take to trading, others labour upon the rice and tea plantations, a third lot—in the north of the island—dive for pearls together with negroes, going down to the bottom of the ocean and arising thence with bloodshot eyes; a fourth group replace horses,—they carry Europeans over the towns and their environs, over dark red footpaths, shaded by enormous vaults of forest verdure over that very *kabouk* out of which Adam was created. Horses bear but illy the sultriness of Ceylon,—even Australian horses; every wealthy resident who keeps a horse sends it away for the summer to the mountains, into Candy, into Nurillia.

Upon the rickshaw-man's left arm, between his shoulder and elbow, the Englishmen, the present lords of the island, put a badge with a number. There are ordinary numbers, and there are special ones. To one old Senegalese rickshaw-man, living in a forest hut near Colombo, had fallen a special number,—seven. "Wherefore," the Exalted One might have said,—"wherefore, monks, did this old man desire to multiply his earthly sorrows?" "Because," the monks might have answered, "because, oh Exalted One, he was moved by earthly love, by that which, from the start of time, summons all creatures into being,—therefore did this old man desire to increase his earthly sorrows." He had a wife, a son, and many little children, dreading not that "he who hath them, hath also the care of them." He was black, very thin and unsightly, resembling both a stripling and a woman; his long hair, gathered in a knot at the nape of his neck and anointed with cocoanut oil, had grown gray; the skin over all his body—or, to put it better, over his bones—had wrinkled; as he ran, sweat streamed down

[47]

from his nose, chin, and the rag tied about his scanty pelvis; his narrow chest drew breath with whistling and gasping. But strengthening himself with the headiness of the betel, working up and expectorating a bloody froth that soiled his moustache and lips, he sped quickly; and the white men rolling in his black lacquered cart through the sun-scorched city, over the dark-red pavements, soft from the sun and smelling of naphtha and the humus of flowers, were satisfied.

Moved by love, not for himself, but for his family, for his son, did he desire happiness, that which was not destined to be his, that which was not given to him. He knew English but poorly; he could not make out at once the names of the places where he was to run to—and frequently ran at a venture. The rickshaw-man's carriage is very small; it has a top that can be thrown back, its wheels are narrow and high, each shaft is no thicker than an average cane. And lo! A big man, his eyes almost all whites, all in white, with a white sun helmet, in rough but expensive footgear, clambers into it, seats himself snugly therein, crosses one leg over the other, and, restrainedly commanding, deep in his throat, hoarsely croaks his destination. Seizing his shafts, the old man bends down to the ground and flies forward like an arrow, scarce touching the ground with his light feet. The man in the helmet, holding a stick in his hands covered with tow-like hair, has gone into deep thought over his affairs, staring vacantly,—when suddenly he rolls his eyes in wrath: why, the fellow's rushing in an altogether wrong direction! To put it shortly, not a few sticks had fallen upon his back, upon his black shoulder blades, always hunched up in presentiment of a blow. But also not a

[48]

few extra cents had he snatched from Englishmen,— checking himself at full speed at the entrance of some hotel or office and dropping the shafts, he would so wrinkle his face, so hurriedly throw out his thin arms, his moist, monkey-like palms cupped, that it was impossible not to give him something additional.

One day he ran home at an altogether unaccustomed hour in the very heat of noonday, when those lemon-coloured birds which are called sun-birds flutter through the forest like golden arrows; when so gaily and shrilly scream the parrots, darting from the trees and flashing like rainbows through the dappled boskage of the forests, through their shade and gleaming light; when, within the enclosures of ancient Buddhistic sanctuaries, roofed with terra-cotta tiles, the plum-coloured blossoms of the leafless Tree of Sacrifice, that resemble little tuberoses, yield such a sweet and heavy odour; when thick-throated chameleons play with such vivid primary colours as they flash over smooth-trunked trees, as well as over trees that are as ringed as an elephant's trunk; when so many huge, gorgeous butterflies soar and float without motion in the sun; and when the hot, fawn-coloured ant-hills swarm and spout, as though with agate grain. All things in the forests chanted and praised Maru, the God of Life and Death, the God of the "Thirst of Being"; all creatures were pursuing one another, rejoicing with a brief joy even as they destroyed one another; but the old rickshaw-man, no longer athirst for anything but a cessation of his sufferings, lay down in the stuffy murk of his mud-hut, under its parched-up roof of leaves arustle with little red snakes, and toward evening was dead—from icy cramps and watery dysentery. His life was extinguished together with the sun, that went down beyond the lilac smoothness of great watery expanses, retreating toward the west, into the purple, ashes, and gold of the most magnificent clouds in the universe. And night came,—a night on which, in the forests near Colombo, all that was left of the rickshaw-man was only a little contorted corpse, that had lost its number, its name, even as the river Kellani loses its appellation when it reaches the ocean. The sun, upon sinking, changes to a wind; but into what does he that has died change? . . . Night was rapidly extinguishing the roseate and green colours of the fleeting twilight,—colours as tender as those of some fairy tale; the flying foxes darted noiselessly underneath the branches, seeking shelter for the night; and the forests were filling up with a black, warm darkness, were bursting into flame with myriads of fire-flies, and were mysteriously, languishingly murmurous with cicadas and with the flowers of which the tiny tree frogs make their home. In the distant forest idol-temple, before a little sacred lamp barely glimmering upon a black altar for offerings that was drenched with cocoanut oil and strewn with rice and withered flower petals, upon his right side, with one hand laid meekly under his cheek, reposed the Exalted One,—a giant of sandal-wood, with a broad gilded face and elongated slanting eyes of sapphires, with a smile of peaceful sadness upon his thin lips. In the dark cabin, upon his back, was lying the rickshaw-man, and the suffering of death distorted his pitiful features,—for that the voice of the Exalted One had not reached him when it had summoned him to forsake earthly love; for that beyond the grave a new life of sorrow awaited him, as a consequence of his previous unrighteous one. The buck-toothed old woman, sitting at the threshold of the cabin, at the fire under a cauldron, wept on this night, nourishing her grief with the self-same unreasoning love and pity. The Exalted One would have likened her emotions to the copper ear-ring, resembling a little barrel, which hung in her right ear,—the ear-ring was big and heavy; it had so pulled down the slit in the lobe of her ear that a considerable hole had formed. Her short blouse of cotton stuff, put on right over the bare coffee-coloured body, stood out sharply white in the darkness. Near by, naked, imp-like children were playing, squealing, pursuing one another. As for the son, a light-footed youth,—he was standing in the semi-darkness beyond the fire. He had that evening seen his bride,—a round-faced, thirteen-year-old girl from a neighbouring settlement. He was frightened and dumbfounded upon hearing of his father's death,—he had not thought that this would come so soon. But, probably, he was too much aroused by another love, which is stronger than the love men bear for their fathers. "Forget not," saith the Exalted One, "forget not, O Youth, longing to enkindle life with life, even as fire is enkindled with fire, that all the torments of this universe, where everyone is either slayer or slain, that all its sorrows and plaints, come from love." But love had already crept into the youth in its entirety, even as a scorpion creeps into its lair. He stood and gazed into the fire. As with all savages, his legs were disproportionately long. But even Siva would have envied the beauty of his torso, that was of the colour of dark cinnamon. The fire made his blue-black hair glisten,—it was as thick as horse hair, and stretched taut

[51]

and gathered at the top of his head; made his eyes glow from under their long lashes,—and their glow was like the glow of coke near the mouth of a forge.

On the next day the neighbours carried off the dead little old man into the depths of the forest; laid him in a pit, with his head to the west, toward the ocean; hurriedly, but trying not to make noise, cast earth and leaves over him; and hurried away to perform their cleansing ablutions. The little old man was done with his running; the brass badge was taken off the thin arm that had grown gray and wrinkled,—and, admiring it, distending his thin nostrils, the youth put it upon his own, that was rounded and warm. At first he only followed the experienced rickshaw-men, trying to catch the destinations of their passengers, memorizing English words and the names of the streets; then he began carrying passengers independently, began earning money himself; he was preparing for a family, for a love of his own,—the desire for which is a desire for sons, just as the desire for sons is a desire for property, and desire for property—a desire for well-being. But one day, having come home, he came upon other horrible tidings: his bride had vanished,—she had gone to Slave Island, to purchase something, and had not returned. The bride's father, who knew Colombo well, having frequently gone there, searched for her for three days, and he must have found out something, because he returned reassured. He sighed and cast down his eyes, expressing his submission to fate; but he was a great hypocrite, a sly old man, like all those who have property, who trade in the city. He was corpulent, with breasts like a woman's; he had hoary hair, carefully combed, and ornamented with an expensive comb of tor-

toise shell; he walked about bare-footed, but under a
sun-shade; he girt his hips with a piece of gaudy material,
of good quality; his blouse was of *piqué*. It was impossible to get the truth out of him; furthermore, all
women, all maidens, are frail, even as all rivers are full
of turnings and windings; and the young rickshaw-man
understood this. After sitting at home for two days in
a daze, without touching food, only chewing betel, he
finally came to himself and again ran off into Colombo.
He seemed to have forgotten entirely about his bride.
He ran with the rickshaw, he covetously hoarded money,
—and it was impossible to understand which he was more
in love with: his running, or those circles of silver which
he gathered for it. One Russian seaman had had a
photograph taken of himself and the rickshaw-man, and
had presented him with one of these pictures. For a
long time after that the young rickshaw-man joyously
marvelled at his image: he was standing between his
shafts, his face turned toward the imaginary spectators,
and everyone could recognize him immediately,—even the
badge on his arm had come out. With all good fortune,
apparently even with happiness, he had laboured thus for
about half a year.

And one morning he was sitting with other rickshaw-
men underneath a many-trunked banyan tree that stood
upon that lengthy street which extends from Slave Island to Victoria Park. The hot sun had just appeared
from behind the trees, from the direction of Maradana.
But the banyan tree had grown high, and there was no
longer any shade about its roots, strewn over with parched
leaves. The little carriages grew hot from the heat,
their thin shafts lay upon the dark-red, heated earth,

that smelt both of naphtha and of freshly-ground coffee. With this odour were blended the pungent sweet odours of the surrounding, ever-blossoming gardens, the odours of camphor, of musk, and of that which the rickshaw men were eating,—and they were eating bananas,—small, warm, tenderly roseate, in aureate skins; they were eating those orange fruits, with a tang of turpentine, the meat of which has the appearance of the flesh of children. They were chattering as they sat on the ground, their knees raised in sharp angles up to their chins, with their arms on top of the knees, and with their feminine heads on top of their arms. Suddenly, in the distance, near the white enclosing walls of a bungalow, dappled by the light and shade, appeared a man clad in white. He was walking in the middle of the street with that determined and firm step with which only Europeans walk. And, jumping up as quick as lightning from the ground, the entire flock of these naked, long-legged men dashed toward him, racing to get ahead of one another. They darted upon him from all sides, and he yelled threateningly, swinging out with his cane. Timid and sensitive, they checked themselves at full speed, gathering around him. He glanced at them,—and number seven, with his pitch-black, horse-like hair, appeared to him stronger than the others. And so his choice fell upon number seven.

He was short and strong, in gold spectacles, with black eyebrows grown together over the bridge of his nose, with a short black moustache, with an olive complexion; the sun of the tropics and liver trouble had already left their sallow trace upon his face. His helmet was gray; his eyes, in some strange way, as though they beheld nothing, looked out of the coal-black darkness of his eye-brows and lashes, from behind the shining lenses. He sat down like one accustomed to rickshaws,—immediately finding in the little carriage that spot which makes it the easiest for the rickshaw-men to run, and glancing at the little watch in a leathern socket strapped around his wrist,—it was tattooed, and the hand was powerful and stubby,—called out "York Street!" His expression-less voice was firm and calm, but his eyes had a strange look. And the rickshaw-man snatched up the shafts and flew off at a considerably greater speed than was called for, every moment clicking the bell that was fastened at the end of the shaft, and shuffling in and out among pedestrians, tilted *arba* carts, and other rickshaws that were running back and forth.

It was the end of March,—the most sultry period. Not even three hours had passed since the rising of the sun,—yet it already seemed as if noon were near, so hot and bright was it everywhere, and so thronged in the neighbourhood of the stores at the farther end of the street. The earth, the gardens, all that tall, spreading vegetation which was growing green and blossoming over the bungalows, over their chalky roofs, and over the old black stores,—all these had cloyed the air with warmth and fragrance, whereas the rain-trees had curled up tightly their little cup-like leaves. The rows of shops, —or, rather, of sheds,—roofed with black tiles, their walls hung about with enormous bunches of bananas, with dried fish, with sun-cured shark-meat, were filled with buyers and sellers,—both alike resembling dark-skinned bath-attendants. The rickshaw-man, bending forward, his long legs twinkling, was running rapidly, and as yet there was not a single drop of sweat upon his back, glistening with cocoanut oil, nor upon his rounded shoulders, between which the slender trunk of his girlish neck gracefully supported his pitch-black head, upon which the blazing sun beat down. At the very end of the street, he came to a sudden stop. Turning his head just the least trifle, he rapidly said something in his own tongue. The Englishman, his passenger, caught sight of the tips of his curved eyelashes, caught the word "betel," and raised his eyebrows. How? Such a young, strong fellow was already wanting betel, after having run only some two hundred steps? Without answering, he struck the rickshaw-man over his shoulder blades with his cane. But the latter, timorous like all Senegalese but at times also insistent, only shrugged his shoulders and flew like an arrow diagonally across the street, toward the shops.

"Betel," repeated he, turning wrathful eyes upon the Englishman, and baring his teeth in a dog-like snarl. But the Englishman had already forgotten about him. And a minute later the rickshaw-man jumped out of a shop, holding upon his narrow palm a leaf of the pepper tree, smearing it over with lime and wrapping within it a bit of the *areca* fruit, resembling a bit of flint. Kill not, steal not, commit no fornication, lie not, nor become intoxicated with aught, the Exalted One hath commanded. Yes,—but what did the rickshaw-man know of Him? Vaguely echoed within him that which had been vaguely accepted by the countless hearts of his forefathers. In the rainy season of the year he had gone with his father to the sacred tabernacles; and there, among the women and the beggars, he had listened to the priests reading in an ancient tongue forgotten of all, and understanding

[56]

nothing, only chiming in in the common joyous acclamation whenever the name of the Exalted One was uttered. More than once it had happened that his father had prayed in his presence upon the threshold of the idol temple; he would bow down before the recumbent statue of wood, muttering its commandments, lifting his joined palms to his forehead, and then would lay upon the altar for offerings the smallest and most worn of his hard-earned coins. But he muttered his prayers with indifference,—for he was merely afraid of the pictures upon the walls of the idol-temple, the depictions of the torment of sinners; he bowed down before other gods as well,—before horrible Hindu statues; in them, too, did he believe, just as he believed in the power of demons, serpents, stars, darkness. . . .

Having thrust the betel into his mouth, the rickshaw-man, fitfully volatile in his emotions, turned amiably smiling eyes upon the Englishman, seized the shafts, and, starting off with a thrust of his left foot, began running again. The sun was blinding; it gleamed on the gold and the lenses of the spectacles whenever the Englishman raised his head. The sun was scorching his hands and knees; the earth was breathing heavily,—one could even see that the air was aquiver above it, as above a brazier,—but he sat immovably, without touching the hood of the little carriage. Two roads led into the city,—or, as the residents called it, into the Fort: one, on the right, passed by the Malay pagoda, over the dam between the lagoons; the other, to the left, led toward the ocean. The Englishman wanted to go by the latter. But the rickshaw-man turned around as he ran, showing his bloodied lips, and pretended that he did not under-

stand what was wanted from him. And the Englishman
again yielded,—he was absent-mindedly looking about
him. The green lagoon, sparkling, warm, filled with
turtles and rotting vegetation, bordered in the distance
by a cocoanut grove, lay on the right. Upon the dam
people were walking, riding, running to the clanging of
bells. Rickshaw-men in fezes, white jackets, and short
white pantaloons were now occasionally met with. The
Europeans sitting in the little carriages were pale after the
exhausting night; they held their white shoes high, putting one knee over the other. A two-wheeled cart, with a
gray humped bullock harnessed to it, rolled by. . . .
Beneath its top, in the light, warm shadow, was sitting a
Parsee,—a yellow-faced old man who looked like an
eunuch, in a gown and a conical velvet skull cap, the latter worked with gold. A giant Afghan, in wide trowsers
to his knees, in soft boots with upturned toes, in a white
casaque and an enormous pink turban, was immovably
standing, bent over the lagoon, gazing at the turtles, at
the warm water. Long covered *arba* carts stretched on
endlessly, dragged along by oxen. Under their narrow
arched tops of straw were piled up bales of goods, and,
at times, there would be a whole cluster of the brown
bodies of young labourers. Shrivelled old men, parched
by the heat, their feet reddened from the red dust, looking like the mummies of old women, paced beside the
wheels. There were stone-cutters pacing along, and stalwart black Tomilas. . . . *"The Pagoda,"* said the
Englishman, referring to a certain tea-house, when they
had come beneath those patriarchal trees that grow at the
entrance into the Fort, beneath the unencompassable

canopies of their verdure, shot with the sun that penetrated through it.

They stopped near the entrance of an old Dutch building, with arcades on its ground floor. The Englishman glanced at his watch and went off to drink tea and to smoke a cigar. As for the rickshaw-man, he made half a turn about the broad, shady street, over the reddishly-lilac pavement, strewn over with the yellow and scarlet blossom of the *ketmias,* and dropping the shafts at the roots of a tree, without checking his impetus, sank down. He raised up his knees and put his elbows upon them, avidly breathing in the steaming, sweetly odorous warmth of noonday, and aimlessly letting his eyes follow the Senegalese and Europeans passing by. Taking a rag from some recess of his apron, he wiped with it his lips, made bloody by the betel, wiped his face, the convexities on his thin chest, and, folding it into a bandage, tied it around his head,—this did not at all look well, giving him the appearance of a sick man; but then, many rickshaw-men do it. He sat, and, perhaps, he may have been pondering. . . . "Our bodies, O Master, are different,—but then, we all have but one heart," Ananda had said to the Exalted One, and, therefore, one can imagine what must be the thoughts or emotions of a youth who had grown up in the paradisaical forests near Colombo and who had already tasted the most potent of poisons,—love for woman; who had already plunged into life,—life, fleetly flying after joys or fleeing from sorrows. Mara had already wounded him,—but then, Mara also healeth wounds. Mara snatches out of the hands of man that which man had seized upon,—but then, Mara also inflames a man to seize anew that which had been taken away, or to seize something else that is like that which had been taken away. . . .

Having had his tea, the Englishman wandered through the street, entering shops, gazing at the show-cases displaying precious stones, elephants and Buddhas made of ebony wood, all sorts of bright coloured stuffs, the golden skins of panthers, spotted with black,—while the rickshaw-man, meditating of something, or, perhaps, merely sentient, was exchanging bright glances with the other rickshaw-men and followed the Englishman, dragging his little carriage after him. Exactly at noon the Englishman gave him a rupee to buy himself some food, while he himself went into the office of a big European steamship line. The rickshaw-man bought some cigarettes, started smoking, inhaling deeply, watching his cigarette, as women do,—and smoked five of them, one after the other. In a delectable daze he sat in the fretted shade, opposite the three-story building where the office was, and suddenly, having raised his eyes, saw that his passenger, and also five other Europeans, had appeared on the balcony under the white awning. They were all looking through binoculars at the harbour,—and now, beyond the roofs of the wharf, appeared two tall, slender masts, slightly inclined backward. The people on the balcony started waving their handkerchiefs, while from beyond the roofs, morosely, mightily and majestically, a whistle began to roar, echoed all over the roadstead and in the city,—the steamer from far-away Europe that the passenger of rickshaw number seven had been awaiting had arrived. With English punctuality did it enter after twenty days' sail to Colombo,—and that

which the rickshaw-man, still filled with hopes and desires, did not at all expect—that dinner, so fatal for him,
to be held in the house near the lagoon, at the steamship agent's home,—was decided upon.

But until dinner, until evening, there still remained
much time. And again this man in spectacles who saw
nothing came out into the street. He said good-bye to
the two men who had come out with him and who had
gone in the direction of the white statue of Victoria, toward the covered wharf; and again the rickshaw-man
started ambling through the street,—this time toward
the hotel, where at this time many tourists and rich residents were eating and drinking in a semi-dark hall, whose
sultry stuffiness was stirred and mixed with the odours
of the food by blades turning near the ceiling. And
again, like a dog, the rickshaw-man squatted down
upon the pavement, upon the petals of the *ketmias*. The
fretted shade of trees whose light-green tips were interlaced spread over the street, and in this shade went past
him the womanish Senegalese, thrusting upon the Europeans coloured postal cards, tortoise-shell combs, precious stones,—one native was even dragging after him
by a cord a little beast in a coat of long quills, trying
to sell it,—and these half-savages, these rickshaw-men,
kept up their ceaseless racing through this rich European
thoroughfare. . . . In the distance, in the centre of an
open square, a woman of heroic size, in marble,—proud,
double-chinned, in crown and royal mantle, seated on her
throne upon a high pedestal of marble,—was blazing in
her whiteness. And those who had just arrived from
Europe were trooping from that direction. Black and
dove-coloured servants jumped out upon tne entrance to

the hotel; bowing, they snatched the canes and small baggage from the hands of the arrivals, who were also met by the bows, restrained and graceful, of a man resplendent with the parting of his pomatumed hair, with his eyes, his teeth, his cuffs, his starched linen, his *piqué* dinner jacket, his *piqué* trousers, and his white footgear. "Men are forever going to feasts, to excursions, to diversions," saith the Exalted One, Who had at one time visited this paradisaical corner of the first men who had come to know desire. "The sight, sounds, taste, and odours of things intoxicate them," He had said; "desire entwines them, even as a creeping plant, green, beautiful, and death-bearing, entwines the tree Shala." Traces of fatigue, of exhaustion from heat, from the rocking of the boat at sea and from maladies, were upon the ashen faces of those going to the hotel. They all had the appearance of being half-dead, they spoke without moving their lips; but they all walked on, looking about them, and one after the other disappeared within the darkness of the vestibule, in order to go to their rooms, to wash up and refresh themselves. And then, having intoxicated themselves with food, drink, cigars and coffee, until their faces flushed crimson, they would roll away in rickshaws to the shore of the ocean, into the Cinnamon Gardens, to the Hindu temples and the Buddhistic sanctuaries. Everyone of them—everyone!—had within his soul that which compels a man to live and to desire the sweet deception of life! And was not this deception doubly sweet to the rickshaw-man, born in the land of the first people? Ladies and gentlemen walked to and fro before him,—elderly, ugly, just as buck-toothed as his black mother, sitting in the distant forest hut; but at

[62]

times young women also went past him,—pleasant to look upon, in white raiment, in small helmets wound with light veils, and, arousing desire within him, they looked intently upon his splendid, upraised eyelashes, upon the rag around his pitch-black head, and upon his blood stained mouth. But then, was she who had disappeared in the city inferior to them? The warmth of the tropical sun had made her grow. She seemed darker on account of her short blouse, white, with little blue flowers, and her skirt, just as short and of the same material, both put directly upon her naked body,—just a trifle full, but strong and small. She had a little rounded head, a convex little forehead, round shining eyes in which childish timidity was already being commingled with a joyous curiosity about life, with a hidden muliebrity, both tender and passionate; there was a coral necklace upon her rounded neck; her little hands and feet were braceletted with silver. . . . Jumping up from his place, the rickshaw-man ran into one of the nearest by-streets, where, in an old, one-storied house under brick tiles, with thick wooden pillars, there was a bar for the lower classes. There he put twenty-five cents on the bar, and for that price gulped down a whole glass of whiskey. Having mixed this fire with the betel, he had assured himself of a beatific exaltation almost until the very evening, until the time when the forests near Colombo, filling with black, sultry darkness, would begin to resound mysteriously with murmurings and moanings of countless cicadas and tree toads, and the thickets of bamboo would be aquiver with myriads of fiery sparks.

The Englishman, too, was intoxicated, as he walked out of the hotel with a cigar,—his eyes were drowsy, his

[63]

face, heightened in colour, seemed to have become fuller.
Glancing at his watch from time to time and thinking of
something, apparently not knowing how to kill time,
he stood a while near the hotel in indecision. Then he
ordered himself carried first to the post office, where he
dropped three postal cards into the box, and from the
post office to Gordon's Garden, which he did not even enter,—he simply glanced in at the gates at the monument
and the pathways; and from the garden he went at ran-
dom: to Black Town, to the market place in Black Town,
to the Kellani River. . . . And then he was whirled on
and on, hither and thither, by the intoxicated rickshaw-
man, who was bathed in sweat from head to foot, aroused
both by whiskey and by betel, and by the hope of receiving a whole heap of pennies, and by certain other dreams
that stir the body and soul and that never forsake a man.
At the most oppressive hour of the afternoon heat and
glare, when, after having sat on a bench under a tree
for two minutes one leaves upon it a dark ring of perspiration, he, to please the Englishman, who did not
know what to do until dinner, ran all over Black Town,—
ancient, populous, redolent of spicy odours; and many
naked coloured bodies and many bright stuffs girt about
hips did the sleepy Englishman see; many Parsees, Hin-
dus, yellow faced Malayans; malodorous Chinese shops,
brick-tiled and bamboo-covered roofs, temples, minarets
and idol-temples; sailors from Europe on shore leave, as
well as Buddhistic monks,—shaven, thin, with insane eyes,
clad in canary-coloured toga-like garments, with the right
shoulder bared, and carrying fans made out of the foliage of the sacred palm. Rapidly, rapidly, did the rickshaw-man and his passenger dash through this teeming

density and dirt of the ancient East, as though they were escaping from some one. Up to the very river Kellani did they run,—the narrow, turbid, and deep Kellani, made too warm by the sun, half-covered with impenetrable green overgrowths that bent low from its banks; the river beloved of crocodiles, who retreat farther and farther into the depths of the virgin forests before the barges with straw-thatched arched covers; barges laden with bales of tea, with rice, cinnamon, precious stones still in the rough,—barges floating with especial deliberation in the golden deep glitter of the sun before evening. . . . Then the Englishman gave orders to return to the Fort, by now deserted, with all its offices, agencies and banks closed; he was shaved in a barber shop and grew unpleasantly younger; he bought cigars, dropped into an apothecary's. . . . The rickshaw-man, grown thinner, all bathed in sweat, was by now gazing upon him inimically, with the eyes of a dog that feels attacks of madness coming on. . . . At six o'clock, having run past the lighthouse at the end of Queen's Street, having run through the quiet and clean military streets, he ran out upon the shore of the ocean, that struck his eyes with its freedom, with its glaucously aureate sheen from the low-lying sun, and started running over Gull Face Place toward Slave Island.

"From longing is born the desire for joy," the Exalted One hath said, "from happiness is born sorrow; out of joy and sorrow doth fear arise." And now within the eyes of the rickshaw-man had already appeared sorrow, and fear, and malice. He had grown daft from running, had more than once, with sad weariness, turned around toward his tormentor; he breathed heavily, putting behind him with his long legs the broad, well-laid road of the Place. At the setting of the sun this Place is vast, empty and melancholy. Having done with business, the Englishmen stroll here before dinner, are driven in costly horse equipages, or drive their wives, mistresses, and children; play tennis and football; and admire the ocean and the magnificent beauty of the tropical sunset,—a sunset not like that of their own land. The rickshaw-man ran on, looking wildly upon these sinewy, red-haired men in short white trunks and gay sweaters, who careered over the Place of their own free will, racing after one another with all their might, jumping up after the soaring balls and kicking them resoundingly with the rough tips of their heavy shoes. The sun was sinking; the sky above the setting sun was growing green; a light, downy cloud, that had been lurking in the skyey depths, became entirely roseate. . . . "Carlton Hotel!" in a lifeless voice said the Englishman, who had all the time been sadly and drowsily gazing toward the west, upon the ocean, upon its softly murmurous surge, scattering into heliotrope foam upon the bowlders on shore. . . . The rickshaw-man, as he ran, would bare his teeth; by now he wanted to gnaw this man who had driven him so hard,—but it was impossible not to run: the Englishman, without changing the expression of his drowsily sad face, more and more often prodded the rickshaw-man with the tip of his cane. And besides, the rickshaw's beatific exaltation had already passed into something else,—into a tense submissiveness, into a coma of ceaseless running. All the hotels in the Fort were filled up, and the Englishman lived in a common one beyond Slave Island,—and now the rickshaw-man once more ran past the banyan tree, under which

[66]

he had sat down this very morning in his greed of earning money from these merciless and enigmatic white men, in his obstinate hope of happiness. Once more the familiar gardens, one after another; the stone enclosures; the Dutch-tile roofs of bungalows,—low, squat, by comparison with the trees spreading over them. . . . Having run into the yard of one such bungalow, the rickshaw-man rested for half an hour near the terrace, while the Englishman was changing his clothes for dinner. His heart was pounding like a poisoned man's, his lips had blanched, the features of his dark brown face had grown sharper, his splendid eyes had grown still blacker and wider, the rag upon his head had become so saturated that he snatched it off and flung it far from him. The odour of his heated body had become unpleasant,—it was now the odour of warm tea mixed with cocoanut oil, and some other, spirituous, ingredient, such as would be produced by taking and rubbing a cluster of ants in one's hands.

Meanwhile the sun had set. An elderly maiden was half-lying under the awning of the terrace in a rocker, reading a prayer-book by the remaining daylight. Having caught sight of her from the street, there noiselessly entered the yard a mute Hindu of Madura,—a tall, dark old man, as thin as a skeleton, with gray hair curling upon his chest and abdomen, in a beggar's turban, in a long apron of stuff that had at one time been red and crossed with yellow stripes. Upon his arm the old man carried a closed basket of palm-wattle. Walking up to the terrace, he salaamed subserviently, putting his hand to his forehead, and sat down upon the ground, lifting up the cover of the basket. Without looking at him, the woman reclining in the rocker waved him away with her

[67]

hand. But he was already taking a bamboo flute out of his belt. And at this point the rickshaw-man jumped to his feet, and in an inexplicable fury yelled loudly at him. The old man, too, jumped up, slammed shut the basket, and, turning about, ran toward the gates. But, for a long while, the eyes of the rickshaw-man were round,—altogether as with that fearful creature whom he pictured to himself,—slowly, like a tightly wound cord, crawling out of the basket and hissingly puffing out its throat, that glimmered with a blue sheen.

The darkness was falling rapidly,—it was already dark when the Englishman, freshly laved, came out upon the terrace in his white dinner jacket, and the rickshaw-man submissively darted toward the shafts. The Englishman called out briskly the name of the place he was to run to, —and who knows if his order found no eerie echo in the heart of the rickshaw-man? It was already night, and an exceptionally hot one,—as always before the oncoming of the rainy season; a night still more fragrant than the day. Still denser had grown the warm and cloying aroma of musk, blended with the odour of the warm earth, pinguid with the humus of flowers. It was so dark in the gardens through which the rickshaw-man was running that only by his heavy breathing and by the scanty light of the little lantern upon the shaft, could one gather that he was bearing down upon one. Then, beneath the black canopies of the trees, came the faint glimmering of the rotting lagoon; and next,—red lights lengthily reflected in it. The big two-storied house in which the agent lived shone through and through in this tropical blackness with the openings of its windows. It was dark in the compound. A large number of rickshaw-men, their bodies blending into the darkness and their loin cloths showing dimly white, had come into this compound with those who had been invited. And the large balcony, open toward the lagoon, was aglow with candles in glass chimneys, clustered about with countless thrips; it was dazzling with the cover of the long table, set with china, bottles, and pails of ice, and was white with the dinner jackets of the people sitting at it, who ate, drank, and without a moment's silence, even though restrainedly, spoke deep down in their throats, as bare-footed corpulent servants, that looked like wet-nurses, waited upon them, their bare soles rustling. And an enormous punkah of Chinese matting, attached by one edge to the ceiling, swayed and swayed over their heads, brought into motion by Malayans sitting behind a partition that did not reach to the ceiling, and kept pouring a constant current of air upon the diners, upon their cold and clammy foreheads. Rickshaw-man number seven dashed up to the balcony. Those seated at the table greeted the newly arrived guest with glad murmuring. The guest jumped out of the little carriage and ran up into the balcony. As for the rickshaw-man, he started off at a gallop to go round the house, in order to get again to the gates, into the compound, to the other rickshaws. And, as he was turning the corner of the house, he suddenly recoiled, as though he had been struck with a stick: standing near an open and illuminated window on the second story,— in a small Japanese kimona of red silk, in a triple necklace of rubies, in broad bracelets of gold upon her round arms,—looking upon him with round shining eyes was his bride: that very girl-woman with whom he had agreed, already a half-year back, to exchange balls of rice! She could not see him below, in the darkness. But he had recognized her instantly,—and, having staggered back, stood stock still on the spot.

He did not fall down, his heart did not burst asunder,— it was too young and strong. Having stood for a minute or so, he sat down on the ground, under an age-old fig-tree, whose entire top, like a tree of paradise, burned and flickered with the dust of fiery-green sparks. For a long time did he gaze upon the dark round little head, upon the red silk that loosely embraced the little body, and upon the arms, raised as she patted her hairdress, of her who stood framed in the window. He squatted on his heels until she had turned about and had gone into the recesses of the room. And when she had disappeared he instantly jumped to his feet, caught the shafts that had been lying on the ground, and flew like a bird through the yard and out of the gates; again did he start running, on and on,—this time knowing unerringly whither he was running, and wherefore, and now himself directing his suddenly liberated will.

"Awake, awake!" clamoured within him the thousands of soundless voices of his mournful ancestors, mouldered for hundreds of generations in this paradisaical earth. "Shake off thee the seductions of Mara, the dream of this brief life! Is sleep for thee,—thou who hast been empoisoned with venom, pierced through with an arrow! An hundredfold doth he suffer who hath that which is an hundredfold dear; all sorrows, all complaints, come from love, from the attachments of the heart,—therefore, slay thou them! Not for long shalt thou be in the tranquillity of rest; anew and anew, in a thousand incarnations, shalt thou be put forth by this thy land of

[70]

Eden, the shelter of the first men who had come to know desire. But still this brief rest shall come to thee, thou that hast too early run forth upon the path of life, passionately setting out after happiness, and that hast been wounded by the sharpest of all arrows,—by the yearning for love and for new inceptions in this ancient universe, where from time out of mind the conqueror stands with a heavy sole upon the throat of the conquered!"

The lights of the open air stalls of Slave Island appeared under the canopies of the trees whose tops were interlaced. The rickshaw-man hungrily ate in one of these stalls a small bowl of rice over-spiced with pepper, and then darted on. He knew where the old man from Madura lived, who had an hour ago entered the yard of the hotel: he dwelt with his nephew, at his large fruit store, in a low house with wooden columns. The nephew, in a dirty European suit of duck, with an enormous mane of black twining wool upon his head, was dragging in the baskets of fruits into the interior of the store, his eyes puckering from the smoke of a cigarette that had stuck to his lower lip. He paid no attention to the insane appearance of the perspiring, heated rickshaw-man. And the rickshaw-man silently hopped up under the shelter of the awning, among the pillars, went to the left, and with his foot pushed a small door behind which he hoped to find the old mute. In his perspiring hand he was clutching a treasured gold-piece, which, while he was still running, he had taken out of a leather pouch that hung at his belt, beneath his apron. And the gold-piece speedily did its work. When the rickshaw-man jumped out again, he bore a large cigar box, tied with a cord.

[71]

He had paid a great price for it, but then, it was not empty: that which it contained was struggling, writhing, knocking against the lid with its tensed coils, swishingly.

Why did he take the little carriage along with him? For take it along he did,—and at an even, powerful pace flew for the shore of the ocean, toward Gull Face Place. The place was empty; darkly did it extend into the distance under the light of the stars. Beyond it were scattered the small and infrequent lights of the Fort, and against the sky was slowly turning the watch-tower of the lighthouse, with its reflectors, throwing fumid stripes of white light in the direction of the roadstead only. The rickshaw-man felt a faint cool breeze blowing from the ocean, whose drowsy murmur was barely audible. Having reached at a run the shore, the middle of the road, the rickshaw-man for the last time threw down the slender shafts, into which at such an early age, but not for long, life had harnessed him, and sat down,—this time not upon the ground, but on a bench; sat down without fear, as though he were a white resident.

In giving a whole pound to the Hindu, he had demanded the smallest and the strongest, the most death-bearing one. And it was,—besides having a faery beauty, being all in black rings, with green edgings, with a dark blue rounded head, with an emerald stripe back of its head, and with a funereal tail,—it was, despite its small size, unusually powerful and malignant; but now, after it had been coiled up in a smelly wooden box, it was especially so. It coiled convulsively, like a steel spring; it writhed, rustled, and knocked against the lid of the box. And he rapidly untied, unwound the cord. . . .

However, who knows just how he did it? Were his hands steady, or did they tremble? Was he rapid, resolute, or no? And did he waver long after untying the cord? Did he gaze for long at the murmurous dark ocean, upon the faint starlight, upon the Southern Cross, the Crow, upon Canopus? Did he bare his teeth in a canine snarl in the direction of the residential quarter, in the direction of the rich hotel with its entrance shining in the distance? Most probably, he had at once unhesitatingly opened the box, and had laid his left hand firmly upon those springy coils, icy as a dead body, that were writhing in the box; he was bitten right in the palm.

And that bite is intolerably searing,—it is like the shock of an electric current, and transpierces a man's entire body with untold pain, with such torture that after feeling it even monkeys cry out piteously and burst into sobs,—childish, passionate, despairingly-imploring. The rickshaw-man, most probably, did neither cry out nor burst into sobs; full well did he know what he had set out to do. But there is no doubt that, having felt this fiery shock, he turned a pin-wheel on the bench, and that the box flew aside. And then, instantly, a bottomless darkness spread out beneath him, and all things darted off somewhere upward, obliquely: the ocean, and the stars, and the lights of the hotel. The surging of the ocean went to his head,—and ceased abruptly: a dead faint always occurs after such a shock. But after such a faint a man always comes quickly to himself,—seemingly only to be nauseated, until blood comes, and to be again plunged into non-being. There are several of these death-swoons, and each one of them, breaking a man, making him gasp, tears away human life, in parts:

[73]

thought, memory, vision, hearing, pain, grief, joy, hatred, —and that ultimate, all-embracing thing which is called love, the yearning to encompass within one's heart all the universe, seen and unseen, and to bestow it anew upon some other.

Some ten days later, on a dark, sultry dusk before a thunder-storm, two pair of oarsmen were racing in a small boat through the harbour of Colombo, toward a great Russian steamship that was about to sail for Suez. The passenger whom rickshaw-man number seven had once carried was half-reclining in the boat.   The steamer was already booming with the rattling of the rising anchor chain, when, getting near the enormous iron wall of the ship's side, he ran up the long trap-ladder to the deck.   The captain at first flatly refused to take him on board: the steamer carried freight only, he declared; the agent had already gone away,—the thing was impossible. "But I beg you,—very, very much!" retorted the Englishman.   The captain looked at him with wonder; he was apparently strong, energetic, but there was the tint of an unwholesome tan upon his face, while the eyes behind the glistening spectacles were unmoving, seeming to see nothing, and perturbed.   "Wait until the day after to-morrow," said the captain; "there will be a German mail-packet then."   "Yes, but to spend two more nights at Colombo would be very hard for me," answered the Englishman.   "This climate exhausts me,— my nerves trouble me.   Besides that, the German packet, as is always the case, will be packed to overflowing, whereas I desire to be alone.   I am done up by these

Ceylon nights, by insomnia, and by all that which a nervous man experiences before thunder-storms at dusk. But just glance at this darkness, at these clouds that have obscured the horizon everywhere: the night will again be a horrible one, the rain season has, properly speaking, already set in. . . ." And, with a shrug of his shoulders, upon reflection, the captain gave in. And a minute later the Senegalese, thin as eels, were already dragging up the trap-ladder a trunk covered with shining black leather, all gay with vari-coloured labels and marked with red initials.

The surgeon's vacant cabin, which was put at the disposal of the Englishman, was very small and stuffy; but the Englishman found it splendid. Having hurriedly disposed his things about it, he passed through the dining cabin up to the deck. Everything was rapidly sinking in the darkness. The ship had already weighed anchor and was heading for the open sea. To the right, other ships, with lights on their masts, seemed to be sailing toward them,—these were the lights of the Fort. To the left, under the high taffrail, the shifting level expanse of the dark water rushed toward the low shore, toward the mounds of coal, and the dark density of the groves of slender trunked palms that were beyond the coal mounds. The water still bounded the darkness and the mournfulness of the clouds, and its shifting rapidity made one's head reel. Constantly veering, constantly increasing, a humid, nauseatingly-fragrant wind was blowing from somewhere. The taciturn clouds suddenly burst into such an abysmal pale-blue light, that, lit up by it, in the very depth of the forest, the trunks of the palms and bananas, and the Senegalese huts underneath them,

[75]

flashed upon the vision. The Englishman blinked in affright; he looked over his shoulder upon the pallid jetty with the little red light at the end of it, by now seemingly sailing upon his left; he looked at the leaden-hued ocean in the distance, beyond the jetty,—and quickly started back for his cabin.

The old steward, a man irritated with fatigue, needlessly suspicious and observant, peeped in several times behind the curtain of the Englishman's cabin before dinner. The Englishman was sitting on a folding canvas chair, holding a thick leather-bound note-book on his knees. He was writing in it with a gold-tipped pen, and his expression, whenever he raised his face, his spectacles flashing, was dull, and, at the same time, wondering. Then, having put his pen away, he went off into a brown study, as though he were listening to the surging and swishing of the waves, ponderously rushing by on the other side of the cabin wall. The steward passed by, swinging a clamorous little bell. The Englishman got up and stripped himself naked. Having sponged himself off with water and eau-de-cologne from head to foot, he shaved, clipped evenly his short, bushy moustache, painstakingly smoothed down with military brushes his straight black hair, parting it at a slant, put on fresh linen and his dinner jacket, and went to dinner with his habitual firm, soldierly bearing.

The ship's personnel, who had long since been seated at table and had been swearing at him for his lateness, met him with exaggerated politeness, showing off before one another with their knowledge of English. He responded with a restrained, but not a lesser, politeness, and hastened to add that he liked the Russian cuisine very much, that he had been in Russia, in Siberia. . . . That, in general, he had travelled a great deal, and had always borne up splendidly on his travels, which, however, could not be said of his last stay in India, in Java and Ceylon; here his liver was affected, his nerves were upset,—he had even come to eccentricities: such, for example, as that which he had shown an hour ago when he had so suddenly appeared on the steamer. . . . At coffee he regaled the ship's men with cognac and *liqueurs;* he fetched a box of thick Egyptian cigarettes and put it on the table, open, for common use. The captain, a man still young, with clever and steady eyes, who endeavoured to be a European in all things, began a conversation about the colonial problems of Europe, about the Japanese, about the future of the Far East. Listening attentively, the Englishman objected or agreed. He spoke well, and not at all with simplicity, but as though he were reading aloud from a well-written article. And at times he would suddenly grow quiet, still more attentively trying to catch the swish of the waves beyond the open door. The thunderstorm had been left behind. Long since the chain of Colombo's lights, that for a long while had been playing like diamonds, had sunk into black velvet. Now the steamer was in infinite darkness, in the void of ocean and of night. The dining cabin was situated on deck, under the captain's bridge, and the darkness was etched in an intense black within the open doors and windows: it seemed to be standing and gazing in into the brightly lit dining room. A humid breeze blew out of this darkness,—the humid, free breath of a something free since the start of time,—and its freshness, reaching those seated at table, made them feel the odour of the tobacco smoke, of the hot coffee, and of the liqueurs. But at times the electric light would suddenly fail,—the doors and the windows then became gleaming pale blue quadrangles; the blue abyss of abysses, noiseless and unutterably expansive, spread out around the steamer; the running swell of the watery spaces gleamed; the horizons were flooded with a blackness as of coal,—and thence, like the grievous murmur of the Creator Himself, still plunged in primordial chaos, came to their ears the roll of thunder, —muffled, sombre and triumphant, shaking all things to their foundation. And at such times the Englishman seemed to be frozen on the spot for a moment.

"This is really frightful!" said he in his lifeless but steady voice after a flash especially blinding. And, getting up from his place, he walked up to the door that gaped into the darkness. "Very frightful," said he, as though he were talking to himself. "And the most frightful thing of all is that we do not think do not feel, and cannot, have forgotten how to feel the full frightfulness of this."

"What, precisely?" asked the captain.

"Why, just this for example," answered the Englishman, "that under us and around us is that bottomless depth, that shifting trough of the sea of which the Bible speaks with such awesomeness. . . . Oh," said he sternly, looking intently into the darkness, "both far and near, everywhere, the furrows of foam flare up, flaming with green, and the darkness surrounding this foam is lilac-black, the colour of a raven's wing. . . . Is it a very eerie thing to be a captain?" he asked gravely.

"Why no, not at all," answered the captain with assumed nonchalance. "It's a tiresome business, and responsible, but, in reality not very complicated. . . . It is all a matter of habit. . . ."

"Better say,—of our callousness," said the Englishman. "To be standing there, up on your bridge, at whose sides these two great eyes,—the green and the red, —look out, blurred, through their thick glass, and to be sailing somewhere into the darkness of night and water, extending for thousands of miles around,—it is madness! But, however, it is no better," he added, again glancing out of the door, "it is no better, on the other hand, to be lying below in a cabin, beyond whose exceedingly thin wall, near your very head, beats and rolls this bottomless deep. . . . Yes, yes,—our reason is just as feeble as the reason of a mole; or, rather, still more feeble, for in the case of a mole, of an animal, of a savage, instinct, at least, has been preserved; whereas with us, with Europeans, it has degenerated, is degenerating!"

"However, moles do not navigate over the entire terrestrial globe," answered the captain smiling. "Moles do not enjoy the benefits of steam, of electricity, of wireless telegraphy. Do you wish to hear me speak with Aden right now? And yet it is a ten days' sail from here."

"And that, too, is frightful," said the Englishman, and cast a stern glance through his spectacles at one of the engineers who had started laughing. "Yes, that too is very frightful. For we, in reality, do not fear anything. We do not fear even death properly: neither life, nor sacred mysteries, nor the depths that surround us, nor death,—neither our death nor that of others! I am a colonel of the British Army, a participant of the Boer War; I, commanding cannons to be fired, used to kill men in hundreds; and here I am, not only neither suffer-

[79]

ing nor going out of my mind because I am a murderer, but never even thinking of these hundreds."

"What about the beasts, and the savages,—do they think of such things?" asked the captain.

"The savages believe that things have to be so, whereas we don't," said the Englishman, and became silent; he started pacing the dining room, trying to step as firmly as he could in his dancing shoes.

The flashes of the distant thunder storm, gleaming roseately over the stars, were by now decreasing. The wind blowing through the windows and doors was stronger and cooler, the impenetrable darkness beyond the door surged more loudly. A large sea-shell that served as an ash-tray was sliding upon the table. Under one's feet, growing unpleasantly weaker, one felt something gathering force below, lifting one up, then falling over on one side, spreading out,—and the floor fell deeper and deeper from under one's feet. The ship's men, having finished their coffee and smoked their fill, sat in silence for several minutes more, casting glances at their queer passenger; then, wishing him good-night, they began picking up their caps. The captain alone stayed on,—he was smoking and following the Englishman with his eyes. The Englishman, with a cigar, was walking, swayingly, from door to door; his dark complexion, his spectacles, and his seriousness combined with absent-mindedness, irritated the old steward, who was clearing the table.

"Yes, yes," said the Englishman, "there is only one thing frightful to us,—that we have forgotten how to feel fear! There is no God, no religion in Europe, long since; we, with all our business activity and greed, are as cold as ice both toward life and toward death. Even if

[80]

we do fear death, it is with our reason or only with the remnants of an animal instinct. At times we even try to inspire ourself with that dread, to exaggerate it,—and still we do not respond, do not feel in due measure those incomprehensible and horrible things of which the life of man is full. . . . Just as I, even I, do not now feel that which I myself have called fearful," said he, pointing toward the open door, beyond which the impenetrable darkness murmured, by now raising high the prow, and tumbling the ship, all of whose partitions were creaking, from one side to the other.

"It is Ceylon that has affected you so," said the captain mechanically.

"Oh, beyond a doubt, beyond a doubt!" agreed the Englishman. "We all,—commercial men, mechanical engineers, military men, politicians, colonizers,—we all, fleeing from our own dullness and vanity, wander all the world over; for you will agree that the number of travelling Europeans is increasing with a magic rapidity; that the entire terrestrial globe is plastered over with motley placards and time-tables. And we try with all our might to be enraptured, now with the mountains and lakes of Switzerland, now with the pauperism of Italy,—her pictures and the broken-up fragments of her statues and columns. Or we wander over the slippery stones which have survived from some amphitheatres in Sicily, or we gaze with simulated delight upon the yellow heaps of rubble at the Acropolis in Greece; or attend, as though it were some show-booth spectacle at a fair, the distribution of the sacred fire in Jerusalem. We pay sums unheard of in order to undergo tortures from guides and fleas in the tombs and clay idol-temples of Egypt. We sail to

[81]

India, to China, to Japan,—and it is only here, upon the soil of the most ancient of mankind, in this Eden which we have forfeited, which we style our colonies and which we covetously despoil, in the midst of squalor, bubonic plague, cholera, fevers, and coloured races whom we have turned into cattle,—only here do we feel, in some slight measure, life, death, godhood. Here, after having remained indifferent toward all these Osirises, Zeuses, Appolons, toward Christ, toward Mahomet, have I more than once felt that I might perhaps have bowed only before them,—these fearful Gods of this cradle of mankind: before the hundred-armed Brahma; before Siva; before the Devil; before Buddha, whose word verily rang forth like the utterance of Methuselah himself, driving nails into the coffin-lid of the universe. . . . Yes, thanks only to the East, and to the diseases contracted in the East; thanks to the fact that in Africa I slaughtered men by the hundreds; that in India, which is being despoiled by England, and, therefore, in part by me, I have seen thousands dying from hunger; that I had bought little girls in Japan to be my wives for a month; that in China I had beaten defenseless, simian old men over their heads with a stick; that in Java and Ceylon I had driven rickshaw-men until I heard the death rattle in their throats; that I had, in my time, contracted a most cruel fever in Anaradhapore, and liver trouble on the shore of Malabar,—only thanks to all this do I still feel and think, after a fashion. Those lands, those countless peoples, which still either live a life of infantile immediacy, sentient with all their beings of existence, and death, and the divine majesty of the universe; or those lands and peoples which have already traversed a long and arduous

path (historical, religious and philosophical), and who
have grown wearied on this path,—such lands and peoples
we, the men of the new age of iron, aspire to enslave, to
divide amongst us, and this we style our colonial problems. And when this division shall come to an end,
then on this world will again be enthroned the might of
some new Tyre or Sidon, a new Rome, English or German. There will be repeated, inevitably repeated, also
that which had been prophesied by Judæan prophets to
Sidon, that, according to the word of the Bible, had
grown to deem itself God; that which had been prophesied to Rome by the Apocalypse; and to India, to the
Aryan tribes that had enslaved it, by Buddha, who has
said, 'O ye princes, ye men in power, rich in treasures,
who have arrayed your covetousness against one another,
insatiably pandering to your lusts! . . .' Buddha understood the significance of the life of Individuality in this
'world of having been,' in this universe, whose meaning
we cannot attain to, and he was horrified with a sacred
horror. Whereas we exalt our Individuality above the
heavens; we want to centre all the world within it, no
matter what may be said of the coming universal brotherhood and equality. And so it is only on the ocean, under
stars new and foreign to us, in the midst of the majesty
of tropical thunder storms; or in India, in Ceylon, where
history is so immeasurable, where at times one glimpses
life veritably primitive, and where on dark, sultry nights,
in the fevered gloom, one feels man melting, dissolving
in this blackness, in these sounds, scents, in this fearful
All-Oneness,—only there do we in a slight measure grasp
the meaning of this our pitiful Individuality. . . . Do
you know," said he, halting again, and flashing his

[83]

spectacles at the captain, "a certain Buddhistic legend?"

"Which one?" asked the captain, who had already yawned surreptitiously and had glanced at his watch.

"Why, this: A raven darted after an elephant who was running down a wooded mountain toward the sea; wrecking all things in his path, breaking down the overgrowths, the elephant plunged into the waves,—and the raven, tortured by 'desire,' fell after him, and, having waited until the elephant had swallowed enough water to kill himself and had floated up on the waves, descended on the carcass with its great ears; the carcass floated on, putrefying, while the raven greedily pecked away at it; but when he came to his senses, he saw that he had been borne far, far from land,—to a distance from which there is no return even upon the wings of a gull, —and he began cawing in a piteous voice, that voice for which Death waits so warily. . . . It is a terrible legend!"

"Yes, it is very significant," said the captain, indifferently.

The Englishman lapsed into silence and again began pacing from door to door. From the surging darkness faintly floated in the sounds of the second bell, abrupt and, as is always the case on the ocean, plaintive. The captain, after having sat for five minutes more out of politeness, got up, shook the Englishman's hand, and went off to his big, restful cabin. The Englishman, reflecting upon something, continued pacing. The steward, having endured for half an hour more in the pantry, entered and with an angry face began switching off the electricity, leaving only one bulb lit. The Englishman, when the steward had disappeared, walked up to the wall and turned off this bulb as well. Darkness descended at once, the surging of the waves at once appeared louder, and the starry sky, the masts, the sail-yards at once appeared in the open windows. The steamer creaked and clambered from one watery mountain to another. It swung wider and wider, rising and falling, —and in its rigging Canopus, the Crow, the Southern Cross swayed widely to and fro, now flying toward the abyss above, now toward the abyss below, and roseate auroras were still flashing above them.

1914.

GAUTAMI

THIS is a tale thrice beautiful in its brevity and un-
pretentiousness, its meaning and the manner of its
telling; a tale of the love of Gautami, the saintly
and the beatified, who, without knowing it herself, did
come under the sheltering shadow of the Blessed One.

Thus have we heard it told:

In a populous hamlet, in a felicitous region, at the
foot of the great Himalayas, in a family poor but worthy,
was Gautami born.

She was tall of stature and rather lean at first sight;
swarthy and pleasant of face was she, and simple and
unpretentious of soul,—therefore did the neighbours bestow an unkind by-name upon her. "Gautami the Lean"
did they nickname her, but she took no offense thereat.
And every order did she obey, and to every order she
made such answer as:

" 'Tis well, dear master; I shall do so. 'Tis well, dear
mistress, I shall do so."

For may plain speech be forgiven us,—not of the wisest
among men and women was Gautami. But neither did
she utter anything foolish,—perhaps because she did not
say much, and laboured at something from morning till
night. And the raiment upon her was always poor, and
always, always the same, but always neat. And so one
day a youth, truly rich and handsome, the son of the great
king of that region, did behold her upon a river bank,

[86]

when she was washing the linen of her sisters and brothers, and he comprehended that she was sensible and submissive, and that there was none to take her part, —not even her parents.

Thus did he think:

" 'There is no help for it,' her parents will say; 'Gautami is not of the wisest, Gautami is not pretty to look upon; she does not resemble a daughter of ours, but rather a servant,— who shall take her to wife? Sooner or later, she shall submit to some man who may desire her,— for Gautami is incapable of refusing. Ah, if only this man prove not without pity, and will give away, to be rightly brought up, the child that will be born of her!' "

Thus did the king's son think.

As for Gautami, having washed and rinsed the linen, she squatted down upon her heels over the water glistening in the sun; having taken off all her raiment, she did swathe all her body from the arm-pits to the knees in an old piece of cloth, and, having spread her long black hair, began to clean her white teeth with a wetted, splintered little stick, began to wash her swarthy limbs, not knowing that the king's son was watching her from behind the clumps of bamboo. And thereupon he did call out to her, and, walking up to her, told her with a smile, yet not unkindly:

"Thou art endearing, Gautami, and not at all as lean as they say you are,—a maid clad in simple raiment, and of tall stature, is often misjudged. I have heard, Gautami, that thou art submissve. Do not resist me, therefore; none shall see our caresses at this sultry hour, near the deserted river."

And Gautami was abashed before him, before his assurances that his wishes were righteous, and she did whisper in answer:

" 'Tis well, dear master; let it be as thou dost will."

And the king's son, having had his joyance of her, saw that she was better than she had seemed, and that her dark eyes, although they were not expressive of thought, and somehow seemed always the same, were never the less full of enchantment. And after that their meetings upon the bank of the river, within the grove of bamboos, became frequent, and so it was that, whenever the king's son would order Gautami to come to him, she always would come, never disobeying; nor did her submissiveness and charm change with the intimacy of their bodies; nor her agreeable manner when their conversation was brief. And when the ordained time had run, she felt herself heavy with child.

Thereupon did the king's son take her as one of his concubines, transferring her with her poor little kit, wherein she kept her modest belongings, the sorry savings of a maiden who works, into his opulent palace, and she lived in the palace until her time was come.

And when her day had approached, one of the king's stewardesses did say to her:

"Gautami! A wife who is about to become a mother goeth to the house of her father to give birth, in fulfillment of the custom. But thou art no wife, but a concubine. Go not therefore to the house of thy parents; but also do not thou transgress against that which is seemly."

And Gautami, having salaamed before her, got up, and went out of the gate of the clay walls that enclosed the palace.

And, having passed over the wooden bridge that spanned a muddy canal, which was near by, she saw one who sat under a tree, with a bowl in his hand,—a blind and an ancient beggar, girt only about his middle with a dirty rag, whereas his arms, his legs, his bosom and his withered, glistening back he had exposed to the blazing sun and the flies.

And the beggar raised his sightless face, hearkening to her steps, and he smiled with the tender and poignant smile of the wisdom of old men.

"Gautami!" spake he to her. "I see thee not but I feel thy approach. Gautami, may thy path be blessed!"

And she kissed the knee of the beggar and went on upon her way; and upon her way, in the hot, sun-filled groves, among the satin trees, she did give birth to her child before its time.

And blissfully, having rested with tears of happiness after her sore travail, she returned with the child in her arms into the palace of the prince and gave full rein to her ceaseless ecstasy and tender delight, to an emotion of bodily love for the new-born, to the delectable disquiet of seeing, scenting, touching, and pressing to her bosom this growing being, that with every day became more and more awake to thought and consciousness.

"My soul hath recalled thee!"—these words had not been uttered by the prince to Gautami when he had become as one with her, even though she had been dear to him, even though they had borne her to the palace of the king with music, upon bullocks adorned with ribbands and flowers, having arrayed her as for a bridal, dressing her black hair smoothly, putting rouge on her cheeks, and blackening her eye-lashes with kohl.

And Gautami, having given birth to the child, received submissively the youth's having grown cold toward her, and removed herself from his sight, that he might not feel troubled and guilty upon meeting her by chance.

And, remaining within the enclosure of the palace, she settled in a simple hut on the banks of the ponds, taking upon herself the duty of feeding the swans that swam in those ponds among the grasses and flowers.

And for a time she was happy, preparing, without herself knowing it, for those great sorrows which were destined to come in ordained replacement of this happiness, and to put her upon the sole true path, into the society of the religious brotherhood of those that go clad in yellow.

Blessed are the meek at heart, who have riven their chain.

In an abode of the highest joy do we dwell, who love nothing in this universe, and like to a bird are we, that beareth nothing with it but its wings.

1919.

M ME. MAROT had been born and had grown up
in Lausanne, in a strict, honest, and industrious
family. She did not marry early, but when
she did, hers was a love match. In the March of 1876,
among the passengers of the old French steamer
Auvergne, sailing from Marseilles to Italy, was a newly
married couple. The days were calm, cool; the sea, all
silvery mirrors, lost itself in the misty spring distances;
the newly-married couple scarcely ever left the deck.
And all admired them, all beheld their happiness with
amiable smiles: he showed his happiness in an alert,
keen glance, in the necessity for motion, in an animated
amiability to all those around him; she, by that joyous
interest, with which she assimilated every trifle. . . .
This newly married pair was the Marots.

He was some ten years her senior; he was short in
height, swarthy of face, with curly hair; his hand was thin,
and his voice sonorous. But in her one sensed an ad-
mixture of some blood other than that of the Latins.
She seemed just the least trifle too tall, although her waist
was splendid; though her hair was dark, her eyes were
a grayish blue. They travelled through Naples, Palermo
and Tunis to the Algerian town of Constantine, where
Monsieur Marot had obtained a rather prominent ap-
pointment. And life in Constantine those fourteen years
which had passed since that happy spring, had given

them everything with which people are usually content: a competance, domestic harmony, healthy and handsome children.

During these fourteen years the Marots had changed very much in appearance: his face had become as black as an Arab's, he had grown gray and dried up from work, from travelling, from tobacco, and from the sun, —many took him for a native of Algeria; nor would any one have recognized her as the woman who had been a passenger upon the steamer *Auvergne:* then, even in the shoes she put outside the door at night, there had been the enchantment of youth; now she too had glints of silver in her hair, her skin had grown finer and more aureate, her hands had become thinner, and in her care of them, in the dressing of her hair, in her linen, in her apparel, she already betrayed a certain superfluous nicety. Their relations had changed as well, of course, although none would have said that it was for the worse. And each one led an individual existence: his time was taken up with work,—he still remained as passionate, and, at the same time, as sober a man as he had been before; she had to take care of him, of the children— two very pretty girls, of whom the elder was by now almost a young lady,—and everybody unanimously declared that there was not in all Constantine a better housekeeper, a better mother, or a more charming person to chat with in a drawing room, than Mme. Marot.

Their house stood on a quiet and clean street. From the second story, out of the front rooms, always in semi-darkness on account of the closed Venetian blinds, could be seen Constantine, famed all over the world for its picturesqueness: this ancient Arabian stronghold, which had become a French city, lies upon sloping crags. The windows of the living rooms, shady and cool, looked out upon the garden,—there, in a perpetual blaze and glare, dozed age-old eucalypti, sycamores, palms, behind their enclosures of high walls. The master of the house frequently absented himself on matters connected with his work. As for the mistress, she led that confined existence to which, in the colonies, the wives of all Europeans are condemned. On Sundays she invariably attended church. On week days she rarely went out and restricted herself to a small, choice circle. She read, busied herself with embroidery, chatted with the children or took part in their lessons; sometimes, putting the dark-eyed Marie, her younger daughter, on her knees, and playing on the pianoforte with one hand, she would sing old-fashioned French songs, to make the long African day seem shorter, while the hot wind entered in a flood from the garden through the wide-open windows. . . . Constantine, under the pitiless blaze of the sun and with all its shutters closed, seemed at these hours a dead city: only the roller-birds called out behind the walls of the gardens, and plaintively, with the nostalgia of colonial lands, sounded the trumpets of the buglers on the knolls beyond the city, where at times the cannons made the earth shake with a dull rumble, and one saw the white helmets of the soldiers twinkling.

The days in Constantine passed monotonously, but no one ever remarked that Mme. Marot was oppressed by this. In her character, exquisite and chaste, never appeared any heightened sensitiveness, nor any surplus nervousness. Her health could not be called robust, but it never caused any alarm to Monsieur Marot. Only

[93]

one incident had struck him: once, in Tunis, an Arab magician had put her so rapidly into a profound sleep, that she had great difficulty in coming back to herself. But this had been still at the time of their journey from France; since that time she had not experienced any such sharp declines of will power, any such unwholesome susceptibility. And Monsieur Marot was happy, tranquil, and convinced that her soul was undisturbed and like an open book to him. And so it really was, even during the last—the fourteenth—year of his domestic life. . . . But now there appeared in Constantine a certain Emile du Buys.

Emile du Buys, son of Mme. Bonnet, an old and close friend of the Marots, was only nineteen years of age. Mme. Bonnet, the widow of an engineer, had also a daughter, Eliza, besides Emile, who was born of the first marriage. He had grown up in Paris and was already reading law; but, above all, he was taken up with the composition of verses which were comprehensible to him alone, and had attached himself to a non-existent school of poetry, "The Seekers." In the May of 1889 Eliza was preparing for the altar, but took sick and died a few days after. Emile, who had never up to now been in Constantine, had come for the funeral. It is easy to understand how touched Mme. Marot was by this death, —this death of a girl who was already trying on the bridal veil; everyone also knows how under such circumstances intimacy is established even between people who have scarce come to know one another. In addition, Emile was in reality only a boy to Mme. Marot. Shortly after the funeral, Mme. Bonnet went to France, to her relatives. Emile remained in Constantine, at the suburban county house of his late stepfather,—at the Villa Hassim, as it was called in the town,—and began to visit the Marots almost daily. No matter what sort of a chap he may have been, or whatever he may have pretended to be, he was, never the less, very young, very sensitive, and had need of people with whom he might seek shelter for a time. "And isn't it strange," said some, "Mme. Marot has become unrecognizable! How animated she has become; how she has improved in looks!"

However, these allusions were unfounded. At first all it amounted to was that her existence became a trifle gayer, and that her girls became more playful and coquettish, for Emile, every minute forgetting his grief and that virus with which, as he thought, the *fin de siècle* had envenomed him, fussed for hours at a time with them, altogether as their equal. Of course he was, after all, a man, a Parisian, and not altogether of an ordinary nature; he had participated in that life which Parisian writers lead, so inaccessible to common mortals; frequently, with a certain somnambulistic expressiveness, he would read strange but sonorous verses; and, perhaps, it was precisely thanks to him that the step of Mme. Marot became lighter and quicker, her house apparel just the least trifle smarter, and the nuances of her voice kindlier and more mocking; there may have been, after all, a drop of purely feminine joy in her soul over the fact that here was a man whom it was possible to lord it over somewhat, with whom it was possible to speak with a half jesting sententiousness, with that freedom which was so naturally permitted by the difference in their years. And also over the fact that here was one who was so devoted to her entire household,—where,

however, the first person for him (this, of course was
revealed very quickly) was still none other than she.
But then, how commonplace all this is! Yet for the
most part he was merely pitiful to her.

He, who sincerely deemed himself a poet born, wanted
to resemble a poet in appearance as well; he wore his
hair long, and tossed back; he dressed with an artistic
sobriety; he had fine brown hair, which went well with
his pale face, just as his black clothes did; but this pallor
was too anæmic, with a yellow tinge; his eyes glittered
constantly, but, because of his enervated face, they
seemed feverish; and his chest was so thin and flat, his
legs were so thin, his hands so bony, that one became
somewhat ill at ease when he would grow immoderately
lively and would run through the street or garden, bending somewhat forward, as though he were sliding, in
order to hide his defect,—he had one leg shorter than
the other. In society he was disagreeable, supercilious;
he tried to be enigmatic, negligent; or, at times, exquisitely impertinent, audacious, at others disdainfully
absent-minded and independent in all things; but only
too frequently he did not sustain his rôles to the end,—
he would forget his part and begin speaking with a certain naïve candour and impulsiveness. And, of course,
he could not manage to hide his feelings for long, to
dissemble as an unbeliever in love and happiness on this
earth: the entire house soon knew of his being in love.
He had already begun to bore the master of the house
with his visits; he began to bring, every day, bouquets
of the rarest flowers from his villa, to sit at the Marots'
from morn till night, to recite verses more and more incomprehensible,—the children heard him, more than

once, adjuring some one to die with him; while at nights he took to disappearing in the native quarters, in those dives where the Arabs, wrapped up in their dirty white *bournouses*, avidly watch stomach dances and drink the most pungent of liquors. . . . To put it briefly, not even a month and a half had gone before his inamoration had passed into God only knows what.

His nerves ceased entirely to serve him. Once he sat through almost an entire day in silence; then got up, took his hat, and went out,—and half an hour later was brought in from the street in a dreadful condition: he was writhing in hysterics; he was sobbing so vehemently that he frightened both the children and the domestics. But Mme. Marot, it seemed, did not attach any special significance even to this transport. She herself was restoring him back to consciousness, herself hastily untying his cravat and persuading him to be a man, and she only smiled when he, without any restraint whatsoever before her husband, caught at her hands, covering them with kisses and vowing his disinterested devotion. Still, it was necessary to put an end to all this. And so when Emile, whom the children had soon missed, again made his appearance several days after the fit, already calmed, even though he resembled a man who had gone through a severe illness, Mme. Marot gently told him all that is usually said in such cases.

"My friend, you are really like a son to me," she had said to him, uttering for the first time this word, "son," and really feeling almost a maternal tenderness toward him. "Do not, then, put me in a ridiculous and painful position."

"But I swear to you that you are mistaken!" he ex-

[97]

claimed, with earnest vehemence. "I am only devoted to you; I only want to see you, and no more!"

And he suddenly fell down on his knees,—they were in the garden on a calm, sultry, dusky evening,—impulsively seized her by the hips, on the verge of fainting from passion. . . . And gazing upon his hair, upon his white, slender neck, she, with anguish and rapture, reflected:

"Ah,—yes, yes, I could have had a son almost the same as he!"

Still, from that time until his very departure for France, he committed no more insane actions. Essentially this was bad; it may have signified that his passion had become deeper. But outwardly everything had changed for the better,—only one other time he could not restrain himself. After dinner one Sunday, in the presence of several strangers, he said to her, without at all reflecting that this might attract attention:

"I most earnestly entreat you to grant me one minute. . . ."

She got up and went with him into the empty, half-dark parlour. He walked up to the window, through which the evening light penetrated from outside in narrow longitudinal streaks, and, looking her straight in the face, said:

"To-day is the anniversary of my father's death. I love you!"

She turned to go away. Frightened, he hastened to add as she was going away:

"Forgive me,—this is the first time and the last!"

And truly, she heard no new admissions from him. "I was enchanted by her confusion," he wrote in his diary that evening, in his choice and grandiloquent style; "I vowed to violate her peace no more: for am I not beatified even as it is?" He continued going into the town,— he only slept at the Villa Hassim; and his behaviour varied, but he always observed a greater or lesser degree of seemliness. At times he was, as formerly, inappropriately playful, naïve, romping with the children in the garden; most frequently of all, however, he sat near her and "drank in her presence," read newspapers and novels to her, and "was happy because she listened to him." "The children did not interfere with us," he wrote of these days, "their voices, laughter, bustle, their very beings, seemed to serve as the finest of conductors for our emotions; thanks to them these emotions were still more enchanting; we held the commonest of every day conversations, but something else could be heard in them,— our happiness; yes,—yes; she, too was happy, I affirm this. She liked to hear me declaim; of evenings, from the balcony, we contemplated Constantine lying at our feet in the blue radiance of the moon. . . ." Finally, in August, Mme. Marot insisted upon his going away, returning to his studies,—and won; and *en route* he entered in his diary: "I am going away! Going away, empoisoned by the bitter delight of parting! She has bestowed upon me, in parting, a bit of velvet ribbon that she had worn about her neck as a girl. When the last minute came, she gave me her blessing, and I saw a humid sparkle in her eyes when she said: 'Farewell, dear son of mine! . . .'"

Whether he was right in his conjecture that Mme. Marot also was happy in August, is not known. But that his departure proved painful to her is beyond a doubt. This word "son," which had stirred her even previously, now took on such a sound for her that she could not hear it in peace. Even formerly, upon meeting friends on her way to church, who would jestingly say to her: "What should you pray about, Mme. Marot; you are without sin and happy as it is!" she had, more than once, replied with a sad smile: "I complain to God because he has deprived me of a son. . . ." Now the thought of a son, of that happiness which he would have ceaselessly given her by his mere existence in this world, never left her. And once, shortly after the departure of Emile, she had said to her husband:

"Now I have comprehended everything! I now know surely, that every mother ought to have a son; that every woman who has no son, if she will but ponder upon herself, will check up her entire life, will see that she is unhappy. You are a man, you cannot feel this, but it is so. . . . Oh, how tenderly and passionately one can love a son!"

She was very kind to her husband that fall. Occasionally, when she would be left alone with him, she would shyly say to him:

"Hector, listen. . . . I am ashamed now to ask you about it,—but still. . . . Do you ever recall the March of 'seventy-six? . . . Ah, if only you and I had a son!"

"All this confused me very much," Monsieur Marot would say subsequently,—"it confused me all the more because she began to grow very thin. She was growing weaker, was becoming more and more silent and gentle in manner. She went less and less often to her friends, —she avoided going to the city unless it were unavoidable. . . . I do not doubt that some dreadful and incomprehensible ailment was taking possession of her soul and body!" While the *bonne* added that, whenever Mme. Marot went out of the house that fall, she always put on a thick white veil,—something she had never done before; that, returning home, she would immediately raise her veil in front of a mirror and would intently scrutinize her tired face. It is superfluous to explain that which went on in her soul at this time. But did she want to see Emile, did he write to her, and did she reply to him? He presented two dispatches at court, purporting to be addressed to him, in answer to his letters. One was dated the tenth of November: "You are driving me mad. Calm yourself. Let me have immediate news of yourself." The other, the twenty-third of December: "No, no, do not come, I implore you. Think of me, love me, as a mother." But the certainty of these dispatches having been sent by her could not be proven, of course. One thing only is certain,—that from September until January Mme. Marot led a distressed, troubled, painful existence.

The late autumn of that year in Constantine was cold and rainy. Then, as is always the case in Algeria, a ravishing spring came on. And an animation,—that beatific, exquisite headiness which is experienced at the time of the blossoming of spring by people who have already left their youth behind them,—again began to return to Mme. Marot. She again began to go out; rode out a great deal with her children, went with them to the garden of the deserted Villa Hassim; she contemplated an excursion to Algiers,—to show her children Blidah, near which, in the mountains, there is a wooded ravine, a spot beloved of monkeys. . . . And so things went right up to the seventeenth of January in the year of 1890. On the seventeenth of January, she awoke from some unusually joyous and tender emotion, which, so it had seemed to her, had stirred her all night long. In the large room where she slept alone during the absence of her husband, who had gone away for a long time on matters connected with his post, it was almost dark because of the Venetian blinds and the window curtains. Still, by that blueish pallor which penetrated from behind them, one could gather that it was still early. And, in confirmation, the little clock on the night-table pointed to six. With an enjoyable sense of the morning freshness entering from the garden, she rolled up in a light blanket and turned to the wall. . . . "Why do I feel so fine?" she thought, dozing off. And, like dim, beautiful visions, pictures of Italy, of Sicily, began to appear before her, pictures of that distant spring when she was sailing in a cabin whose windows looked out on deck, upon the chill silvery shimmer of the sea; a cabin with portieres of red silk, shrivelled and faded by time, and with a high threshold glittering with brass that had been worn down by many years of cleaning. . . . Then she saw the limitless bays of the sea; lagoons; lowlands; a great Arabian town, all white, with flat roofs, and with undulating mistily blue knolls and foot-hills beyond it. This was Tunis, in which she had been but once, on that very same spring when she had been in Naples, and in Palermo. . . . But here a wave of cold seemed to go through her,—and, with a shiver, she opened her eyes. It was already going on nine o'clock; one could hear the voices of the children, the voice of their *bonne*. She arose, threw on a *peignoir*, and, stepping out on the balcony, descended into the garden and sat down on a rocker, standing in the sand near a round table underneath a mimosa in blossom, spreading its golden canopy overhead, its fragrance heavy in the sun. The maid brought her coffee. She again began to think of Tunis, and recalled that strange experience she had gone through, that sweet fear and that beatific abnegation of her will which was like that of pre-mortal moments,—an experience she had undergone in that pale blue city in the warm, rosy dusk, half-reclining in a rocker on the roof of a house, vaguely seeing the dark face of the Arab hypnotist and magician who was squatting on his heels before her, lulling her to sleep with his barely audible, monotonous sing-song, and the slow movements of his thin hands. And suddenly, even as she was thinking thus and mechanically gazing with eyes wide-open upon a bright silvery spark with which a teaspoon in a glass of water was aflame, she suddenly lost conscience. And when she came to with a start, Emile was standing over her. All that took place subsequent to this unexpected meeting is known from the words of Emile himself,—from his story, from his answers to interrogations. "Yes, I dropped into Constantine as though from heaven!" he had said. "I had come because I had comprehended that the powers of heaven itself could not stop me. On the morning of the seventeenth of January, straight from the station, without any word of warning, I appeared at the house of Monsieur Marot and ran into the garden. I was dumbfounded by that which met my eyes; but I had scarce made a step when she came to. She, it seemed, was also amazed, both by the unexpectedness of my appearance, and that which she had just been through; but she did not even emit an exclamation. Having looked at me, like a person just awakened from a deep sleep, she got up from her seat, putting her hair in order.

" 'That's the very presentiment I had,' she said, somehow without any expression. 'You did not obey me!'

"And with an accustomed gesture, having buttoned the *peignoir* at her breast, she took my head in both her hands and kissed me twice on the forehead.

"I lost my head from rapture and passion, but she gently put me aside and said:

" 'Let us go; I am not dressed,—I shall return at once, go to the children. . . .'

" 'But, for God's sake, what was the matter with you?' I asked, ascending after her to the balcony.

" 'Oh, a mere nothing—a slight trance. I had gazed too long at a glittering tea-spoon,' she was answering, getting control of herself, and beginning to speak with more animation. 'But what have you done, what have you done!'

"I did not find the children anywhere; the house was empty and quiet; I sat down in the parlour. Suddenly I heard her begin singing in a distant room in a strong, sonorous voice, but I did not then comprehend all the horror of that sound, because I was all atremble with a nervous ague. I had not slept all night; I had counted the minutes as the train had sped me toward Constantine; I jumped into the first *fiacre* I had met upon running out of the depot; I did not expect to reach the height of the city. . . . I knew, I, too, had a premonition, that my arrival would be fatal for us; but still I could not expect that which I had seen in the garden, this mystical meeting, and such a sharp change in her attitude toward

[104]

me! After ten minutes, she came out with her hair dressed, in a light-gray dress of an iris tint.

"'Ah,' said she, as I was kissing her hand, 'but I had forgotten that to-day is Sunday, and that the children are in church; but then, I have over-slept. . . . The children will go to the pine grove after church,—were you ever there?'

"And, without waiting for my answer, she rang, ordered some coffee to be served to me, and, sitting down, began to look at me intently, and, without listening, began to question me as to how I had lived, what I had been doing. She started to speak about herself, of the fact that after two or three months, which had been very bad for her, during which she had aged dreadfully,—these words were uttered with sort of incomprehensible smile,—she was feeling well, as young as never before. . . . I replied, I listened, but did not understand a great deal; both of us said anything but that which we wanted to say; my hands grew chill from the nearness of that other fearful, inevitable hour. I do not deny that I was struck as if by lightning when she had said 'I have aged. . . .' I suddenly saw that she was right: in the thinness of her hands, and of the faded, even though really rejuvenated face, in the slenderness of certain outlines of the body, I caught certain signs of that which compels our hearts to contract so painfully, and even somehow awkwardly,—yet all the more passionately,—at the sight of an aging woman. 'Ah, yes, how rapidly and sharply she had changed!' I reflected. But she was beautiful, never the less. I was growing intoxicated as I gazed upon her. I had grown accustomed to dreaming of her without end; I had not forgotten that moment, when on

[105]

the evening of the eleventh of July, I had first embraced her knees. Her hands, too, were slightly trembling, when she was putting her *coiffure* in order, smiling, and gazing at me; and suddenly—you will understand all the catastrophic force of this moment!—suddenly, this smile was distorted, somehow; and, with difficulty, but firmly, she uttered:

" 'Still, you ought to go home, to rest up from the journey; your appearance is dreadful; you have such suffering, fearful eyes and such burning lips, that I no longer have the strength to see them. . . . Do you wish me to?—I shall go there in your company. . . .'

"And, without letting me answer, she got up and went away to get her hat and cloak. . . .

"We arrived quickly at the Villa Hassim. I lingered near the entrance, in order to pluck some flowers. She did not wait for me, opening the door herself. I had no servants; there was only the caretaker,—he did not see us. When I stepped into the ante-room, hot and half dark because of the closed Venetian blinds, and offered her the flowers, she kissed them, then embracing me with one hand, she kissed me. From emotion her lips were hot, but her voice was clear.

" 'But listen . . . how shall we . . . have you anything with you?' she asked.

"I did not at first understand her,—so had this first kiss, this first familiar 'you' overwhelmed me,—and I mumbled:

" 'What do you want to say?'

"She took a step back.

" 'What!' she said in astonishment, almost sternly.

'Can you possibly have thought that I . . . that we can live after this? Have you anything with you that we may die?'

"I recovered my wits and hastened to show her a revolver loaded with five bullets, with which I never parted.

"She rapidly went on, from room to room. The semi-darkness was everywhere. Hearing only the rustle of her silken skirts, I followed after her, with that confusion of all the senses with which a naked man goes on a sultry day into the sea. Finally we arrived at the end of our journey; she threw off her cloak and began to untie the ribbons of her hat. Her hands were still trembling, and once more I remarked through the dusk something pitiful and tired in her face. . . .

"But she died without wavering. During the last moments she became transformed. Kissing me, and leaning back in order to see my face, she told me, in a whisper, a few words so tender and touching that I have not the strength to repeat them.

"I wanted to go to pluck some more flowers, in order to strew our funeral couch with them. She did not let me, she was hurried, she was saying: 'No, no, it is not necessary . . . there are plenty of flowers . . . here are your flowers'—and she kept on repeating:

" 'And so, I charge you, by all that you hold sacred, that you kill me!'

" 'Yes, and then myself,' said I, not for a second doubting my resolution.

" 'Oh, I believe you, I believe you!' she answered, by now as if in a trance. . . .

[107]

"A minute before her death she said, very quietly, but simply: 'My God, this is a deed without a name!'

"And again:

"'Where are the flowers you gave me? Kiss me—for the last time.'

"She herself put the muzzle of the revolver up to her temple. I wanted to shoot, but she stopped me:

"'No, that isn't right,—let me show you the right way. Here, so, my child. . . . And *afterward* make the sign of the cross over me, and lay the flowers upon my breast. . . .'

"When I fired, she moved her lips slightly. I fired once more. . . .

"She lay there, calm; in her extinguished gaze there was some bitter beatitude. Her hair was spread out; a tortoise shell comb was thrown upon the floor. Swaying, I got up, to put an end to myself. But, despite the Venetian blinds, it was light in the room; and in this light, and amid this quiet which had suddenly arisen all about me, I distinctly saw her face, already grown pallid. . . . And here a sudden madness possessed me,—I dashed to the window, throwing apart, flinging open the shutters, and began to shout, and to shoot into the air. . . . The rest you know. . . ."

In the spring, five years ago, travelling over Algeria, the writer of these lines visited Constantine. He often recalls now those evenings, rainy and chill, but spring evenings never the less, which he passed by the fireplace in the reading room of a certain old and homelike French hotel. Upon the heavy, elaborate *étagères* there lay tattered illustrated journals—in them one could find

some faded portraits of Mme. Marot, at different ages,—
among them, one taken in Lausanne, when she was a
girl. . . . Her story is told here again, through a strong
desire of telling it in my own way.

1916.

THE SON

LIGHT BREATHING

IN the graveyard, over the fresh clayey mound, stands
a new cross of oak,—strong, heavy, smooth,—of the
sort that is pleasant to contemplate.

It is April, but the days are raw; the monuments of
the graveyard—a spacious, truly provincial one,—can be
seen through the bare trees even from afar, and the chill
wind makes the porcelain wreath at the foot of the cross
tinkle again and again.

As for the cross itself,—a rather large bronze medallion has been set into it; while in the medallion is a
photographic portrait of a well dressed and alluring
high-school girl, with eyes joyous, strikingly alive.

This is Olliya Meshcherskaya.

As a girl she did not in any way stand out among that
noisy crowd of short brown dresses which so discord-
antly and youthfully hums in the corridors and class-
rooms; what could be said of her save that she was one of
a number of rather pretty, wealthy, and happy girls, that
she was bright, but mischievous and very much uncon-
cerned about whatever admonitions were made to her by
an instructress? Then she began to blossom out, to de-
velop, not by the day but by the hour. At fourteen,
while her waist was slender and her little feet graceful,
she already had well-defined breasts and all those con-
tours, the enchantment of which human speech has never
yet expressed; at fifteen she was famed as a beauty.

[110]

How painstakingly did certain of her mates dress their hair, how meticulous about their persons they were, how carefully watchful of their restrained motions! But she feared nothing,—neither ink spots on her fingers, nor a flushed face, nor disheveled hair, nor a knee bared in a running fall. Without any cares or efforts on her part, and somehow imperceptibly, to her came all that which distinguished her from all the rest of the high-school during her last two years there,—elegance, good taste in dress, cleverness, a radiant, yet an understanding sparkle in her eyes. No one danced like Olliya Meshcherskaya; no one raced on skates as well as she did; no one was sought after at balls as much as she; and, for some reason, no one was so liked by the lower grades as she was. Imperceptibly, she became a young lady, and imperceptibly her fame in school became secure; and there were already rumours that she was inconstant, that she could not live without admirers; that Shenshin, a student in the boys' high-school, was madly in love with her; that apparently she was also in love with him, but so changeable in her treatment of him that he had made attempts at suicide. . . .

During her last winter, Olliya Meshcherskaya lost her head entirely from her pursuit of pleasure,—so they said in the high-school. The winter was snowy, sunny, frosty; the sun sank early behind the tall fir grove of the snow-covered school garden, but it was invariably serene, many-rayed, holding forth a promise of both frost and sunlight for the morrow as well; to say nothing of strolling through Cathedral Street, of skating at the rink in the city park on a rose-tinged evening, to music, and amid this throng gliding in all directions, among which

Olliya Meshcherskaya seemed the best dressed, the freest from care, the happiest. And then one day, during the main interval, as she was careering like a whirlwind through the assembly hall escaping from the little girls of the first grade who were pursuing her and squealing for joy, she was unexpectedly summoned to the directress. She stopped in full career; giving a single deep sigh, with a rapid and by now accustomed movement she put her hair in order, hitched up the little corners of her apron at the shoulders, and, her eyes radiant, ran upstairs. The directress, a small woman, young looking but gray haired, was calmly sitting with some knitting in her hands, at a writing table underneath a portrait of the Tsar.

"How do you do, Mlle. Meshcherskaya," she said in French, without raising her eyes from the knitting. "It is to be regretted that this is not the first time I am compelled to summon you here, in order to speak to you about your conduct."

"I am listening, Madame," answered Meshcherskaya, approaching the table, looking at her radiantly and in animation, but without any expression on her face, and she sat down with that lightness and grace of which only she was mistress.

"You will listen but badly to me,—I have, it is to be regretted, become convinced of that," said the directress, and drawing a thread and making the ball of wool roll over the polished floor, upon which Meshcherskaya had cast a glance of curiosity, she raised her eyes: "I shall not repeat myself; I shall not speak at length," she said.

Meshcherskaya liked very much this unusually tidy and large study; on frosty days its atmosphere was so cozy from the warmth of the glistening Dutch stove, and the freshness of the lilies-of-the-valley upon the writing table. She glanced at the young Tsar, drawn at full length in the midst of some resplendently glittering hall; at the straight parting of the milky, neatly waved hair of the directress, and kept an expectant silence.

"You are no longer a little girl," said the directress with much significance, secretly beginning to grow irritated.

"Yes, Madame," answered Meshcherskaya simply, almost gaily.

"But not yet a woman," said the directress with still greater significance, and her dull-coloured face began to glow slightly. "First of all,—what sort of a coiffure is that? That is a woman's coiffure!"

"Madame, I am not to blame if I have nice hair," answered Meshcherskaya, giving the slightest of pats with both hands to her attractively dressed head.

"Ah, so that is it,—you are not to blame!" said the directress. "You are not to blame for your coiffure, nor to blame for these expensive combs, nor to blame for ruining your parents with buying little slippers at twenty roubles![1] But, I repeat to you, you lose sight of the fact that as yet you are only a high-school girl. . . ."

And at this point, Meshcherskaya, without losing her simplicity and calmness, suddenly interrupted her with politeness:

"Pardon me, Madame, you are making a mistake: I am a woman. And—do you know who is responsible for this? Papa's friend and neighbour, and also your

[1] A rouble, before the revolution, was equal to about half an American dollar. *Trans.*

[113]

brother, Alexei Mikhailovich Maliutin. This happened last summer in the country. . . ."

And a month after this conversation an officer of the Cossacks, homely and of plebeian appearance, having absolutely nothing in common with that circle to which Meshcherskaya belonged, shot her on the platform of a railroad station, among a large crowd which had just arrived with the train. And the incredible confession of Olliya Meshcherskaya, which had dumbfounded the directress, was fully confirmed; the officer had declared to the examining magistrate that Meshcherskaya had enticed him, had had a *liaison* with him, had sworn to be his wife; but at the depot, on the day of the murder, when she was seeing him off to Novocherkassk, she had suddenly told him that she had never even as much as thought of loving him, that their talks about marriage were all merely a mockery of him, and she let him read that page in her diary which dealt with Maliutin.

"I ran over these lines, went out on the platform where she was promenading, waiting till I should finish reading, and shot her," said the officer. "The diary remained in the pocket of my uniform coat; just glance at what was written on it on the tenth of July of last year."

And the examining magistrate read something approximately as follows:

"It is now two o'clock at night. I had fallen fast asleep, but had immediately awakened. . . . This day I have become a woman! Papa, mamma, and Tolliya had all gone to the city, and I was left alone. I cannot express how happy I was over being alone! In the morning I strolled by myself in the garden, in the fields; I was in the forest,—it seemed to me that I was all alone in the entire universe, and my thoughts were more pleasant than they have ever before been in my life. I even dined alone, then I played for a whole hour; to the sounds of the music I felt as if I would live without end and would be as happy as never before! Then I fell asleep in papa's study. And at four Katiya woke me up, saying that Alexei Mikhailovich had arrived. I was very glad he had come; it was so pleasant for me to receive and entertain him. He had driven up on his pair of very handsome horses, of a special small breed, and they stood all the time near the steps; but he remained, because it had been raining, and he wanted the ground to be dry toward evening. He was very sorry that he had not caught father in, was very animated, and bore himself like a gallant toward me; he joked a lot about having been in love with me for a long time. When we were strolling before tea in the garden, the weather was splendid again, the sun glistened through the entire wet garden, although it had become really downright chilly, and he walked about with my arm through his, and said that he was Faust with Marguerite. He is fifty-six, but he is still very handsome, and always very well dressed,— the only thing I did not like was that he had come in a kind of cape; he is all scented with English eau-de-cologne, and his eyes are altogether young,—and black; and his beard is attractively divided in two long parts and is perfectly silvery. At tea we sat in the glass enclosed veranda; I felt somehow unwell and laid down upon a low couch, while he smoked; then he changed his seat to where I was, and again began telling me some nice things; then to examine and kiss my hand. I

[115]

covered my face with a silk handkerchief, and he kissed me several times on the lips through the handkerchief. . . . I cannot understand how it could have, happened; I lost my mind, I never thought that I was that kind! Now there is only one way out for me. . . . I feel such loathing for him, that I cannot live through this! . . ."

The town during these April days has become clean, dry, its stones have grown white, and it is easy and pleasant to walk over them. Every Sunday, after mass, a little woman in mourning, in black kid gloves, with an ebony umbrella, starts out walking through Cathedral Street, which leads to the city gates. She passes by the engine house, crosses, by means of a paved road, the dirty square where there are many sooty smithies, and the air from the fields is blowing fresher; farther on, between the monastery and the jail, the cloudy horizon shows white, and the spring fields gray; and then, when one has treaded his way among the puddles under the wall of the monastery and turns to the left, one sees something like a large, low garden, surrounded by a white enclosure, above the gates of which enclosure is painted the Assumption of the Mother of God. The little woman rapidly makes a sign of the cross several times, and like one who knows the way walks through the main path. Having reached the bench opposite the cross of oak, she sits in the wind and the spring chillness, for an hour, for two hours, until her feet in their light shoes and her hands in their tight kid gloves grow entirely benumbed. Listening to the birds of spring, sweetly singing even in the cold, listening to the tinkling of the wind through the porcelain wreath, she thinks at times that she would give half her life, if only that dead wreath might not be before her eyes. The thought that it was Olliya Meshcherskaya whom they had buried here, in this very clay, throws her into astonishment verging on stupefaction: how can one associate that sixteen year old school girl, who only some two or three months ago was so full of life, enchantment, gaiety, with this clayey hummock, and this oaken cross? Can it be possible that underneath it is the same girl whose eyes shine so deathlessly out of this bronze medallion, and how reconcile with this pure gaze that dreadful thing which is connected now with the name of Olliya Meshcherskaya? But deep in her soul the little woman is happy, as all people in love, or devoted to some passionate idea in general, always are.

This woman is a teacher of Olliya Meshcherskaya, a girl of over thirty, who has long lived upon some fiction or other that supplants her actual life. At first her brother, a poor ensign and in no way remarkable, was such a fiction,—all her soul was bound up with him, with his future, which for some reason appeared to her brilliant, and she lived in a strange expectancy, that her fate would somehow change magically, thanks to him. Later, when he was killed at Mukden, she assured herself, that she, to her great good fortune, it would seem, was not like others; that the lack of beauty and femininity were in her case compensated for by brains and higher interests; that she was a toiler in the world of ideas. The death of Olliya Meshcherskaya captivated her with a new dream. Now Olliya Meshcherskaya is an object of her ceaseless thoughts, of rapture, of joy. She goes to Olliya's grave on every

[117]

AN EVENING IN SPRING

ON St. Thomas' week, on a clear evening barely tinged with rose, at that enchanting time when the earth has just been freed from the snow, when, in the little hollows upon the steppes, underneath the young bare oaks, some gray, hardened snow still lingers, an old beggar was going from house to house in a certain village in the Eletz province,—of course, he had no hat, and there was a long linen wallet slung over his shoulder.

This village was a large one, but quiet, lying far out among the fields. And besides, it happened to be a quiet evening. There was nobody near the flooded, clayey pond, that one could not see the limits of; nor upon the level common where, in the shade of the huts and hayricks, this old man was walking. His head was bald, yet still black-haired; he held a long walnut staff in his hand, and looked like a primitive bishop. The common was of a clear, vivid green; the air was freshening; the pond, concavely-full, its tone that of a flashing flesh colour, was slightly crimson, and there was a certain beauty about it, despite a bottle-green block of ice, covered with rusty manure, that still floated about in it. Somewheres on the other side, warmly and caressingly lit up against the low-lying sun,—somewhere far-off, it seemed,—a child, strayed behind some corn-kiln or storehouse, was crying, and its plaintive, monotonous wailing was not unpleasant to the ear in the evening

[119]

glow. . . . But the folk thereabouts were none too generous of alms.

There, at the entrance to the village, near an old, well-to-do farm, where age-old oaks covered with the nests of rooks stood beyond the three-roomed *izba* of dark-red brick, a young gray-eyed married woman had given something, but even that had been a trifle. She had been standing near the stone threshold amid the drying spring mire upon a hard-beaten path, holding a pretty little girl, whose little eyes did not show any glimmer of intelligence, perched in her arms; the child had on a little patchwork cap, and, pressing her close against her, the woman was dancing, stamping her bare feet, and, as she turned, her cotton skirt would swell out.

"There's an old man; I'll give you to him to put in his little wallet," she was saying through her teeth, her lips feasting on the little girl's cheeks:

> "I'm a-goin' to dance
> So's the floor will creak. . . ."

And, turning, completely around, she changed her voice to a ringing, coquettish tone, evidently imitative of some one:

"Old man, old man,—don't you need a little girl?"

The girl was not a bit frightened; she was calmly sucking a round cracknel, and the mother began coaxing the little girl, in all sorts of ways, to give it to the smiling beggar who had come up:

"Give it to him, my little babe, give it to him; for you and I are all, all alone on this whole farm; so we have nothing to give alms with. . . ."

And the little girl stolidly stretched out her short

holiday,—she had formed the habit of going to the graveyard and of wearing mourning since the death of her brother. For hours she does not take her eyes off the oaken cross; she recalls the pale little face of Olliya Meshcherskaya in her coffin, among the flowers—and also that which she had once happened to overhear: once, during the main recess, strolling through the school garden, Olliya Meshcherskaya was saying, all in one breath, to her favourite mate,—the stout, tall Subottina:

"In one of papa's books,—he has a lot of old-fashioned funny books,—I read what sort of beauty a woman ought to have . . . you understand, there is so much said there that one can't remember everything: well, of course, black eyes, like boiling pitch,—honest to God, it is written just so!—like boiling pitch,—eye-lashes as black as night; a softly mantling blush, a slender waist, a hand longer than the ordinary,—you understand, longer than the ordinary!—a little foot, a moderately large bosom, a regularly rounded calf, a knee the colour of a sea-shell, sloping—but high—shoulders. . . . I learned most of this by heart, that's how true all this is! But do you know what the chief thing is?—Light breathing! . . . But then, I have it,—you just listen how I sigh,—really, haven't I got it?"

Now this light breathing has been scattered anew upon the universe, upon this cloud-covered sky, upon this chill spring wind. . . .

1916.

[118]

little arm, with the saliva-moistened cookie clenched in her little fist. And the beggar, smilingly shaking his head at other folks' happiness, took it and munched it as he went on his way.

He held his stick lightly, in readiness, as he went; now it would be a wicked, snarling watch-dog that would roll up in a ball underneath your feet,—and having rolled right up to you, would suddenly become quiet; or else a yellow, downy hound would ferociously tear the ground and throw it up with his hind feet, standing near a hay rick and growling, growling and gasping, with fiery eyes. . . . Upon approaching the little window of a hut, the beggar would make a humble bow and would tap lightly against the frame with his staff. But often no one would respond to this tap; many were still finishing up their sowing, finishing up their plowing, many were out in the fields. And his soul, the soul of a peasant from of old, even rejoiced in secret: the folks are out in the field . . . this is the time that feeds the whole year . . . no time for beggars. . . . And at times, on the other side of the panes upon which the beggar tapped, a fair-faced peasant woman carrying a child at breast in her arms, would lean over as she sat on a bench. Through the sorry little window, she appeared very big. Not at all abashed because the beggar could see her soft breast, as white as wheat-flour, she would wave him away with her large hand, covered with silver rings, while the infant, without letting the sweet nipple out of its mouth, lay back and looked up at her with its dark, clear eyes, scratching hard its bare little outspread legs, all dotted with pink from flea-bites. "God will give you alms,—don't be angry with us," the peasant woman would say calmly. As for the old women, each one of them would wrinkle up her face painfully, inevitably leaning out and complaining for a long time, constantly re-iterating that she'd be glad as glad could be to give alms, but there wasn't anything . . . everybody was out in the fields . . . and to give without asking she was afraid,—she, being an old woman, had had her head bitten off long ago, as it was. . . . The beggar would agree with her, would say, "Well, forgive me, for the love of God," and would go on farther.

He had done thirty versts[1] that day, and was not a bit fatigued; only his legs had grown benumbed, dulled, and had begun to wobble. His long bag was half-filled with crusts and some odds and ends; while under the patched long coat, narrow belted and long skirted, under the sheepskin jacket and the much worn blouse, under the shirt next his skin, there had long been hanging upon his crucifix an amulet wherein were sewn ninety-two roubles in bills. And his soul was at rest. Of course, he was old, thin, all weather-beaten,—his mouth contracted, parched, until it was all black; his nose was like a bone; his neck all in wrinkles resembling cracks, criss-crossing one another, as though his neck were made of cork. But he was still spry. His eyes, which once upon a time had been black, were now rheumy and dimmed by thin cataracts; but still they could see not only the full-flooded pond, but, as well, the roseate tint upon its farther side, and even the clear, pale sky. The air was getting fresher; more loudly, but seemingly from a still greater distance, came the receding cry of the child; there was a scent of the chilling grass in the air. . . . Two pigeons

[1] A verst is about two-thirds of a mile. *Trans.*

[122]

soared together over the roofs, fell to the clayey little bank of the pond, and, raising their little heads, began to drink. . . . Just a little before, in a lonely farm near the great road, some women had grown generous and had given him a big piece of calico and a pair of good trousers,—oh, good as new, you might say; a young fellow that belonged to their farm had made them for himself, but he had been crushed in a pit, in the quarry where the *moujiks* had been digging for clay. Now the beggar was walking along and deliberating: should he dispose of them, or put them on himself, and throw away those he had on—which, by now, were really none too presentable,—near the edge of some field?

Having come to the end of the village, he entered a short little lane that led out into the steppe. And into his eyes glanced the many-rayed, fair-weather sun of April, sinking far beyond the plain, beyond the gray fallow-lands and the newly tilled fields of spring-corn. At the very end of the village, at a turn of the well-beaten, glistening road, leading to that distant, humble hamlet where the beggar was thinking of passing the night, stood a new hut, not large, well-roofed with new thatch, which was lemon-coloured and resembled a well-combed head. Keeping aloof from everybody, a man and his wife had settled here a year ago,—there were shavings and chips still knocking about here and there. They were a thrifty, hard-working, agreeable couple, and sold vodka on the sly. And so the beggar went straight toward this hut,—there was a possibility of selling the new trousers to its owner,—and besides, he liked just to enter it; he liked it because it seemed to be living some especial life, all its own, quiet and steadfast, standing at the end leading out of the village and gazing with its clear little windows upon the setting of the sun, while the sky-larks were finishing their song in the chilling air. Near the blind wall that gave out upon the by-lane lay a shadow, but its front wall was gay. Last fall its owner had planted three acacia bushes beneath the little windows. Now they had taken root and were already downy with a yellowish verdure tender as that of a willow. Having skirted them, the beggar walked in through the entry into the main room.

At first, after the sunlight, he could not see anything, although the sun was looking in here as well, lighting up the blue transparent smoke floating over the table, that stood underneath a hanging tin lamp. To gain time while his eyes grew accustomed, he bowed and crossed himself for a long time in the direction of the new tinselled icon hanging in a corner. Then he laid down his bag and his staff on the floor near the door, and made out a large-bodied *moujik* in bast shoes and a tattered short sheepskin coat, sitting with his back to the door, on a stool near the table; the well-dressed mistress he saw sitting on a bench.

"The Lord's blessing be with you," said he, in a low voice, bowing once more. "Greetings of the holiday just past."

He wanted to sing the paschal *Christ Is Risen*, but felt that it would be out of place, and reflected:

"Well, I guess the master is not at home. . . . What a pity."

The mistress was not at all bad-looking, with a very shapely waist, with white hands,—just as though she were no mere peasant woman. She was in a gala-dress,

[124]

as always; in a pearl necklace, in a blouse of coarse calico, with thin puffed-out sleeves, with an apron broidered in red and blue, in a skirt of indigo wool with terra-cotta checks, and in half-boots, rough but well-sown and made to fit the foot, their heels shod with steel. With her neat head and clear face bent down, she was embroidering a blouse for her husband. When the beggar had greeted her, she raised her steady but unglittering eyes, threw an intent glance upon him, and nodded amiably. Then, with a light sigh, she laid her work aside, deftly stuck her needle in it, went toward the oven, her half-boots clacking over the wooden floor and her flanks swaying, and took a small bottle of vodka and a thick cup with blue stripes out of a little cupboard.

"I have gotten tired, though . . ." said the beggar, as if he were talking to himself,—both in apology for the vodka and because he was confused by the silence of the *moujik*, who had not turned around toward him.

Stepping softly in his bast-shoes, humbly walking around him, the beggar sat down upon another stool, at an opposite corner of the table. As for the mistress, she put the cup and the small bottle before him, and went back to her work. Then this stalwart, tattered son of the steppes raised his head heavily,—there was a whole greenish demijohn standing before him,—and, narrowing his eyes, he fixed his gaze upon his humble bottle-companion. He may have been pretending just a trifle; but still, his face was inflamed; his eyes were drunken, filled with the dull glitter of tipsiness; the lips, grown soft and flabby, were half-open, as in a fever,—evidently, this was not the first day of his spree. And the beggar grew a little more wary, and carefully began filling his

[125]

cup. "After all, now, he'll drink his and I'll drink mine. . . . This is a tavern, and we don't bother one another," he was thinking. He raised his head, and his mistily-black eyes, the colour of ripe sloe-thorn, as well as his whole visage, made rough and weather-beaten by the steppe, were void of all expression.

"Where was you tramping?" asked the *moujik*, roughly and crazily. "Have you come to steal, seeing as how all the folks are out in the fields?"

"Why should I be stealing?" the beggar replied, evenly and meekly. "I've had six children of my own, and my own house and goods. . . ."

"You're blind and you're blind, but, never fear, many's the feather and the twig you've carried to your nest!"

"Why should you be saying that? I've worked hard as could be for ten years in the quartz mines. . . ."

"That ain't work. That's. . . ."

"Don't you be saying anything out of the way," said the mistress, without elevating her voice, without raising her lashes, and bit off the thread. "I don't listen to anything unseemly. I ain't heard it from my husband yet."

"Well, that will do; I won't do it any more . . . lady!" said the *moujik*. "'Scuse me . . . I'm after asking you," said he to the beggar, frowningly, "what can you get out of the ground, now, when it ain't been ploughed nor sown?"

"Well, now, of course. . . . Whoever has the land, for example. . . ."

"Wait,—I'm smarter than you be!" said the *moujik* slapping the table with his palm. "Answer what you're asked: did you serve for a soldier?"

[126]

"I was a non-commissioned officer of the Tenth Grena-
diers Regiment of Little Russia, under Count Rumiyant-
zev-Zadunaisky. . . . What else should I be doing but
serving for a soldier?"

"Keep still, don't gabble more'n you're asked! What
year was you took?"

"In 'seventy six, in the month of November."

"Wasn't you ever at fault?"

"Never."

"Did you obey the officers?"

"There was no way of my doing otherwise. I had
taken an oath."

"But what's that scar doing on your neck? Do you
understand what I'm driving at now? I am testing
him," said the *moujik*, with his eye-brows working
surlily, but changing his commanding voice for a more
simple one, and turning toward the mistress his crazed
face, aureately illumined through the tobacco smoke by
the sunset; "I may be poor, all right, but I've caught
more than one fellow like that! I know enough to come
in out of the rain!"

And again he put on a frown, looking at the beggar:

"Did you bow down before the Holy Cross and the
Gospel?"

"That I have," answered the beggar, who had managed
to take a drink, to wipe his mouth with his sleeve, to sit
up straight again, and to impart to his face and his
misty eyes a dispassionate expression.

The *moujik* surveyed him with glazed eyes.

"Stand up before me!"

"Don't raise any fuss. Am I talking to you, or am I
not?" the mistress quietly intervened.

[127]

"Wait, for the love of God," the *moujik* waved her away in vexation. "Stand up before me!"

"Honest to God, what are you up to. . . ." the beggar began to mumble.

"Stand up, I'm telling you!" yelled the *moujik*. "I'm a-going to examine you."

The beggar stood up and shifted from foot to foot.

"Hands at the sides! So. Got a passport?"

"But are you an inspector, or something?"

"Keep still,—don't you dare to jaw back at me like that! I'm smarter than you be! I went all through this myself. Show it to me this minute!"

Hastily unhooking his long overcoat, then his sheepskin jacket, the beggar submissively rummaged within the bosom of his shirt for a long time. Finally he pulled out a paper wrapped up in a red handkerchief.

"Give it here," said the *moujik* abruptly.

And, unwrapping the little handkerchief, the beggar handed him a small frayed gray book, with a large wax seal. The *moujik* awkwardly opened it with his gnarled fingers and pretended to read it, putting it at a distance from him, leaning back, and looking at it for a long time through the tobacco smoke and the red light of the evening glow.

"So. I see now. Everything ship-shape. Take it back," he said, his parched lips moving with difficulty. "I am poor as poor can be; it's the second spring, you might say, that I'm neither ploughing nor sowing; folks have done for me. . . . I fell down at his feet, the dog that he is. . . . And yet I'm beyond a price, you might say. . . . But you just tell me all that you've stolen, or

[128]

else I'll kill you right off!" he yelled ferociously. "I know everything; I've gone through all sorts of things. . . . I've been boiled in pitch, you might say,—that's how I've suffered. . . . It is the Lord that gives us life, but any vermin can take it away. . . . Give the bag here, and that's all there is to it!"

The mistress merely shook her head, and leaned back from her embroidery, contemplating it. The beggar went toward the door and gave the *moujik* the bag, just as he had given him the passport. The *moujik* took it, and, as he laid it near him on the stool, he said:

"That's right. Now sit down,—let's chat a bit. I'll get to the bottom of all this here. I'll make an inspection of my own, don't you fret!"

And he became silent, staring at the table.

"Spring . . ." he muttered. "Ah, but what a sorrowful sabbath-day it is, that a man may not work in the fields. . . . Go on!" he cried out to some imagined person, trying to snap his fingers:

> "Oh, the lady starts to dance,
> And her fingers is all blue. . . ."

And he relapsed into silence. The mistress was smoothing down the embroidery with her thimble.

"I'm going out to milk the cow," said she, getting up from her seat. "Don't blow up the fire whilst I am out, or else you'll burn us out in your drunkenness."

The *moujik* came to with a start.

"Lordy!" he exclaimed, in hurt tones. "Little mistress! How can youse say that. . . . You've grown aweary for your husband, never fear?"

"That's none of your worry," said the mistress. "He's in town, on business. . . . He don't go traipsing around no inns."

"You'd go traipsing, too!" said the *moujik*. "Well, what would you have me do, now,—go out on the wayside, or what? You rich devils are all right. . . ."

The mistress, picking up a milk-pail, went out. It was growing dark in the hut; everything was quiet, and the roseate light was suffused in the soft, spring obscurity. The *moujik*, with his elbows on the table, was dozing, as he pulled at an extinguished, crudely made cigarette. The beggar was sitting peacefully, with never a sound, leaning against the dark partition, and his face was almost invisible.

"Do you drink beer?" asked the *moujik*.

"I do," came the low answer out of the dusk.

The *moujik* was silent for a while.

"We are vagabones, you and me" said he, morosely and meditatively. "Poor wayside rubbish. . . . Beggarmen. . . . I feel weary in your company!"

"That's right. . . ."

"But as for beer,—I like it," said the *moujik* loudly, after another silence. "She don't keep it, the carrion! Otherwise I would have drunk some beer . . . and would have had a snack of something. . . . My tongue's all soaked,—I want to eat. . . . I would have had a snack and drunk something. . . . Yes. . . . But she, the mistress, ain't got such a bad face! If I was harnessed up with one like her, I would. . . . All right, never mind, sit down, sit down . . . I got respect for the blind. Whenever a grand holiday used to come around, I would take twenty of these here blind men, now, and seat them at table,—you would have had to look and look to find another household like ours! And they would sing a stave for me, and make me a bow to boot. . . . Do you know how to sing staves? About Alexei, the Man of God? I do take to that stave. Pick up your cup,—I'll treat you to some of mine."

Having taken the cup from the beggar's hands, he held it up to the faint light of the evening glow and half-filled it. The beggar got up, made a low bow, drained the cup to the bottom, and again sat down. The *moujik* dragged the beggar's bag upon his knees, and, untying it, began to mutter:

"I sized you up at once . . . I've got enough money of my own, brother; you're no mate for me. . . . I go through my money in cold blood . . . I drink it away . . . I drink away a horse a year, and send a good ram up in smoke. . . . Aha! So you've run up against a bit of a *moujik*,—do you understand who I am? But still, I feel sorry for you. I understand! There's thousands of the likes of you roaming about in spring-time. . . . There's mire, and sloughs, and never a path or a road,—but you've got to keep on going, bowing before everybody. . . . And you can't never tell whether they'll give you anything or no. . . . Eh, brother! Don't I understand you?" asked the *moujik* with bitter sorrow, and his eyes filled with tears.

"No, this time of the year is not so bad, it's all right," said the beggar quietly. "You walk along a field, over a big, abandoned tract that had once been planned for a road. . . . All alone, with never another soul nigh. . . . Then, too, there's the dear sun, and the warm

[131]

weather. . . . True, there's many a thousand of the likes
of me roaming about. Half of Russia is roaming so."

"I've drunk away two horses," said the *moujik*, rak-
ing the crusts out of the bag, pulling out a waist-coat,
the calico, the trousers, and a bast shoe. "I'm goin' to
go all through all your miserable pickings, and old rags.
. . . Hold on! Pants! I must buy them from you, soon
as I come into a little money. . . . How much?"

The beggar thought for a while.

"Why, I'd let it go for two. . . ."

"I'll give you three!" said the *moujik*, getting up,
placing the trousers under him, and sitting down upon
them. "They're mine! But where's the other shoe? It
will pass for new,—that means you must have stolen it,
for sure. But then, it's better to be thieving, than to be
grieving your heart out in the springtime, the way I
am a-doing now; to be perishing from hunger, to be coming to the end of your rope,—when you take the very
least of the shepherds, and you'll find him at work. . . .
I have drunk a horse away,—but a beastie like that is
worth more nor any man. . . . But am I no ploughman,
no reaper? . . . And now you sing a stave, or I'll kill
you right off!" he cried out. "I feel weary in your
company!"

In a quavering, modest, but a practiced voice the
beggar began to sing out of the obscurity:

"Once upon a time there lived and were two brethren—
Two blood-brethren, two brethren in God and Christ. . . ."

"Eh, two brethren in God and Christ!" the *moujik*
chimed in, in a high-pitched and piteous tone, straining
his voice.

[132]

The beggar, with even churchly chanting, continued:

> "One dwelt in cold and poverty,
> Rotting in his leprosy. . . ."

"And the o-other was rich!" out of tune, drowning out the beggar, with tears in his voice, the *moujik* caught up the song. "Put more heart in it!" he cried out, as his voice broke. "Grief has swallowed me up; all men are having a holiday, all men are sowing,—but here I be, biting the earth; it's the second spring that my mother earth has been barren. . . . Let me have your cup, or I'll kill you right off! Open the window for me!"

And again the beggar submissively gave him his cup. Then he started to open the window. Being new, it had swollen and would not yield for a long while. Finally it did yield, and flew open. A fresh, pleasant odour of the fields floated in. It was completely dark out there now, the roseate night glow had become extinguished, barely shimmering over the soft darkness of the quiet, joyous, fecundated field. One could hear the half-drowsy sky-larks finishing their very last songs.

"Sing, Lazarus,—sing, my own brother!" said the *moujik*, extending a full cup to the beggar. "We're two of a kind, you and me. . . . Only what are you alongside of me? A vagabone! Whereas I am a working man, that gives food and drink to all those that suffer. . . ."

He sat down suddenly, losing his balance, and again dug into the bag.

"And what might you have here?" he asked, examining the calico, which had turned the faintest pink in the barely perceptible light of the evening glow.

"Oh, that's just so. . . . Some women gave it to me,"

[133]

said the beggar quietly, feeling everything floating before him from tipsiness, and that it was time to be going, and that it was necessary to extricate the trousers from underneath the *moujik* somehow.

"How can that be! You lie!" cried out the *moujik*, banging the table with his fist. "It's a shroud,—I can see! It's a grave-shroud!" he cried out with tears in his voice, and was silent for a while, hearkening to the abating songs of the sky-larks. Then he shoved the bag away from him, and, shaking his tousled head, began to cry: "I have risen in my pride against God!" said he bitterly, weeping.

And then, straining himself, he began to sing loudly, keeping good time:

> "Oh my mother gave me birth and she guarded me,
>   Though I now a sinner be, unforgivable!
>   All the torments have I borne,
>   All the sorrows have I borne,—
>   Nowheres found I joy for me.
>   Oh, my mother spoke to me
>   And she cautioned me;
>   If she only knew, if she only saw,
>   She could never bear
>   Such calamity. . . ."

"Oh, my soul is a sinner and a creeping thing!" he cried out wildly, weeping, and suddenly started clapping his palms with an elderitch laughter: "Beggar-man, give me your money! I know you through and through; I feel you through and through,—give it to me! I know you have it! It can't be otherwise,—give it to me for love of the Lord God Himself!"

And, swaying, he arose, and the beggar, who had also

[134]

arisen, felt his legs giving away from fear, felt a dull ache start in his thighs. The tear-stained face of the *moujik*, barely discernible in the twilight, was insane.

"Give it to me!" he repeated, in a voice suddenly grown hoarse. "Give it to me, for the Love of the Queen of Heaven! I can see, I can see,—you're grabbing at your bosom, at your undershirt; that means you've got it,— all your kind has! Give it to me,—it ain't of no use to you, anyway, whereas it will set me on my feet forever! Give it to me of your own will,—brother, don't lead me into sin!"

"Can't do it," said the beggar, quietly and dispassionately.

"What?"

"Can't do it. I've been saving for twenty years. Can't bring myself to do it."

"You ain't goin' to give it to me?" asked the *moujik* hoarsely.

"No . . ." said the beggar, barely audible but unshaken.

The *moujik* was silent for a long while. The beating of their hearts could be heard in the darkness.

"Very well," said the *moujik*, with an insane submissiveness. "I will kill you; I'll go and find me a stone and then kill you."

And, swaying, he went toward the threshold.

The beggar, standing erect in the darkness, made a sweeping and slow sign of the cross. As for the *moujik*, he, with his head lowered like a bull, was already walking about under the windows.

Then there came a crunching sound,—evidently he was pulling a stone out of the foundation.

[135]

And a minute later the door slammed again,—and the beggar drew himself up still more.

"For the last time I'm a-telling you . . ." the *moujik* mumbled out with his cracked lips, walking up to him with a big white stone in his hands. "Brother. . . ."

The beggar was silent. His face could not be seen. Swinging back with his left arm and catching the beggar by his neck, the *moujik* struck hard his shrinking face with the chill stone. The beggar tore away, backward, and, as he fell, catching the table with his bast-shoe, he struck the back of his head against a stool, and then against the floor. And falling upon him, the *moujik*, squeezing the breath out of his chest, frenziedly began to batter in his throat with the stone.

Ten minutes later he was already far out in the dark, even field. There were many stars out; the air was fresh; the earth gave forth a metallic odour. Completely sobered up, he was walking so rapidly and lightly that he seemed capable of covering a hundred versts more. The amulet, torn off the beggar's crucifix, he was holding tightly clenched in his hand. Later, he flung it from him into a dark, freshly ploughed field. His eyes were staring fixedly like an owl's; his teeth were tightly clenched, like a lobster's claws. Although he had looked for his cap for a long while, he had been unable to find it in the darkness; the chillness beat upon his bared head. His head seemed to him to be of stone.

1914.

THE SACRIFICE

SIMON NOVICOV, who was living in Oats Ford with his brother Nicon,—Nicon of the withered arm,—was burned out in midsummer, about the fast of St. Peter. The brothers decided to divide their property, and Simon, intending to leave the Ford, was putting up a hut for himself near the great highway.

On the evening before Elijah's Day the carpenters had asked for leave to go home. After supping with the large family of his brother, in the midst of flies and the clamour of children, he lit his pipe, put on his short sheepskin coat, and said to his folks:

"It's stuffy in here. I'm going to the building,—I'll sleep the night there. I'm afraid the tools might be stole."

"You ought to take the dogs with you, at least," one of the women counselled him.

"Get along with ye!" said Simon, and went out.

There was a full moon out that night. What with his thoughts of his future household, Simon did not even notice how he had climbed up hill by the broad path to the pasture lands that led out of the village, and, after putting about a verst behind him on the big road, had come right up to his hut, which had a ceiling but was, as yet, unroofed. It stood at the edge of the fields of grain, in the midst of an empty field. Its sashless windows gaped blackly, and it was dully glistening against the light of the moon with the ends of its new corner-beams, with the tow sticking out of its joints, and the sticks and shavings about its threshold. The aureate July moon, which had risen far beyond the ravines of the Ford, hung low and was turbid. Its warm glow was diffused over everything. The ripe grain glimmered whitely ahead,—dully, sombrely, like stretches of sand. But toward the north the sky was altogether overcast, —a cloud was gathering there. A soft breeze, blowing from all sides, would at times gather strength and run fitfully over the rye and oats,—and they would rustle crisply, disquietingly. The cloud toward the north appeared immovable, but it was frequently shot with an eerie, fleeting, golden sheen.

Simon, stooping at the threshold through habit, entered the hut. It was dark and stuffy within it. The yellow moonlight, looking in at the unglazed windows, did not blend with the darkness, but only intensified it. Simon threw down his short sheepskin coat upon the shavings in the middle of the hut, directly in the path of one of the rows of light, and lay down on his back. After drawing at his extinguished pipe for a space, he put it in his pocket, and, after thinking for a little while longer, fell asleep.

But now the wind began blowing in at the windows, and, by way of the entry, through the door. The thunder began muttering dully in the distance. Simon sat up. The wind increased—it was now running over the feverishly murmuring grain without cease, and the light of the moon had become still dimmer. Simon walked out of the hut, and, turning the corner, was among the crisp and sultry swishing of the oats, which were as pallid as a shroud. He glanced at the cloud,—the colour of dark slate, it had taken up half the heavens. The wind was blowing straight in his face, tugging at his hair and tangling it, interfering with his vision. The flashes of lightning, too, interfered with his vision and blinded it, as they flared up, more and more ominous and fiery. Simon, making the sign of the cross, got down on his knees: in the distance, in the midst of the sea of oats, standing out against the bank of the cloud, a small throng was advancing toward him. Their heads were bared; in white girdles, in new short sheepskin coats, they were with difficulty bearing a seven-foot altar-piece, painted by some ancient master. The throng was mistily-spectral, but the image was very plain,—an awesome, severe countenance, showing red upon a black panel, which was burnt by candles, dripped over by wax, and bound at the edges by old, blue-coloured silver.

The wind had parted the hair upon Simon's brow, pleasantly blowing it back, and Simon, in fear and joy, bowed down to the ground before the image. When he finally did raise his head, he saw that the crowd had halted, awkwardly supporting the image, which was majestically leaning backward; while upon the cloud was limned, as in a church picture, a towering, enormous visage: the mighty, hoary-bearded Elijah himself, clad in chitons of fire, and sitting, like God-Sabbaoth, upon the lifelessly-blueish tiers of the lower clouds, while two greenish-orange rainbows were flaming above him, against the slate-coloured background. And, flashing his lightning-like orbs, blending his voice with the distant rumble of the thunder, Elijah spake to Simon:

"Stand up straight, Simon Novicov. Hearken, ye

princes and peasants! I am about to judge him, Simon
Novicov,—a peasant tenant of the Eletz province, of the
Predtechev District, of the little village of Oats Ford."

And the entire field, glimmering as white as sand
all around, with all its ears of grain together with the
tares darted forward, bowing down before Elijah, and
amidst their murmur Elijah began to speak:

"I was wroth with thee, Simon Novicov,—I wanted
to punish thee."

"Wherefore, Father?" questioned Simon.

"It is no fitting thing for thee, Simon Novicov, to be
questioning me, Elijah. Thou art the one to make answer."

"Well, forgive me; let it be as thou dost will," said
Simon.

"Summer before last I did kill Pantelei, thy eldest son,
with a stroke of lightning; wherefore didst thou bury him
in the ground up to his waist, bringing him back to life
through black magic?"

"Forgive me, Father," said Simon, bowing, "I felt
sorry for the young lad. Judge for thyself,—why, he
would be the one to give me food and drink in my old
age."

"Last summer I did mow, I did trample down thy
rye with hail and with whirl-winds: why didst thou get
knowledge of it beforehand, and sell this rye while it
yet stood uncut?"

"Forgive me, Father," said Simon, bowing. "My
heart felt a forewarning; need did force me to it."

"Well, was it not I that burned thee out but just now,
at St. Peter's fast? Wherefore dost thou hasten to build
anew, to divide thy goods with thy brother?"

[140]

"Forgive me, Father," said Simon, bowing. "My brother of the withered hand is unlucky; I thought all the misfortunes were coming from him."

"Shut thy eyes. We shall ponder, we shall take counsel, as to thy punishment."

Simon shut his eyes; he bowed down his head. The wind was noisy,—under cover of its noise he was trying to eavesdrop, on the sly, what Elijah and the peasants were whispering together about. But there came a heavy peal of thunder near at hand,—not a thing could he hear.

"No, we can't think of anything," said Elijah with all his voice. "Thou thyself must counsel me."

"And may I open my eyes?" asked Simon.

"There is no need of that. A blind man thinks all the surer."

"Thou art a queer fellow, Father," Simon smiled thoughtfully. "Well, what is there to think about? I shall place a three-rouble candle before thee. . . ."

"Thou hast not the wherewithal. Thou hast spent everything on building."

"Well, in that case I shall go on a pilgrimage to Kiev, or to Belgorod," said Simon, irresolutely.

"That's just loafing, and a waste of shoe-leather. Who's going to take care of the household?"

Simon went into deep thought.

"Well, then, slay my little girl Anphiska. She's just going on three. The girl, to tell the truth, is a kindhearted, endearing little creature,—we will all feel sorry for her; but then, there's no help for it. . . . One can't get everything with just a little!"

"Lend ear, ye faithful," said Elijah loudly. "I agree."

And the cloud was rent by such a flame that Simon's

lids almost caught fire, and the heavens were split by such a peal that all the earth quivered beneath him.

"Holy, holy, holy is the Lord God-Sabbaoth!" whispered Simon. "Heaven defend us!"

When he came to, opening his eyes, Simon beheld only the dust-laden cloud, the deserted, agitated grain, and himself, standing on his knees in the midst of its ears. The wind was whirling in a pillar over the road, and the moon had grown entirely dimmed.

Simon jumped up on his feet. Forgetting all about his short coat, about the axes and the planes, he started off for home, for the village, braving the whirl-winds. The heavy rain caught him out on the common. The dark clouds had piled up above the darkened ravines. The red moon was sinking beyond them. The village was in heavy slumber, but the cattle in the yards were stirring uneasily, the roosters were crowing in alarm. And, running up to his old, half-burned-down hut, Simon heard the wailing of women within. Nicon of the withered arm was standing at the threshold, in his sheepskin coat and without a hat; scrawny and wrinkled beyond his years, he was looking about dully and confusedly.

"There's been a calamity at your house," he said, and one could tell by his voice that he was not yet thoroughly awake.

Simon ran into the hut. The women-folk were running about in the darkness, screaming, looking for the sulphur matches. Simon snatched a small box of them out from behind the image, and lit a tallow-wick. The cradle, which was hung near the oven, was swinging from side to side,—the women had been striking against it

[142]

when they were running about. And within it lay the little girl, dead. She had turned all livid, and a quilt work cap was smouldering on her head.

Simon has been living happily, ever since.

1913.

AGLAIA

IN that community, in that forest village where Aglaia
was born and had grown up, she was called Anna.
She was bereaved of her father and mother at an
early age. The small-pox visited the village one winter,
and many of those who had gone to their rest were carted
off then to the churchyard in the settlement beyond
Sviyat-Oziero.[1] Two coffins in one day stood in the hut
of the Skuratovs as well. The little girl had experienced
neither fear nor pity; she had only come to remember
forever that odour which emanated from them, which is
like nothing else on earth and is unknown and oppressive
to the living, and that winter freshness, that cold of the
Lenten thaw before Easter, which had been let into
the hut by the peasants who were carrying the coffins out
to the wide sledge standing under the windows.

In that forest-covered region the villages are few and
small; their crude, log-enclosed yards are scattered without any order, just as the clayey hummocks permit and as
near as possible to the little rivers, to the lakes. The
folk thereabouts are not so very poor and watch after
their goods, their ancient way of living,—notwithstanding
the fact that they have been going out to hire since time
out of mind, leaving the women to plough the step-
motherly earth, where it is free of the forest; to mow the

[1] Holy Lake. *Trans.*

[144]

grasses in the forest; and in winter to whirr at the weaving loom. Toward that way of living did Anna's heart incline in her childhood; endeared to her were both the black hut and the burning rush light in its cresset.

Katherine, her sister, had long been married. She it was who managed the house,—at first together with her husband, who had been taken into the household; and later, when he began going away for a whole year at a time, all by herself. Under her eyes the girl grew, steadily and rapidly; never did she cry, never did she complain of aught; only she had constant fits of pensiveness. If Katherine called to her, asking what the matter with her was, she would answer simply, saying that her neck was creaking, and that she was listening to it. "There," she would say, turning her neck, and her fair little face, "do you hear it?" "And what are you thinking of?" "Oh, just so. I don't know." During her childhood she never had anything to do with girls of her own age, and never did she go anywheres,—only once had she gone with her sister to that old settlement beyond Sviyat-Oziero, where in the churchyard, under pine trees, crosses of pine wood stick up out of the ground, and where stands a little church of logs, roofed with blackened tiles of wood that look like scales. That was the first time that she had been dressed up in bast slippers and a *sarafan* of bright coloured linen, and that a necklace and a yellow kerchief had been bought for her.

Katherine grieved about her husband and wept; wept, too, about her childlessness. But, having shed all her tears, she gave a vow to have no more knowledge of her husband. When her husband would come, she would

[145]

meet him joyously, speaking with him cheerily, painstakingly looked over his shirts, mending all that stood in need of mending; she bustled about the oven, and was pleased when he liked anything; but they slept apart, like strangers. And when he would go away, she would again become wearied and quiet. More and more frequently did she leave the house, staying at a near-by nunnery, visiting the holy old man Rodion, who was striving for his soul in a hut within a forest that was beyond that nunnery. She was perseveringly learning to read, bringing saintly books from the nunnery, and would read them aloud; not in her usual voice, but pitching it in high sing-song. She would be sitting at a table, her eyes castdown, holding the book with both hands, while the girl stood near by, listening and picking a splinter from the table, looking all about the hut, which was always in the best of order, Drinking in the sounds of her own voice, Katherine read on of saints, of martyrs, who had contemned the dark things of our earth for things heavenly, desirous of crucifying their flesh with its lusts and its passions. Anna listened attentively to the reading, as to a chant in an unknown tongue. But as soon as Katherine would shut the book, she would never ask her to read some more: the book was always beyond her understanding.

In adolescence she grew not by days, but by hours. When she was about thirteen, she became exquisitely slender, tall, and strong. She was gentle, fair of face, blue-eyed, but the work she liked was of the commonest, of the roughest. When summei came on, when Katherine's husband returned, when the entire village went to the mowing, Anna, too, went with her people and worked like a grown-up. Only, there is not a great deal of summer work in that region. And once more the sisters would be soon left alone, once more they would return to their placid existence; and, once more, having done for the day with the live stock, with the oven, Anna would be sitting at her sewing, or the loom, the while Katherine read aloud: of seas, of deserts, of the city of Rome, of Byzantium, of the miracles and deeds of the first Christians. In the black hut in the forest sounded then words that enchanted the ear: "In the land of Cappadocia, in the reign of the devout Byzantian emperor, Leo the Great . . . In the days of the patriarchship of the most holy Joachhim of Alexandria, in Æthiopia, which is most distant from us. . . ." Thus did Anna come to know of the virgins and youths, torn to pieces by wild beasts at pagan circuses; of the heavenly beauty of Barbara, beheaded by her cruel, ferocious, unnatural parent; of the relics of saints, guarded by angels on the Mount of Sinai; of the warrior Eustacius, converted to the true God by the call of the Crucified Himself, who burst out like a refulgent sun between the horns of a deer that he, Eustacius, had been pursuing in the chase; of the labours of Sabbas the Sainted, that dwelt in the Vale of Fires; and of many, many others, who had spent their bitter days nigh desert springs, in crypts, and in mountain cenobies. . . . During her adolescence she had beheld herself in a dream, clad in a long linen shift and with a crown of iron on her head. And Katherine had told her: "That stands for dying, sister,—for an early death."

And when she was going on fifteen, she became altogether maidenly, and folks marvelled at her loveliness; the aureately-white colour of her face was just the least

[147]

bit tinged with a delicate blush; her eyebrows were bushy, of a light flaxen colour, her eyes blue; she was light, well-made,—unless it were that she was disproportionately tall, slender, and long of arm; quietly and beautifully did she raise her lashes. The winter that year was a rigorous one. The forests, the lakes, were snowed under; the openings in the ice were thickly frozen over; the frosty wind burned; and of dawns, two mirror-like, rainbow-tinged suns were flashing at the same time. Before the Christmas holidays Katherine ate bread-and-*kvass* pudding, and dried oatmeal; but Anna would nourish herself only with bread: "I want to fast till I get another prophetic dream," she had told her sister. And toward the New Year again did she have a dream: she saw an early, frosty morning; the blinding, icy sun seemed to have just rolled out from beyond the snow-drifts, and a cutting wind was making her catch her breath; she was flying upon skiis against the wind, toward the sun, over the white plains, in pursuit of some wondrous ermine,—but she suddenly tumbled off into some abyss, and was blinded, stifled in the cloud of snow dust swirling up at the edge of the precipice from under the skiis.

She could understand nothing of this dream; but Anna, during all New Year's day, did not once look into her sister's face. The priests were going through the village; when they came to see the Skuratovs in their turn, she hid behind the curtains of the sleeping place above the big oven. During that winter, not having yet become settled in her intentions, she was frequently dreamy, and Katherine would say to her: "I have long been calling you, to go to Father Rodion,—he would ease you of all your worries!"

She read to her that winter of Alexis, the Man of God; and of John, who dwelt in a hut of branches,—both had died in poverty at the gates of their well-born parents; she read of Simeon Stylites, who had rotted alive while standing upon a pillar of stone. Anna asked her: "But why doesn't Father Rodion stand on a pillar?" And she answered, that the tasks of holy people are varied, that our Russian martyrs had sought salvation, for the most part, in the caverns of Kiev,—and, later on, within impassable forests; or else had attained the Kingdom of Heaven as naked, useless innocents. During that winter did Anna find out about the Russian saints as well,—her spiritual forefathers: about Matthew the Clear-Seeing, upon whom was bestowed the gift of seeing only the dark and base things of this world, of penetrating into the innermost hidden recesses of filth in the hearts of men, of beholding clairvoyantly the visages of underground devils and of hearing their impious counsellings. She heard of Mark the Grave Digger, who had dedicated himself to the burial of the dead, and who through his incessant proximity to Death had gained such sway over it that it trembled at the sound of his voice; she heard of Isaac the Anchorite, who had clad his body in the undressed hide of a goat which had grown to his skin forever, and who gave himself up to mad dances with evil spirits, that enticed him of nights into skipping and reeling to their noisy calls, reeds, tympani and dulcimers. . . . "From him, from Isaac, started all these innocents," Katherine had told her. "And how many there were of them afterward, none can reckon up! Father Rodion said thus: 'There have been none of them in any other land save ours; only to us did the Lord send them as a visitation for our great sins, and through His great grace.' " And she added what she had heard in the nunnery,—the grievous tale of how Russia had retreated out of Kiev into impassable forests and morasses, into its little towns of bast, under the cruel rule of the princes of Muscovy; what Russia had endured from seditions, from internicine wars, from ferocious Tartar hordes and from other chastisements of God: from plague and famine, from fire and heavenly portents. There was then, said she, such a vast multitude of the folks of God, suffering and acting the innocent for the sake of Christ, that the holy songs were not to be heard for their squealing and clamouring in the churches. And a considerable number among them, said she, were canonized among the heavenly throng. There was Simon, from the forests of the Volga regions, who wandered over desert waste lands, hiding himself from the sight of man, clad only in a torn shift, and afterward, dwelling in a city, he was castigated every day by its citizens for his uselessness, and expired from the wounds inflicted during such castigations. There was Procopius, who took upon himself ceaseless tortures in the town of Viatka, for that he would, in the night-time, clamber up into belfries and ring the bells in quick alarum, as though there were a fiery conflagration. There is a Procopius that was born in the region of Ziryan, amongst savages, amongst hunters after beasts; all his life did he go about with three coal-rakes in his hands; he did adore the desert places, the mournful wooded banks of the Sukhona, where, perched upon a little bowlder, he did with tears pray for those that sailed upon it. There was Jacob the Beatified, who sailed in an oaken log, hollowed out into a coffin, upon an ice block, down the river Msta to the benighted dwellers of that poor region; there is John the Hairy, from near Rostov-the-Greater, whose hair was so unruly that it threw into a panic all whosoever might behold it; there was John of Vologda, called Big Cap, small of stature, wrinkled of face, all hung over with crosses,—until his very death he never took off his head covering, that was like to a pot of cast-iron; there was Basil, that went about naked, who wore for apparel, in winter cold and summer heat, only iron chains and a little handkerchief that he bore in his hand. . . . "Now, sister," Katherine had said, "they are standing before the face of the Lord, rejoicing among the throng of His Saints; as for their imperishable relics, they repose within shrines of cypress and of silver, in the holiest of cathedrals, by the side of kings and prelates!"

"But why doesn't Father Rodion be an innocent?" again asked Anna. And Katherine answered that he had followed in the steps of those who imitated not Isaac, but Sergius of Radonezh; he had followed in the steps of the men who had founded monasteries in forests. Father Rodion, said she, had at first sought salvation in an ancient and famed desert place, located in the same regions where, in the midst of a dreary forest, in the hollow trunk of an oak, three centuries old, a great saint had once dwelt. There had Father Rodion served a strict novitiate and taken the habit; had merited through the tears of his repentance, and through his mercilessness toward the flesh, a sight of the countenance of the Queen of Heaven Herself; he had fulfilled his vow of seven years' seclusion and seven years' silence, but he was not satisfied with that,—he left the monastery, and had come,—it was now many, many years ago,—into these forests. He had put

[151]

on shoes of bast, a white robe of sack-cloth, a black stole with an eight-pointed cross upon it, with a depiction of the skull and bones of Adam; he subsists only upon water and uncooked swamp-grass; he has barred the little window of his cabin with a holy icon; he sleeps in a coffin, under an ever-lit holy lamp, and at the hour of every midnight he is incessantly beset by howling beasts, by throngs of ravening dead men, and by devils. . . .

On her fifteenth birthday, at that very age when a maid ought to become a bride, Anna forsook the world forever.

Spring that year came early and was a warm one. The berries ripened in the woods beyond number; the grasses were waist-high, and at the beginning of the Fast of St. Peter[1] the entire village went out to mow them. Anna worked with a will; became sunburned among the grasses and the flowers; the blush flamed darker upon her face; the kerchief, pushed lower over the forehead, hid her warm glance. But once, in the meadow, a great glistening snake with an emerald head wound itself around her bare foot. Seizing the snake with her slim and long hand, tearing away its icy and slippery plait, Anna cast it far from her without even lifting her face. But she was very much scared,—she had become whiter than linen. And Katherine said to her: "This, sister, is the third sign for thee: dread the Arch-Tempter, a dangerous time is coming for thee!" And it may have been the fright, or it might have been these words,— but for a week after that the deathly pallor did not depart from Anna's face. And just before St. Peter's Day, suddenly and unexpectedly, she begged to go to the

[1] In midsummer. *Trans.*

nunnery to hear the all-night mass,—and did go, and did spend the night there, and in the morning was found worthy of staying in the crowd of humble folk near the threshold of the recluse. And a great grace did he show to her: out of all the crowd did he remark her and did beckon her to him. And she came out of his cabin with her head bent low, covering half her face with her kerchief, having pushed it down over the fire of her flaming cheeks, and in the confusion of her emotions did not see the ground beneath her. And a chosen vessel, a sacrifice to God, had he called her; had lit two little wax tapers, and, taking one himself and giving the other to her, had stood a long while in prayer before an image. And afterwards he had ordered her to kiss that image,—and had given her his blessing to enter the nunnery for a novitiate within a short while. "My joy,—thou simple sacrifice!" he had said to her. "Be thou a bride not of this earth but of heaven! I know, full well, thy sister hath prepared thee. I shall concern myself with this also, sinner that I am."

In the nunnery, in the monastic atmosphere, abandoning the world and her own will for the sake of her spiritual godfather, Anna, who has been named Aglaia upon taking the veil, passed three and thirty months. And when the thirty-third month was almost run, she did depart this life.

How she had lived there, how she had sought her salvation, is known to none, for the remoteness of time. But still some things have remained in the memory of the people. Once upon a time, some peasant pilgrim women, from various and distant places, were bound for that wooded region where Anna had been born.

[153]

Near a small river which they had to cross, they met the usual wanderer over holy places, in appearance ill-favoured, tattered,—even, to put it plainly, queer, for the reason that his eyes, underneath a derby that had once been high in the world, were bandaged with a kerchief. The women began questioning him about the ways, the roads to the nunnery; about Father Rodion himself, and about Anna. He, in answering them, spoke a bit about himself at first: "I, now, little sisters, don't know such a terrible lot, myself; however, I can chat a bit with you, for I am returning from those very parts. You," he said, "must feel uncanny in my company, and I don't wonder at it: I'm not a sweet sight to many; whoever I meet, whether he be afoot or on horseback, seeing a little old pilgrim going through a forest, hobbling along all by his lonesome with a white kerchief over his eyes, and, to boot, chanting psalms to God,—of course, he's taken aback. But then, for my sins, far too greedy and quick are my eyes; my sight is so rare and penetrating, that I can see even at night, like a cat; and being in general sharp-sighted beyond measure, because I don't travel with other folk but keep to myself,—well, for that reason have I resolved to curb a little my corporeal sight. . . ." Then he began telling them how great a distance, by his reckoning, the pilgrim women had left to go; toward what regions they should direct their way; where they might have lodgings and rest; and what sort of a place the nunnery was.

"First," said he, "will come the settlement near Sviyat-Oziero; then that very village where Anna was born; and then you'll see another lake, belonging to the convent, which lake, though shallow, is of a decent size, and you'll have to sail over this lake in a boat. And, as soon as you get out of the boat, right there is the convent itself, so near you might almost reach it with your hand. Of course, there's no end of woods on the other shore as well, and through the trees you can see, as always, the walls of the convents, the domes of chapels, the cells, the hostels. . . ."

Then, for a long while, he related to them the life of Rodion, the childhood and adolescence of Anna, and, in the end, he told them of her stay in the nunnery:

"Oh, her stay was not a long one," said he. "It is a pity you say, with such beauty and youth? Of course, to such fools as we, it would be a piteous thing. But it's plain to be seen Father Rodion knew well what he was about. For he was that way with everybody,— kindly, and meek, and gladsome, yet set on having his way, unto mercilessness; but he was especially so with Aglaia. I, my little ones, have been at the spot where she is resting. . . . A long little grave, beautiful, all grown over with grass, all green. . . . And I won't hide anything,—I won't hide that it was there, at her grave, that I thought of tying up my eyes; it was Aglaia's example that gave me the idea; for she, I must tell you, during all her stay in the nunnery, did not for a single hour raise her eyes; even as she had pushed the veil down over them, so did it remain, and she was so sparing of her speech, so evasive, that even Father Rodion himself wondered at her. And yet, come to think of it, it was no easy matter for her to bear her task—to bid eternal farewell to the world, to the face of mankind! And her work in the nunnery was the very hardest that she could find, while her nights she spent standing in prayer.

[155]

But then, how Father Rodion had come to love her! He marked her out from all the rest, let her come every day into his little cabin; held long converse with her about the future fame of the nunnery; even revealed his visions to her,—with a strict order of silence. Well, and so she burned out, like a candle, in the briefest time. . . . Again do you sigh, being sorry? I do agree with you, it is a sad thing! But I will tell you something far greater; for her great humility, for her disregard of this world, for her silence and for her toiling beyond her strength, he wrought a thing unheard of: toward the end of the third year of her striving, he invested her with the habit, and afterward, after prayer and holy meditation, he did summon her to him on a certain fearsome hour and commanded her to her end. Yes, that is just the way he spoke to her: 'My joy, thy time has come! Remain thou in my memory just as glorious as thou now art, standing before me in this hour; depart to God!' And what think ye? Within four and twenty hours she did forsake this life. She lay down, burning as with a fire,—and passed out. True, he did console her,—he confided to her before her end that by reason of her not having been able, during the first days of her novitiate, to keep just a few things of his secret discourses, only her lips would be rotted. He offered up silver coins for her funeral, and coppers to be given out at her burial; a bundle of candles for a forty days' mass for her; a yellow candle worth a whole rouble for her coffin; and the coffin itself,—rounded out, of oak, hollowed out of one piece. And he blessed her as she was laid out, slender and just a trifle too tall, within that coffin, with her hair all let out, in two shroud-shifts. She was in an under-cassock of white, with a black selvage all around, and in a black mantle with white crosses on top of it; upon her little head they put a green little cap of velvet, broidered with gold; on top of the cap a small skull cap; and after that they tied a blue shawl with tassels upon her head, and then they put a leathern rosary into her dear hands. . . . Oh, I can't tell how fine they arrayed her. And yet, little ones, there is a spiteful rumour which is of the devil, that she did not want to die,—oh, how she didn't want to!

"Departing in such youth and in such beauty, she took her farewell of everybody, so they say, with tears, saying to all, in a loud voice, 'Forgive me!' And at the very last she closed her eyes and said distinctly: 'And against thee, Mother-Earth, have I sinned in body and soul,—wilt thou forgive me?' And those words are fearful words: touching their foreheads to the earth, men uttered them in the prayer for repentance throughout ancient Russia, before Whitsuntide, before the heathen day of the water nixies."

1916.

A CERTAIN Ivlev was once travelling, in the beginning of June, to a distant region of his provence.

The *tarantass*, with its dusty top all awry, had been given him by his brother-in-law, at whose estate he was passing the summer. The *troika* [1] of small but well-broken horses, with thick matted manes, he had hired in the village, from a wealthy *moujik*. They were driven by a son of that *moujik*, a lad of eighteen, —a plodding fellow, a good husbandman. He was all the time cogitating about something with displeasure, seemed to be offended at something, could not take a joke. And, having become convinced that there was no possibility of getting into talk with him, Ivlev yielded to that peaceful and aimless observation, which chimes in so well with the beat of hoofs and the jangling of little bells.

The drive was very pleasant at first: the day was warm, grayish: the road a much travelled one; the meadowlands were full of flowers and sky-larks; from the grain-fields, from the dove-coloured fields of rye, spreading onward as far as the eye could see, a pleasant little breeze was blowing, bearing flower pollen over slanting masses of the grain and rye, at times making this pollen dust swirl like smoke,—and the distance even

[1] Three horses, harnessed abreast. *Trans.*

[158]

seemed misty from it. The lad, in a new cap and a clumsy jacket made of lustrine, was sitting upright; the fact that the horses were completely entrusted to him, and that he was wearing his best clothes, made him especially serious. As for the horses, they coughed and ran along without hurrying; the off-horse at times made the whiffle-tree scrape against the wheel, at others strained in his harness, and one horse-shoe was constantly flashing under him with its white steel.

"Will we stop at the count's?" asked the lad, without turning around, when a village came into view ahead of them, enclosing the horizon with its hedges and garden.

"What for?" said Ivlev.

The lad was silent for a time, and having knocked off with a whip a large gadfly that had stuck to a horse, answered sombrely:

"Why, to drink tea. . . ."

"It isn't tea you've got on your mind," said Ivlev, "you're always trying to save the horses."

"It isn't travelling that worries a horse,—it's food," answered the lad with conviction.

Ivlev looked about him: the weather had turned bleaker, discoloured clouds had gathered from all sides, and drops of rain were already falling,—these unassuming days always wind up with a downpour. . . . An old man in spectacles, who was ploughing near the village, said that only the young countess was at home, but they drove up never the less. The young fellow pulled a long coat over his shoulders, and satisfied with the fact that the horses were resting, was calmly getting soaked under the rain upon the driver's seat of the *tarantass*,

[159]

which had been drawn up in the middle of the dirty yard, near a stone trough that had sunk into the ground, which ground was all trampled over by the hoofs of cattle. He was inspecting his boots, was adjusting with his whip-stock the breech-band of the shaft-horse; while Ivlev sat in the drawing room, which was darkening from the rain. He was chatting with the countess and awaiting tea. There was already a smell of shavings burning; the thick green smoke of the samovar, which a barefooted wench on the steps was stuffing with bundles of brightly burning sticks, pouring kerosene over them, floated past the window. The countess was in a capacious pink dressing gown, which showed her powdered bosom; she smoked, inhaling deeply; she patted her hair frequently, baring her firm and rounded arms to the shoulders; inhaling the smoke and laughing, she kept on leading the talk around to love, and, among other things told him about her near neighbour, the landowner Khvoshchinsky, who, as Ivlev had known ever since childhood, had all his life long been a maniac over his love for his chambermaid Lushka, who had died in early youth. "Ah, this legendary Lushka!" Ivlev had remarked jestingly, slightly confused over his confession. "Because this queer fellow had made a divinity of her, had dedicated all his life to insane dreams of her, I, in my youth, was almost in love with her: I fancied, in thinking of her, God knows what; although, they do say, she was not at all good-looking." "Yes?" said the countess, without listening. "Why, he died this winter, you know. And Pisarev,—the only one whose visits he tolerated, because of their old friendship,—affirms that in everything else he was not in the least insane, and I be-

[160]

lieve it,—he was simply different from the run of the men of to-day. . . ." Finally the barefooted wench with unusual carefullness served him with a glass of strong gray tea out of a teapot, and with a small basket of fly-specked tea cookies.

When they started off again, the rain had set in in earnest. It was necessary to raise the top, to cover up with the calcined, shrunken apron, to sit all hunched up. The horses clattered their muffled bells; little streams ran over their dark and glistening haunches; the grasses swished succulently under their wheels as they passed some boundary or other, among the fields of grain, through which the young fellow had driven in the hope of shortening the way; the warm rye-scented air gathered underneath the top, blending with the odour of the old *tarantass*. . . . "So that's how things are,—Khvoshchin-sky has died," Ivlev was thinking. "I absolutely must drive up, just to have a glance at this deserted sanctuary of the mysterious Lushka. . . . But what sort of a man was this Khvoshchinsky? A madman, or simply some sort of an overwhelmed soul, all centred in one thing?" To judge by the stories of old land-owners, who were of the same age as Khvoshchinsky, he had at one time passed for an extraordinarily clever fellow in this prov-ince. And suddenly there fell upon him this love, this Lushka; then her unexpected death came,—and every-thing went to rack and ruin. He locked himself up in the house, in that room where Lushka had lived and died, and had sat there through more than twenty years,— not only not going out anywhere, but not showing him-self to anybody even on his own estate. He had sat a hole through and through the mattress on Lushka's bed,

[161]

and ascribed literally everything that took place in the world to Lushka's influence: if there were a thunderstorm,—it was Lushka who sent it; if a war were declared,—it meant that Lushka had so decided; if the harvest happened to be bad,—the peasants had not succeeded in pleasing Lushka. . . ."

"You're driving to Khvoshchinsky's, aren't you?" called out Ivlev, putting his head out in the rain.

"To Khvoshchinsky's," came from the lad, indistinctly through the noise of the rain; water was running down from his drooping cap by this time. "Going up Pisarev's hill. . . ."

Ivlev did not know any such road. The settlements were constantly becoming poorer and farther away from the world. The boundary came to an end, the horses were going at a walk, and brought the careening *tarantass* through a washed-out hollow to the bottom of a little hill, into some still unmown meadows, the green declivities of which stood out mournfully against the low-lying clouds. Then the road, now disappearing, now finding itself anew, began to wind in and out, along the bottoms of gullies, through ravines filled with alder bushes and branching osiers. They came upon somebody's little apiary—several small logs standing upon a slope, among tall grass with wild strawberries glimmering red through it. . . . They made a detour of some old dam, sunk among nettles, and a pond long since dried up—a deep hollow, grown over with burdocks taller than a man in height. . . . A pair of black snipe with a mournful cry darted out of them towards the rainy sky. . . . But upon the dam, amidst the nettles, an old, big bush was blossoming out with little pale pink flowers,—that charming little tree which is called God's Own Tree,[1]—and Ivlev suddenly recalled the localities, recalled that he had ridden through here more than once on horseback in his youth, with a gun slung over his shoulders. . . .

"They do say that she drowned herself right here," said the young fellow unexpectedly.

"You're talking about the mistress of Khvoshchinsky, aren't you?" asked Ivlev. "That isn't so; she didn't even think of drowning."

"No,—she did drown herself," said the lad, "only, they think that he went mad from his poverty, most likely, and not on account of her. . . ."

And after a silence, he roughly added:

"Well, we ought to be driving on again. . . . For this same Khvoshchinskoë now. . . . Look at how petered out them horses be!"

"Suit yourself," said Ivlev.

Upon the hillock whither the road (now lead-coloured from the rain) led, upon a clearing from which the trees had been carried away, among the wet, rotting chips and leaves, among the stumps and young aspen growths, with their bitter and fresh scent, a solitary hut was standing. There was never a soul around,—only the singing green-finches, sitting under the rain upon tall flowers, rang through the entire thin forest that stretched upward beyond the hut. But when the *troika*, splashing through the mud, had come abreast of its threshold, a whole pack of huge hounds dashed out from somewhere,—black, chocolate, and smoke-coloured,— and with ferocious baying swirled around the horses,

[1] Abrotanum; southern wood. *Trans.*

[163]

jumping up to their very muzzles, turning head over heels as they ran, and even spinning up to the very top of the *tarantass*. At the same time, and just as unexpectedly, the sky over the *tarantass* was split by a deafening peal of thunder, which had not sounded once during the day, while the young fellow began in a rage to lash the dogs with his whip, and the horses dashed away at a gallop among the aspen trunks that began flashing before the eyes. . . .

The village of Khvoshchinskoë could already be seen beyond the forest. The hounds lost ground and at once grew quiet, trotting back in a business-like manner; the forest gave way and again fields opened up ahead. Evening was coming on, and one could not determine now whether the storm-clouds, on three sides, were dispersing or encroaching. On the left was one almost black, with blue openings through which light showed; on the right, a hoary one, rumbling with ceaseless thunder; while toward the west, from Khvoshchinsky's estate, from beyond the sloping hills over the river valley, was a turbidly blue one, with dusty streaks of rain through which could be seen the roseate mountains of clouds piled in the distance. But the rain was abating about the *tarantass*, and Ivlev, standing up, all bespattered with mud, threw back with pleasure the top, now grown heavy, and freely breathed in the fragrant dampness of the field.

He was looking at the approaching estate, was beholding, at last, that of which he had heard so much; but, even as formerly, it seemed to him that Lushka had lived and died not twenty years ago, but almost in times immemorial. Looking out over the bottom-land, all

trace of the shallow little river was lost in the lush vegetation, over which a white king-fisher was soaring.
Further on, on a mound, lay rows of hay, grown dark
from the rain; among them, far apart from one another, were spread out ancient silvery poplars. The
house, rather a large one and at one time white, with
its wet roof glistening, stood upon an absolutely bare
spot. There was neither garden, nor any outbuildings
around it,—only two pillars of brick in lieu of gates,
and with burdocks growing in the ditches. When the
horses had crossed the little river by a ford and had gone
up the hill, some woman, in a man's summer overcoat with
its pockets hanging down, was driving a few turkey hens
through the burdocks. The *façade* of the house was unusually bleak; it had few windows, and all of them were
small, and set within thick walls. But then, the sombre
front entrances were enormous. From one of them a
young man in the gray blouse of a high-school student,
belted with a broad strap, was looking with wonder at
the arrivals; he was black-haired, with handsome
eyes, and of very pleasing appearance, although his
face was pale, and as spotted with freckles as a bird's
egg.

It was necessary to explain the visit in some way.
Having climbed up to the entrance and given his name,
Ivlev said that he wanted to see, and perhaps to buy,
the library that, so the countess had said, had been left
by the deceased. And the young man, flushing deeply
and pulling down his blouse from behind, at once led
him into the house. "So this, then, is the son of the
famous Lushka!" reflected Ivlev, throwing a rapid glance
at everything that met his eyes. He looked back fre-

quently and said anything that came to mind first, just so as to have an additional glance at the master of the house, who appeared too youthful for his years. The latter answered hurriedly, but monosyllabically; he was evidently confused both by his bashfulness and his greed. That he was fearfully glad over the possibility of selling the books, and that he had conceived the notion of not parting with them at a cheap price, was apparent from his very first words, from that awkward hastiness with which he announced that books such as those in his possession could not be gotten for any amount of money. Through the half-dark entry, which was spread with straw rusty from dampness, he led Ivlev into a large ante-room.

"So this is where your father lived?" asked Ivlev, entering and taking off his hat.

"Yes, yes,—here," the young man hastened to answer. "That is, of course, not just here . . . for they used to sit in the bedroom most of all . . . but, of course, they came here also. . . ."

"Yes, I know,—for he was ill," said Ivlev.

The young man flared up.

"That is, ill in what way?" he said, and manlier notes sounded in his voice. "That's all gossip; he was not at all ailing mentally. . . . he simply read all the time, and did not go out anywhere, that is all. . . . But no, don't you take your hat off, please,—it's very cold here, for we don't live in this half of the building. . . ."

True, it was far chillier in the house than it was out in the air. In the dismal ante-room, its walls pasted with newspapers, upon the sill of a window, dismal from the storm clouds, was standing a quail cage made out

[166]

of bast. A little gray bag was hopping over the floor of its own volition. Bending down, the young man captured it and put it down on a bench, and Ivlev understood that there was a quail imprisoned in the little bag. They next entered the parlour. This room, with its windows toward the west and toward the north, took up almost half the entire house. Through one window, against the gold of the evening glow that showed through the clearing clouds, could be seen a century-old weeping birch tree, all black; through the remaining window, a tall, withering acacia tree. The front corner was taken up by a shrine without glass, with images standing and hanging within it; among them stood out, both by its great size and its antiquity, one trimmed with silver, and upon this image, their wax gleaming yellow like dead flesh, were lying wedding candles tied with pale-green bows.

"Pardon me, please," Ivlev was about to ask, overcoming his scruples, "but, did your father really. . . ."

"No, that's just so," mumbled the young man, instantly grasping his meaning. "He bought these candles after her death already. . . . And he even wore a wedding ring all the time."

The furniture in this parlour was crude. But then, in the spaces between the windows stood exquisite whatnots, crowded from top to bottom with porcelain knickknacks, crystal, tea china, and goblets rimmed with gold. As for the floor, it was entirely strewn over with dead bees, that crackled under foot. The empty parlour, as well, was strewed with the bees. Having traversed it, and also some other sombre room with a sleeping ledge built against the side of a stove, the young man came

[167]

to a stop before a low little door and took a big key out of his trousers'-pocket. Having turned it with difficulty in the rusty key-hole, he threw open the door, mumbling something,—and Ivlev saw a cubby-hole with two windows: against one wall stood a bare iron cot without any bedding; against another—two little book-cases of bird's-eye birch.

"So this is the library?" asked Ivlev, walking up to one of these.

And the young man, having hastened to answer in the affirmative, helped him to open the little book-case, and began to follow his hands covetously.

The strangest of books did this library consist of! Ivlev would open the thick bindings, would turn over a rough, gray page, and would read: *The Forbidden Ground.* . . . *The Morning Star and Night Dæmons.* . . . *Reflections on the Mysteries of Creation.* . . . *A Marvellous Journey into a Magick Region.* . . . *The Latest Dream Book.* . . . And yet his hands would persist in trembling slightly. So this was what that lonely soul, which had secluded itself forever from the world in this little room and had but lately quitted it, had nurtured itself upon? . . . But perhaps this soul had not really been insane, after all?

" 'There is a state. . . .' " The lines of Baratynsky came into Ivlev's mind:

> There is a state,—
> But what name shall it be given?
> 'Tis neither dream nor waking, wavering twixt both;
> And comprehending it within him, man
> To frenzy's verge is driven. . . .

[168]

It had cleared up in the west; gold was peeping out from behind the beautiful lavender-coloured clouds and strangely illumined this humble sanctuary of love,—a love beyond understanding, which had transformed into some ecstatic existence a whole life that perhaps was destined to be a most commonplace one had there not happened to be a certain Lushka, mysterious in her enchantment. . . .

Taking a little foot-stool from under the cot, Ivlev sat down before the cabinet and took out his cigarettes, imperceptibly scrutinizing and memorizing the room.

"Do you smoke?" he asked the young man who was bending over him.

The latter again blushed. "I do," he mumbled, and tried to smile. "That is, I don't exactly smoke,—rather, I try to jolly myself. . . . But, however, if I may,— very much obliged to you. . . ."

And, having clumsily taken a cigarette, he lit it with his hands trembling, walked over to the window-sill and sat down upon it, barring out the yellow light of the evening glow.

"And what is this?" asked Ivlev, bending down to the third shelf, upon which lay only a single volume, very small, resembling a prayer-book, and where also stood a casket whose corners were trimmed with silver, grown black with time.

"That's just . . . the necklace of my late mother," answered the young man, after a confused hesitation, but trying to speak negligently.

"May I have a look?"

[169]

"If you please . . . although it really is very simple
. . . it won't interest you. . . ."

And opening the casket, Ivlev saw a much worn bit
of cord, a string of very cheap little round blue globules,
resembling stone ones. And such emotion possessed him
upon glancing at these globules, which had at one time
lain upon the neck of her whose lot it was to be so beloved, and whose dim image could no longer be anything
but beautiful, that his eyes grew dim from the beating
of his heart. . . . Having looked his fill, Ivlev carefully
put the casket back in its place; he then took up the
little book. This was a tiny, beautifully made *Grammar
of Love, or the Art of Loving and of Being Loved in
Return*, published almost a hundred years ago.

"This book, to my regret, I cannot sell," said the young
man with difficulty. "It's very valuable. . . . He even
put it under his pillow."

"But perhaps you will let me have just a look at
it?" said Ivlev.

"If you please," said the young man in a whisper.

And, overcoming his compunctions, vaguely oppressed
by the young man's gaze, Ivlev began slowly turning the
leaves of *The Grammar of Love*. It was all divided into
short chapters: *Of Beauty, Of the Heart, Of the Mind,
Of Deportment, Of Love's Signs, Of Attack and Defense,
Of Falling Out and Reconciliation, Of Platonic Love.*
. . . Each chapter consisted of very brief, elegant, at times
very subtle, sentences, and some of them were very
lightly marked by a pen in red ink. "Love is not a
mere episode in our Life," Ivlev read. "Our Reason
contradicts the Heart and doth not convince the latter."
"Women are never so strong as when they arm themselves

[170]

with Weakness." "We adore Woman because she holds sovereign sway over our Ideal Dream." "Vanity chooses; True Love,—never." "A Woman of Beauty must take second place; the first belongs to the Woman of Charm. It is the latter that becomes the Sovereign of our Heart: before we have rendered our Heart an account of Her, our Heart becomes a Captive to Love for Eternity. . . ." Then followed *An Explanation of the Language of Flowers*, and again here and there were marked passages:

Wild Poppy—Sadness.
Priest's Cap—Thy alluring beauty is imprinted on my heart.
Periwinkle—Sweet Remembrances.
The Mournful Geranium—Melancholy.
Worm-wood—Eternal Bittnerness.

While upon a blank page at the very end, in tiny, bead-like characters, was a stanza of eight lines, written in the same ink. The young man stretched out his neck as he peeped into *The Grammar of Love*, and said with a forced smile:

"He wrote that himself."

Half an hour later, Ivlev bade him good-bye with relief. Out of all the books he had bought only this small volume at a high price. The turbidly-golden evening glow was fading in the clouds beyond the fields, yellowly reflected in the puddles; the fields were wet and green. The lad was not in any hurry, but Ivlev did not spur him on. The young fellow was saying that that woman who had been driving the turkey hens through the burdocks before was the deacon's wife; that young Khvoshchinsky has been living with her for a long time now, that he already has children. Ivlev was not listening. He was constantly thinking of Lushka; of her necklace, which had left a complex feeling within him, resembling that which he had once experienced in a little Italian town upon beholding the relics of a female saint. "She has come into my life forever!" he reflected. And, taking *The Grammar of Love* out of his pocket, he slowly read over, by the light of the evening glow, the verses written upon its last page:

> We were assigned a thorny wreath
> In this world, where all evils be;
> The love I bore was unto death,—
> It died with me.
>
> But—"Live thou in legends of Love's bliss!"
> Shall greet it hearts that with Love strove;
> And to their grandchildren shall show this
> *Grammar of Love.*

1915.

A NIGHT CONVERSATION

I

THE sky had been silvery with stars all night long, the fields beyond the garden and the threshing floor was darkling evenly, and the wind-mill, with the two horns of its wings, showed sharply black against the clear horizon. But the stars gave out sparks, trembling, frequently cutting the sky with narrow green streaks; the garden was fitfully murmurous, and already chill autumn could be heard in its murmurings. From the direction of the mill, from the sloping plain, from the desolated stubble-field, a strong wind was blowing.

The farm hands had sated themselves at supper,—it was the holiday of the Assumption of the Holy Virgin, —and had avidly smoked their fill on their way through the garden to the threshing barn. Having thrown on their long great coats, tight at the waist, and falling in folds over their short sheepskin coats, they were going there to sleep, to guard the heaps of grain. Following behind the farm hands, dragging a pillow, walked the master's son, a tall high-school student, with three white *borzoi* hounds running at his heels. Upon the threshing floor, in the fresh wind, there was a pleasant smell of chaff, of new rye straw. They all lay down comfortably in it, in the very biggest stack of all, as near as possible to the piles of grain and the corn kiln. The dogs fussed

[173]

about, rustled for a while at the feet of the workers, and also quieted down.

Over the heads of the recumbent men the broad Milky Way, dividing into two smokily-translucent branches, glimmered whitely and faintly, filled with the fine star dust suspended within them. It was quiet and warm in the straw. But a north-east wind, again and again, ran disquietingly through the brushwood that was darkling along the ditch to the left, with its rampart of earth; and increasing, it neared with an inimical noise. Then a cool breath would reach the face, the hands, together with a bad odour from the lanes between the heaps of grain. And over the horizon, beyond the irregular black blotches of the brushwood, icy diamonds vividly flared up; the Capella was bursting into vari-coloured fires.

Having settled down, they all shut their eyes, after a yawning spell. The wind was dreamily rustling the prickling straws that stuck out above their heads. But its coolness reached their faces, and they all felt that they did not want to sleep as yet,—they had slept their fill after dinner. The high-school student alone was languishing from a sweet longing for sleep. But the fleas would not let him sleep. He started scratching, let his thoughts run on wenches, on the widow through whom he, with the help of the farm hand Pashka, had lost his innocence that very summer, and he also became broad awake.

This student was a thin, awkward stripling with an unusually soft colouring—his face was so white that even sunburn had no effect upon it; he was blue-eyed, with outrageously big hands and feet, with a big Adam's-apple. He had not parted company with the farm hands

[174]

all summer,—at first he had carted manure, then the
sheaves; he put in order the piles of grain, he smoked an
atrocious cheap tobacco, he imitated the *moujiks* in
speech and in his roughness with wenches, who always
started laughing at him in chorus, greeting him with cat-
calls and cries of "Veretenkin! Veretenkin!" [1]—a stupid
nickname invented by Ivan, who was a helper at the
threshing machine. He passed his nights now at the
threshing floor, now in the horse stable; he did not change
his linen and his canvas clothes for weeks at a time, nor
would he take off his tarred boots; he raised blood-blisters
on his feet, unaccustomed to coarse foot-cloths; he lost all
the buttons on his summer uniform overcoat, which had
been soiled by wheels and manure, had broken the letters
and the little silver leaves on his uniform cap.

"He has broken away from the house entirely!" his
mother would say of him, with a caressing, kindly regret,
enraptured even by his defects. "Of course, he'll pick
up, become stronger,—but just look what a matted choate
he is,—he doesn't even wash his neck!" she would say,
smiling to her guests and pulling his soft, chestnut locks,
trying to get at the soft little spiral, curling like a girl's,
at the nape of his neck,—dark, contrasting with the
childishly white flesh visible under the blouse that buttoned at the side, contrasting with the large vertebræ
under the fine, smooth skin. But he would sulkily turn
his head away from under her caressing hand, frowning
and blushing. He grew not by the day but by the hour,
and as he walked he stooped, whistling meditatively, an-
gularly lumbering from side to side. He still ate linden
blossoms and the gum of cherry trees; he carried, al-

[1] "Spindle-Shanks! Spindle-Shanks!" *Trans.*

[175]

though by now secretly, a sling shot to shoot sparrows with, but he would have been consumed with shame had this been revealed, and he constantly kept his hands in his pockets. Only last winter he had played Redskins with his little sister Lily. But in the spring, when through all the streets of the town streams were running and shimmering with a blinding dazzle; when the white window-sills in the class-rooms were aflame with the sun; when the teacher's room was shot through and through with the sun, and the principal's cat was lying in ambush for the first finches in the high-school garden, still filled with silvery snow,—in the spring he had gotten the notion that he had fallen in love with the slender little Youshkova, a bookish, serious-minded high-school girl; he had struck up a close friendship with Simashko, a spectacled six-termer, and had determined to dedicate his entire summer vacation to self-culture. But in the summer his dreams about self-culture were already forgotten; a new resolve was taken,—to study the common people; which resolve had soon passed into a passionate infatuation with the *moujiks*.

On the evening before the Assumption, the high-school boy was heavy with sleep while still at supper. Toward the end of every day, when his head would grow heavy and fall down on his chest,—from fatigue, from talking with the farm hands, from his rôle of a grown-up,— his boyishness returned: he wanted to play a bit with Lily, to have a brief reverie, before falling asleep, of some distant and unknown lands, of extraordinary manifestations of passion and self-sacrifice, of the lives of Livingston and Baker, and not of the *moujiks* written about by Naumov and Nephedov, whom he had given his word of honour to Simashko to read; he wanted to sleep, for at least one night, at home, instead of getting up before the sun, in the cold morning light, when even dogs yawn and stretch so languorously. . . . But the maid entered, saying that the farm hands had already gone to the threshing floor. Without listening to his mother's calls, the high-school lad threw his uniform overcoat with its bobbing belt over his shoulders, and put on his cap; grabbing the pillow out of the maid's hands, he caught up with the farm hands in the lane. He staggered from drowsiness as he walked, dragging the pillow by a corner, and, as soon as he had stumbled up to the heap of straw and had crawled under an old raccoon overcoat lying there, he sailed off into some sweet, black darkness. But the tiny dog-fleas began to burn him as with fire; the farm hands began talking among themselves. . . .

There were five of them: Khomut,[1] a kindly, shaggy old man; Kiriushka, a lame, white-eyed, irresponsible lad, who gave himself up to a childish vice, which fact everybody knew and which made Kiriushka still more irresponsible, making him bear in silence all sorts of jeers about his short leg, twisted at the knee; Pashka, a good-looking *moujik* of twenty-four and recently married; Theodot, an elderly *moujik*, from another region, somewhere near Liebedyana, nick-named Postnii;[2] and Ivan, —a very stupid fellow, but one who deemed himself an amazingly clever, cunning, and mercilessly-scoffing man. This last held in contempt all work, save work with agricultural machines; he wore a blue blouse and had im-

[1] "Horse-collar." *Trans.*
[2] "Lenten." *Trans.*

pressed everybody with the idea that he was a born machinist, although everybody knew that he did not know a blamed thing about the construction of even a simple winnowing machine. He was always narrowing his morosely-ironic little eyes and pursing up his thin lips, never letting a pipe out of his teeth. He generally kept a portentous silence; but whenever he did speak, it was only to annihilate somebody or something with a comment or a nick-name. He scoffed at absolutely everything: at sense and folly, at simplicity and slyness, at despondency and laughter; at God and his own mother, at the gentry and the *moujiks*. The nick-names he bestowed were absurd and incomprehensible, but he uttered them with such an enigmatic air that it seemed to everybody that they had both a meaning and a caustic aptness. He had not spared even himself, and had given himself a nick-name: "Rogojkin," [1] he had said once in reference to himself, hinting at something so weightily, so maliciously, that everybody rolled from laughter, and afterwards he was never known as anything but Rogojkin. He had christened the high-school student as well, had said something nonsensical about him as well: "Veretenkin."

The school-boy,—so he thought,—had come to know these people well during the summer, had become attached to all of them in different ways,—even to Ivan, who unmercifully made fun of him. He was learning one thing or another from them, was adapting their pronounciation,—absolutely, as it proved, unlike the speech of the *moujiks* in books; adopting their unexpected, absurd, but unshakable conclusions, the uniformity of their

[1] "Made out of matting." *Trans.*

[178]

ready wisdom, their coarseness and indifference, their capacity for work and their dislike of it. And, had he gone to the city after the vacation, without reverting to his infatuation for the life of the *moujiks* during the next summer, he would all his life have thought that he had observed the common people of Russia very well,—if, by accident, a lengthy, frank conversation had not sprung up among the farm hands on this night.

It was started by the old man who was lying alongside of the school-boy and who was scratching more than anybody else.

"Pestering the life out of you, young master, hey? They're nothing but a misery, Khomut!" said he,—the word "Khomut" he used to characterize not only his entire existence, but also all its weariness, all its unpleasantness.

"Can't stand it," replied the school-boy. "The women and wenches now, the devil take them, they won't touch. But who would you think they ought to be biting if not them?"

"Main thing is, whether a body wear drawers or no, it makes no difference to them fleas," indifferently agreed the old man, giving off, as he tossed about, a strong odour,—of a body long unwashed, and of a worn peasant's coat that had become permeated with the smoke of a chimneyless hut.

The others kept silence. Usually, they were jocose before falling asleep, questioning Pashka about his conjugal life, while he answered them with such unperturbed and gay shamelessness that even the school-boy, who was constantly entranced by him, never taking his eyes off his intelligent and animated face, was vexed over any one's being able to speak so of one's own young wife. Now no one seemed about to begin questioning, and the student wanted to do so himself, in order to excite his imagination, forever empoisoned by the widow, and to hear the self-assured voice of Pashka,—when the latter stretched himself, sat up, and began rolling a crude cigarette. The old man raised up his head, covered with a cap, and shook it.

"Eh, but you'll burn this place down some day, young fellow!" said he. "Watch out. It don't take much to bring on trouble."

"Well, I'll get out of it by blamin' the young master," answered Pashka, a trifle hoarse from a cold; and, having cleared his throat, he started laughing. "He's smoking all the time himself. Wonderful night to-night, young master," said he, changing his tone to a serious one and turning around to the school-boy. "What's the only thing lacking on this night, you might say? Why, the moon."

They all felt that he wanted to tell something. And, truly, having kept silent for a while, without eliciting any reply, he suddenly added:

"Are you asleep, young master? What hour might it be now?"

The school-boy raised himself up, pulled his silver watch out of his trouser's-pocket, and began inspecting it by the light of the stars.

"Half-past ten," said he, bending over.

"Well, now, I just knew it was that," concurred Pashka, gaily and self-assuredly, lighting his cigarette, which was rolled somewhat in the form of a pipe; it was gripped in one corner of his mouth between his teeth, and he lit it with a stinking sulphur match flaming within his cupped hands. "Just exactly at this time last year I killed a man."

And the school-boy at once straightened up, letting his hands drop,—and he seemed to be turned to stone during all the time that the others talked. At rare intervals he would put in a word, but it was as though it were not he, but some other who was talking in his stead. Then everything within him began to shiver in an icy ague fit inducive of senseless laughter, and his face began to burn, as though it were aflame.

II

Ivan, as always, maintained a portentous silence. Kiriushka was not at all interested in whatever they were talking about; he lay thinking his own thoughts,— mostly about an accordeon, the purchase of which was his most cherished dream. Theodot, too, who lay leaning upon his elbow, was silent for a long while. He was a strong, flat-chested *moujik*, who at the beginning of the summer had not been considered by the farm hands as one of them, because he wore a short sheepskin coat, without a waistline and without folds in its skirts,—which was the kind worn by the Tartars of Kazan. He had seemed a stranger to the school-boy as well. Just as he liked the cheerful composure of Pashka, the smoothness of his mannerisms, his sun-burned face, so he was not disposed to intimacy by the face of Theodot, also calm but devoid of any expression, large, ashen-gray, wrinkled, with sparse moustaches, always wet from the slavering caused by his pipe; his whitish, weather-beaten lips were

[181]

turned considerably outward. Theodot was listening attentively, but did not put in a single word during Pashka's narrative,—only now and then he would give a consumptive cough and spit into the straw. And at first the conversation was sustained only by the dumbfounded school-boy and the old man.

"What are you lyin' about nothin' at all for?" said the old man indifferently, upon hearing the boastful declaration of Pashka. "What sort of a man could you have killed? Where?"

"Bust my eyes if I'm lyin'!" responded Pashka warmly, turning in the old man's direction. "Last year, on Assumption. Not only was it wrote up in all the papers,—it was even in the order sent to the regiment."

"Well, where was it you killed him?"

"Why, in the Caucasus, in the Zukhdens. Honest to God! Of course, I ain't agoin' to lie about it; I didn't do it all single-handed,—Koslov also fired a shot; he's also one of ours, from the Eletzkaya province. I wasn't the only one that got the thanks for it; the division commander thanked him too, in front of all the men lined up, and rewarded us with a rouble each, right off; but then, I know without any mistake that it was me that winged him."

"What him?" asked the high-school student.

"Why, a convict; this Cheorchian, now."

"Hold on," the old man interrupted him. "You just tell the whole thing sensibly. Where was you stationed?"

"There he goes again!" said Pashka with assumed vexation. "There's a queer fellow,—won't believe

[182]

nothing. We was stationed at these New Ceniyaks, now. . . ."

"I know the place," said the old man. "We, too, was stationed there for eighteen days."

"There, you see now,—that means I ain't just making it up as I go along, for I can tell you how this happened, just about. We wasn't stationed for no eighteen days then, brother, but for a whole year and seven months; as for these here convicts, we was in duty bound to escort them up to the very Zukhdens. These here convicts, now, was the most important criminals what could possibly be,—rebels, they was. So then, ten of them in all was caught in the mountains and put in our keeping. . . ."

"Hold on," interrupted the high-school student, imitating the old man, and feeling his hands turning to ice; "but how was it you told me that you'd never get to shooting any rebels,—that you'd liefer shoot any officer who might order you to fire at them?"

"Well, I wouldn't let my own father off, when need be," answered Pashka, throwing a furtive glance at the student, and again turning to the old man. "Maybe I'd never have laid a finger on him, even, if he hadn't taken it into his head to ruin us all; but no, he went in for foxiness and we might all have been sentenced to hard labour for a whole year. But as it turned out, it was all for the best; we got thanks and turned out to be a bit smarter than him. Just you listen, now," he said, pretending that he was addressing the old man only. "We was leading them along, all fair and square. We didn't have any of these carryings on, like beating them, now, for example, or

[183]

urging them on with the butt-end of a gun. . . . But one of them,—a sort of a skinny fellow, short of stature,—was walking along and complaining about his stomach all the time, asking us all the while to let him do something. . . . He just barely managed to tinkle along in his leg-irons. Then, at last, he approaches the superior officer: 'Let me lie down in the cart.' Well, he was allowed to do so, like he was real sick. Only by now we come to the Zukhdens. And the night's as black as pitch, and it's raining cats and dogs. We made 'em sit down on the front entrance, and watched 'em; each one of the soldiers had a little lantern in his hands, of course, while the superior officer went off into the room, to try the bars at the windows to see if they was all right, now, and hadn't been filed away by some hidden file."

"Absolutely," said the old man. "According to law he's got to take over everything in good shape."

"That's just what I'm talkin' about," confirmed Pashka, again hastily hiding a lit sulphur match in his cupped hands. "You know all this business, now, and that makes it interestin' to be telling you about it. Well, the superior officer had gone off," he went on, squeezing out the match and letting the smoke out of his nostrils, "he'd gone off, inspecting things, while we stand around, nodding our heads,—we wanted to sleep something dreadful,—when this here Cheorchian suddenly jumps up, and off 'round the corner with him! That means, you understand, that he had all this business figured out, while he was still in the cart; he had cut the strap around his legs that held the shackles, with the first thing that had come to his hand; had loosened them upon him, then picked 'em up in his hand, so,—" Pashka bent over and, spread-

[184]

ing his legs, demonstrated how the prisoner had grabbed up the shackles, "and then had taken to his heels! But me and Koslov was no fools; we dropped our lanterns and took after him: Koslov ran around the corner too, whilst I went straight ahead to cut him off. I keep on running, but all the time I'm trying to catch the clink,— where his chains might be clanking, that is. It ain't even worthwhile to be shootin' at haphazard, thinks I. At last, I catch the sound,—and bang! I feel it go past him. I fire another shot,—again I hear it go by him. But Koslov is popping away right and left; like as not to get me any minute. . . . Then I got riled: 'Ah,' thinks I, 'may your eyes bust out!' I put the gun to my shoulder and I let 'er go: glory be to the Lord, I got him,— I hear by the sound that he must have fallen down. I let out two more shots toward the same spot, and ran; and there he was sitting on his bottom on the ground. He's sitting down, propped up with his hands in the dirt; his teeth are bared, and he's rattlin': 'Quick,' says he, 'quick, Russ, stick your bayonet into me right here. . . .' Meaning his chest, that is. I charged with my bayonet on a run,—straight through his heart. . . . Why, the bayonet went right out at his back!"

"Good work!" said the old man. "Let's have just one good puff. . . . Well, and where was Koslov at now?"

Pashka inhaled some smoke, deeply and quickly, and thrust the fag-end into the old man's hand.

"Why, Koslov," he answered, hurriedly and gaily, flattered by the praise, "why, Koslov is running, yelling with all his might: 'Did you do for him?' 'I've done for him' says I, 'let's drag the carcass away. . . .' We took him by the shackles at once and dragged him back,

[185]

to the porch. . . . I cut him down like a weed," said he, changing his tone to a calmer and more self-satisfied one.

The old man cogitated for a while.

"And you say the officer rewarded you with a rouble each?"

"That's straight," answered Pashka. "He gave it to us right out of his own hands, with all the battalion lined up on parade."

The old man, shaking his cap-covered head, spat into his palm and extinguished the cigarette end in the spittle.

Ivan, leisurely, through his teeth, drawled out:

"Well, it's plain to be seen there's lots of fools among the soldiers too."

"How do you make that out?"

"Why, here's how," said Ivan, "you durn fool! What should you have done? You oughtn't to have dragged him, but should have sent your mate with a report, and stood guard with a gun over the dead body. D'you understand now, or don't you?"

III

Theodot began speaking even more plainly, after a general silence and a muttering of: "Ye-es . . . well done. . . ."

"Well, now," he began slowly, lying back on his elbow and casting an occasional glance at the dark figure of the student, motionlessly stuck before him against the background of the starry sky; "well, now, I sinned absolutely over nothing. I killed a man over a mere trifle, you might say; all on account of a she-goat I had."

"What do you mean,—over a she-goat?" the old man, Pashka, and the school-boy interrupted him in unison.

"Honest to God, that's the truth," answered Theodot. "But you just listen a while to what sort of bane this she-goat was. . . ."

The old man and Pashka again lighted cigarettes and began to stamp down the straw, in preparation to listening. The student, too, wanted to light up, but his icy hands would not stir, would not come out of his pockets. As for Theodot, he continued seriously and calmly:

"The whole trouble was just on account of her. I didn't do the murder on purpose, of course. . . . He was the first to beat me up. . . . And there was quarrelling, going to court. . . . He came, drunk, whilst I jumped out, all heated up, and hit him with a whet-stone. . . . But what's the sense of talkin' about it; as it was, I done penance for half a year at a monastery on account of him; but if there hadn't been this here she-goat, nothing at all would have happened. Main thing was, none of us had ever kept these here goats; they ain't in the *moujik's* line, and we can't understand the handling of them; and then, to top it all, the goat turned out to be a bad one, and frisky. What carrion she was,—the Lord save me from such another! Just the same as a little *borzoi* bitch, she was. Maybe I wouldn't have wanted to get her,—everybody was laughing, talking me out of it as it was; but I was downright forced to it by need. We ain't got any large, well-managed farms, nor any sort of free land or forests. . . . We ain't had a common pasture land of our own from time out of mind, and as to what small live-stock we might have, it simply

[187]

has to find forage on the waste-lands. As for large cattle,—we used to put the cows into the big owner's grounds, and for all that sort of thing us little fellers was supposed to mow, and bind in sheaves, two acres of grain, and plough two acres of fallow-land; and put in three days with the old woman at mowing, and three days at threshing. . . . Count it up,—and what don't it come to?"

"The Lord deliver us!" the old man supported him sympathetically.

"Whereas to buy a she-goat," Theodot went on, "well, that meant scraping off seven, or say eight, roubles to give away for her; on the other hand, if she tried hard, she'd yield four bottles, no less, of milk, and the milk she'd give was thicker and sweeter nor cow milk. The hard part about her was, of course, that you couldn't keep her together with the sheep; a she-goat fights with them a lot, when she's carrying a kid, and once she starts in she gets fiercer'n a dog,—just can't bear to look at them. And what a creature she was for climbing,—it didn't mean nothin' to her to get up on top of a hut, or a clump of willows. Wherever there was a willow, she was dead sure to strip it bare, would strip off all its tender bark—there was nothing she liked better'n that!"

"But you wanted to tell us how you killed a man," the school-boy uttered with difficulty, looking all the while at Pashka, at Pashka's face, indistinct in the light of the stars; he was incredulous that this very Pashka was a murderer, and he was picturing to himself a small, dead Georgian, whom two soldiers were dragging along by his chains, through the mud, surrounded by a dark rainy night.

[188]

Gawd knows how I grieved; however I went to ploughing,—it was just ploughing time then. I took a bit of
bread with me, wrapped up in a kerchief, laying it down
near the edge of the field where I was working. Now,
on another mound, there was one of our village lads
ploughing,—suddenly, I hear him shouting something,
pointing with his hand. I look around and just gasp:
there was the she-goat! She had dragged out the little
bundle, seizing it in her teeth; she had shaken it loose
and was standing, jerking her beard, and eating the
bread. . . . I dropped my plough as fast as I could and
went for her. I go after her, and she goes away from
me. I go after her, and she goes away from me,—she'd
run a little ways, and stop, and munch the bread,—a
lot she cared! And such a happy and a clever carcass
she was,—she watched every move I made. I had my
heart set on her, I sure wanted to catch her. I just
could have smashed her to bits, it seems! She gobbled
down the bread and went off; she'd turn around and
give me a look, shaking her tail,—well, just making fun
of me!"

"No use talking,—it's a carefree creature!" said the
old man.

"That's just what I'm saying!" exclaimed Theodot, en-
couraged by the sympathy. "That's just what I'm talking about,—that she downright ruined us! There hadn't
even a week passed, when everybody had it in for me:
'Your goat,' says they, 'as good as lives amongst our
grain.' She trampled down a whole eighth of an acre of
my own, tearing down all the ears of oats. Then one
day a thunder-storm came up; the lightning started in
flashing, and the rain poured down,—I looked and I see

my white she-goat sailing along with all her might straight toward our place, bleating like she was scared out of her own voice—and then she pops straight into our doorway. I started off as fast as my legs would carry me after her; I got her into a tight corner, drew a cord that I used for a belt over her horns, and began letting her have it. . . . The thunder rumbles, the lightning flashes, but I keep on lambasting her, I keep on lambasting her! I must have beat her for more than an hour, without lying. Then I put her up on the brewing vat, tied her up with the rope girdle . . . but who knows whether the girdle was rotted, or whether it was something else,— only when we look in the morning, the goat's gone again! Then—would you believe it?—I was so vexed, that I just burst into tears!"

IV

Theodot's tone had become so simple, so sincere, so filled with the tones of husbandry aggrieved, that it would never have entered anybody's head that here was a murderer, confessing his sin. Then, too, he was listened to in a spirit of simplicity. Kiriushka was lying flat on his belly, his head covered with his great coat; his feet, in big bast sandals and thickly wrapped in foot cloths, were sticking out. Ivan, with his cap shoved down over his forehead, his hands tucked into his sleeves, was lying on his side, also without moving; as for his stern and serious silence, he maintained it because he deemed it beneath his dignity to be interested in fools. He was so little concerned whether those before him were murderers or not, that he had even called out once:

"Time to sleep! Finish that gabbing to-morrow!"

As for Pashka and the old man, both half-reclining and biting little straws, they merely shook their heads and grinned occasionally, as if to say: "Well, Theodot sure has known his fill of trouble with that she-goat!" And Theodot, evidently deeming himself already vindicated by this sympathy for his ridiculous and hard situation, lost entirely his diffidence about digressions. And the high-school boy, gritting his teeth both from the wind and from the inner cold, would at times look about him wildly: Where was he, and what queer night was this? But it was still the same simple, familiar country night, of which there had been many. The field was dark, the corn-kiln stood out in a sharp triangle against the starry sky; through the underbrush, beyond which the stars flared up and fell, a wind was blowing; its cool breath, with the pleasant scent of the chaff, reached the face and hands, rustled in the straw, and again grew still, dying away. . . . The hounds—white balls sunk in the straw—were fast asleep. . . . And all the horror lay only in that it was late, that a small cluster of silver stars had risen high in the north-east, that the dark mass of the slumbrous garden was murmuring in the distance, dully, autumn-wise; that the eyes in the faces of those conversing were sparkling in the starlight.

"Yes, little brother of mine," Theodot was saying, laughing over his own ridiculous and sad predicament, "nobody can't say it weren't a misfortune! At last they tell me, now, that a *moujik* in the Prilepakh had driven my she-goat to his place. I start out to get her back; no help for it,—such seemed to be my lot. I come to the village; there's nobody around, wherever I look,—

everybody's out in the fields. A lad is riding off for water; I ask him,—'Where's Bockhov's house?' 'Why,' says he 'right there, where the old woman in the red petticoat is sitting under a bush.' I walk up: 'Is this Bochkov's place?' The old woman waves her hand at me, pointing to a little yard in the blazing sun. . . ."

"Must have gone daft from old age," put in Pashka, starting to laugh so pleasantly that the student looked around at him with amazement and fear, reflecting: "Why no,—it can't be true; he must have told lies about himself!"

"She was gone daft," confirmed Theodot. "Just kept on waving her hand. But I had already been hearing a hog grunting in the little yard. I open the door to a sty, a corner fenced off with plaited willow, where this same pig was kept. I see a big sow pulling a woman around; the woman's thrown her weight upon it, holding it with both hands, pouring out of a pail upon it with the other. And the sow is all black from mud, lugging the woman, dragging her along,—the woman can't manage her nohow, and her clothes is pulled up to her belly. It was both to sin and to grin! Soon as she saw me, she pulls down her skirt,—her legs, her hands was all in manure. . . . 'What d'you want?' 'What do I want? I'm here on business. You drove my she-goat up here; you're keeping strayed cattle, but ain't giving out no notice of it.' 'We ain't keeping any she-goat of yours,' says she. 'We let her go. We drove her into the owner's place.' And she laughs at something. 'So-o,' thinks I, 'that means I'm in hot water again: well, just you wait!' I went out and kept on; I had just gone past the next farm, had turned up a path through some flax, when a

[194]

red-haired little fellow bobs up from somewheres right in my way. 'Did you come for the goat?' 'For the goat,—but why?' Suddenly I hear a woman yelling beyond the hut: 'Where you gone to, Kuzka, damn your eyes!' 'Run quick,' I says, 'here's your mother comin' with some stinging nettles.' And there she was, right on the spot; she sees him and runs: 'Didn't I tell you to look after the little one? But where did you go off to, you so-and-so?' And then she pounces on me! 'Where you from?' 'And what business of yours may that be now?' 'Oh, no, you tell me where you're from!' 'I'm the man in the moon. What are you yelling about? I'm looking for my she-goat.' 'Oh, so it's you, is it, damn your eyes, that don't give any peace to the village with your goat!' And suddenly I see a tall *moujik* rushing toward me from the corn kiln,—without a cap, beltless, in boots. He ran on me at full speed. 'Your goat?' 'Mine. . . .' He unwraps himself, swings back, and lets fly one in my ear."

"Good work!" exclaimed the old man and Pashka in the same breath; as for the school-boy, he even let out a little squeal: this, then, was the most horrible part of all! But Theodot calmly pulled out the skirt of his short coat from under him, and calmly continued:

"Oh, yes, he warmed me up so that my head just begun to hum. I grab him by his hands, and ask him, what that was for? And by now people was running up. . . . Right in front of everybody, I ask them to be witnesses of this here matter; again I ask what it was my goat had gone and done? It turns out that she had knocked a child off its feet, had broken its head, making it bleed; had chewn up a shirt, and had trampled some rye. Very

well,—complain to the court about it; there I'll be called
to account and you won't be let off either. 'Now,' says
I, 'you ain't a-goin' to get a durn thing off me!' I put
on my cap and went as fast as I could to the owner's
yard. I grew a trifle cheerier: the goat, thinks I, won't
get away from me now; and you can't sue me now,—
you should have waited before you started in fighting
with me. I draw near and I see, on a pony with a clipped
tail, a lad in a satin cap, his legs and arms bare,—a
jockey, they calls it. The horse is playful, and he flicks
it with a little whip. 'How do you do, now; allow me
to ask,—has your grace got my she-goat?' 'And who may
you be?' 'I'm the owner of that there goat.' 'Well, now,
my daddy ordered it to be driven in.' Things are going
along fine; I go on farther and meet a beggar, from
whom I lay in some bread,—for the hounds in the
owner's yard are pretty big. I enter the yard and see
a four-horse carriage standing on the gravelled drive
near the house,—the horses are well-fed, spirited.
There's a flunky at the grand entrance, his beard parted
in two. A grown-up young lady walks out in a hat
trimmed with ribbons, her face all covered up with
muslin. 'Dasha!' she yells to the maid in the house,
'ask the master to come as soon as possible. He's at
the riding-ground.' I start for the riding-ground.
There I see the owner himself standing, in a uniform
frock with a green collar; he wears a medal and carries
his cap in his hand; his bald head simply blazes in the
sun, his belly is all in creases, and he's all red himself.
And there's a little lad perched up on the roof, his arm
plunged in under the roofing, looking for something,—
must be for starlings, thinks I to myself. But no,—he

[196]

was taken up with sparrows. The owner looks on, yelling: 'Catch them, catch, them, the sons of bitches!' And the little boy catches the young sparrows, pulls them out, and knocks them against the ground. The owner catches sight of me: 'What do you want?' 'Why, now,' says I, 'your gardener caught my she-goat at the strawberries. Allow me to take her away, so's I may kill her.' 'This isn't the first time, now,' says he, 'I shall fine you two roubles.' 'I agree with you,' I says, 'I'm at fault, and I admit it. What hard luck!' I says, 'I always have two wenches watching it; but yesterday, as though for spite,—the deuce knows whether they ate too many raw mushrooms, or what it was,—they was rolling around, spewing up; and as for my wife, she also didn't watch out, to tell the truth,—she was lying in the barn, yelling with all her might,—her hand had all swollen up. . . .' A man's got to excuse himself somehow. I tell him all about what a baneful creature my she-goat is, how I was given one in the ear for her,—he laughs and grows good-natured. 'No matter how I chase her,' says I, 'I can't catch her nohow; and I so wanted to ask your grace for a little gunpowder and to borrow a gun from the truck gardener, so's to shoot her with it. Well, of course, he softened a lot, allowed me to take her, and I done for her on the spot.''

"You done for her?" asked the old man.

"Absolutely," said Theodot. " 'Well, take it,' says he, 'only watch out, don't mix it up with mine.' 'That won't happen, nohow,' says I, 'I'd know her amongst a thousand.' We went out to the fold, taking Pakhomka the shepherd along with us. I give one look,—and at once notice her behind the sheep; she was standing, looking at me sharply for some reason, eyeing me askance. Me and Pakhomka got the sheep into a corner as tight as we could, and I began to walk up to her. I make two steps,—she gives one jump over a ram! And again she stands, looking. Again I start for her. . . . And then, she points her head with its horns toward the ground and makes one dash for the sheep, and they all just rush away from her,—they parted like water! Then I got mad. Says I to Pakhomka: 'You just drive her up as easy as you can, the whilst I climb up on the shed, where it's darker, and grab her by the horns.' And it's awful how much manure there was in that yard, right up to the very sheds in some places. I climbed up on the shed, laid down, grabbed a beam as hard as I could, whilst Pakhomka kept on scaring her on toward me. I waited and waited, until finally she came under the very shed,—and then I made a grab for her horns! And then she starts in bleating. I even got scared! I fall off the shed; I dig my feet in, holding on to the horns, while she dashes with me all over the yard, drags me up to a pit; then she squirms out, scraping me with her horn over the beard, over the nose,—till everything turned black. . . . When I look up, she's already up on the roof: she'd jumped up on the pile of manure, from the manure on to the roof, from the roof into the tall grass. . . . We could hear the dogs getting noisy in the yard; the other dogs picked it up, raising a racket in the village. We, of course, jumped out after her. But she's flying along with all her might, and straight for the last hut: there was a new hut being built there; the windows was still boarded up and there was no entry yet, while there was just bare poles laid aslant for the roof. So she clambered up them up to the very ridge—a power like a whirlwind must have carried her up there! We ran up as fast as we could; as for her, she must have felt her death coming,—she was bleating for all she was worth, all scared. I picked up a hefty brick, took aim,—and caught her so neat that she just jumped up in the air, and then started with a swish down the roof! We ran up, but she was just lying there, her tongue jerking in the dust. . . . She'd take a breath and then rattle, take a breath and rattle again,—till the dust rose up near her nose. And her tongue was long, just like a snake. . . . Well, of course, after half an hour or so, she had croaked."

V

There was a silence. Theodot raised himself up to a sitting posture, and, bending down, spreading his hands, began slowly to unwind the cords with which his old, constantly falling foot-cloths were tied up. And a minute later the school-boy with horror and repulsion saw that which he had seen so many times before with perfect calmness: a *moujik's* bare foot, dead-white, enormous, flat, with a monstrously grown great toe lying crookedly on top of the others, and the thin, hairy skin, which Theodot, having unwound and dropped the foot-cloth, began to scratch hard in a delectable fury, tearing it with his nails, as strong as those of a beast. Having scratched his fill and wriggled his toes, he took the foot-cloth with both hands,—it was hardened, bent, and blackened at the heel and sole, just as though it had been rubbed with black wax,—and shook it out, spreading an unbearable stench upon the fresh breeze. "Yes, murder means nothing to him!" reflected the student, shivering. "That is the foot of a real murderer! How horribly he killed this beautiful she-goat! And the man that he killed with a whet-stone . . . he must have been sharpening a scythe . . . and must have struck him straight in the temple, killing him on the stop. . . . But Pashka! . . . Pashka! . . . How could he tell about it so gaily and with such enjoyment, too! 'It came right out at his back!' "

Suddenly, without raising his head, Ivan began speaking morosely:

"Fools are beaten even at the altar. Why, Postnii, it wouldn't be half-enough to beat you to death for this here she-goat. What did you go and kill her for? You should have sold it. What sort of a husbandman do you call yourself after that, you durn ninny, when you don't understand that a *moujik* can't get along without live-stock? It should be valued. If I only had a she-goat, now. . . ."

He didn't finish his sentence, was silent for a while, then suddenly grinned.

"There was an affair in Stanova, now; well that really was something. . . . It wasn't worse than your goat, now; a land-owner by the name of Mussin was keeping a wild bull. This bull just wouldn't let anybody pass; he gored two young cowherds to death. They'd fasten him up with a chain, but still he'd tear loose and go off. Just the very same way, too, like your goat, he'd trample the peasants' grain; but no one dared to chase him off: they were afraid, and would walk a mile around him. Well, of course, they sawed off his horns, gelded

[200]

him. . . . He quieted down a bit. Only the *moujiks*
scored up everything against him. When these here
riots began, here's what they did: they caught him in
the field, tied him up with ropes, threw him off his
feet. . . . They didn't beat him at all, but just took and
stripped him to the last hair. So, all bare, he dashed
into the owner's yard,—he ran in at full speed, fell all
in a heap, and died right on the spot,—losing all his
blood."

"How?" asked the school-boy; "they took his hide
off? While he was alive?"

"No, while he was cooked," mumbled Ivan. "Oh you
Moscow city feller!"

Everybody started laughing; while Pashka, laughing
more than all of them, quickly picked up the conversation.

"Well, there's a lot of murderers for you! And you
was saying, just like that, that we ought to be treated
kindly. No brother, guess you can't get along here
without us marching soldiers! When after the Seniyaks
we was stationed at Kursk, now, we was also restoring
order in a certain settlement. The *moujiks* had gotten it
into their head to ruinate an owner. . . . And the owner,
they do say, was a good sort, at that. . . . Well, the
whole settlement went for him, and, naturally, the women
tagged along. The watchmen came out to meet the
villagers. The peasants went for them with stakes and
scythes. The guards fired one volley, and then, of course,
took to their heels: what the devil sort of strength can
you expect from those dunderheads!—but one bullet did
get a baby in a woman's arms. The woman was left
alive, but he, of course, didn't even let out a squeak,—

just gave one jerk with his little legs. So, good Lord!"
said Pashka, tossing his head from laughter and seating
himself more comfortably, "what only didn't the
moujiks do! They broke everything to smash and
smithereens; chased this same owner into a corner, tram-
pling him down, while this *moujik*, the father of this here
child, ran up to that very spot with this same baby;
he was all gasping and crazed from grief, and he starts
in to beat the owner over his head with this dead baby!
Grabbed him by the little legs and starts in lambasting
the owner. And then the others fall upon him, and, of
course, all for one and one for all, they finished him.
We were rushed up, but he was already beginning to
rot when we got there."

"Well, what are you laughing about, you fool!" the
school-boy wanted to cry out, suddenly feeling a ferocious hatred for Pashka's laughter, for Pashka's voice.
But here Kiriushka suddenly stirred, and, raising his
head, said with childish naïveness:

"But that which took place when Kochergin the land-
owner was bein' wrecked,—*that* was something awful!
I was then living with him as one of his shepherds. . . .
So all their mirrors was thrown into the pond. . . .
Afterwards, people from the village would come over for
a swim, and would always be pulling them out of the
slime. . . . You'd dive, stand up,—and then your foot
would just slide over a mirror. . . . And this, now . . .
how do you call it . . . fortopianner was dragged into
the rye. . . . We used to come. . . ." Kiriushka raised
himself up, and, laughing, leant back on his elbows; "we
would come and there it would be standing. . . . You'd
take a club, and start banging upon it,—upon its keys,

[202]

that is. . . . From one end to the other. . . . Why, it would play better nor any accordeon!"

Everybody laughed once more. Theodot had adjusted his foot-gear, had again criss-crossed his foot-cloths accurately with the cords, and, having set himself to rights, had resumed his former position. And, having waited for a moment of silence, he began to finish his story in measured tones:

"Yes, he gave me one on the ear, and yet put in a suit as well. . . . For all these, now, losses and damages, for the forage, that is. He was called Andrei Bogdanov, —Andrei Ivannov Bogdanov. A tall *moujik*, he was,— red-faced, thin, always evil-tempered, always drunk. Well, now, so he started a suit. It was he that had warmed my ear, and he it was that was suing me to boot. Here the busiest time of the year came along, with nary a breathing space; but I've got to be hiking off fifteen miles away. . . . I guess that's just what the Lord must have punished him for. . . ."

As he gazed at the straw, stifling his cough and wiping his flat lips with the palm of his hand, Theodot's speech was becoming more and more sombre, more and more expressive. Having said "The Lord must have punished him," he was silent for a while, and then went on:

"The suit, of course, came to nothing. A peace was patched up between us. We was both at fault, that is. But only he wasn't content with that. He made up with me, but right after he walked away, drank till he was blind-drunk, started threatening to kill me. He yells before everybody: 'Wait,' says he, 'wait, I ain't drunk yet, now; but when I've drunk enough I'll settle your hash.' I wanted to get away from the mixup,—it made me feel

[203]

sick in the stomach. . . . Then he took to coming to our village: he'd come under my windows, drunk as drunk could be, and would start in to curse me out, saying things about my mother. And I have a grown-up daughter. . . ."

"That weren't right," sympathetically grunted out the old man, and yawned.

"Oh, it was a grand story!" said Theodot. "Well, now, so he comes on an evening before the Kiriki. I hear him making a hubbub in the street. I got up, without saying a word, went out into the yard, sat down on a harrow, and started sharpening a scythe. But I was taken with such a rage that I saw red before my eyes. Then I hear him walking up to the hut, raising a rumpus. Must be wanting to break the panes, thinks I to myself. But no; he just made a lot of noise and was already going somewhere else. That would have been the end of it perhaps,—if only Ollka, my daughter, hadn't jumped out. . . And then she starts in yelling, with a voice not her own: 'Help, father, Andrushka is beating me!' I dashed out with the scythe whet-stone in my hand,—and, all in a passion, hit him once right over his head! He just hit the ground. Folks ran up, started dousing him with water . . . but he lies there, and by now he's only hiccoughing. . . . Maybe something might have been done then. . . . Like putting a cold pack on him, or something like that. . . . He ought to have been carried off to a hospital as fast as possible, and a tenner should have been handed to the doctor. . . . But where was a tenner to be gotten? Well, so he hiccoughed and he hiccoughed, and he passed away toward night. He threshed about and threshed about; then turned over on his back, stretched himself out, and there he was, all ready. And the folks were standing around, looking, all silent. And the lights was already lit by that time."

All atremble with a quick shivering, his face flaming, the high-school student got up, and, sinking in the straw up to his waist, started climbing down the stack. A *borzoi* bitch, frightened by him, suddenly jumped up and gave a jerky bark. The student drew back sharply, falling into the straw, and stood stock still. The chill wind was rustling; a cluster of chill autumn stars showed white above his very head, while from beyond the hillock of rustling straw came the measured, low-pitched voice of Theodot.

"I sat in the barn for two days under guard, and saw the whole thing through a little window. . . . How they cut him up, that is. The people flocked in from all the villages, to have a look at this murdered man,—and me too, for that matter. They used to shove their way right up to the very barn. Two benches was carried out on the common, placed right near the barn, and the murdered man put upon them. A log of wood was put under his head; chairs and a table were brought out for the coroner and the sawbones. The sawbones walks up to him; he tears off his shirt, tears off his drawers,—and I see a corpse lying all naked, already stiff; yellow here and green there, while his face was all like wax; the red beard had become thin, and simply stood out. The sawbones put a burdock over you know what place. Right at hand, as usual, there was a box with all sorts of contraptions. The sawbones walks up, parts his hair from ear to ear, makes a cut, and begins to take off the scalp together with the hair, in halves. Where it was thin, he scraped with a little knife. He tore away a half to either side,—soon as he gets one piece off, he pulls it down over the eye. The whole skull became visible,—like some kind of a little pot, it was. . . . And there's a black spot on it, near the right ear,—black clotted blood; where the blow had come, that is. The sawbones says something to the coroner, and the coroner writes: 'Three cracks on such and such parts.' Then the sawbones starts in sawing through the skull all around. The saw don't work, so he takes a little hammer and a small chisel, see, and goes over the marks that he'd made with the saw, breaking through with the little chisel. And the top of the skull just fell away, like a cup,—the brain was all plain to be seen. . . ."

"What don't they do, the murdering cut-throats!" hoarsely remarked the old man, who had just dozed off.

But Theodot was firmly finishing his say:

"Then he took out a heavy knife, and starts cutting the chest, right through the gristle. He hacks out a three cornered piece, and starts pulling it away,—it even started cracking. . . . All the stomach came to view, and the blue lungs, and all the innards. . . ."

Deafened by the beating of his own heart, the student got up on his feet, standing up to the full of his great height,—in his cap, shoved back on the nape of his neck, in his light uniform overcoat, which was already too short for him. Gray, huge, dreadful in his Mongolian calmness, Theodot was speaking in measured tones, his pipe gripped between his teeth; but the student was no longer listening to him. With all his eyes he was looking at all these men—so familiar and yet so unknown, so incomprehensible,—who had made his whole soul so sick on this night. Pitiful in his vice and his meekness, in all his pastoral primitiveness, Kiriushka was sleeping, covered with his great coat, one thick leg, swathed in white foot-cloths, and twisted at the knee, sticking out from underneath it. Ivan, too, was sleeping; Ivan of the morose, disdainful face, whose mother, a horrible, black old woman, had been dying for three years now, in his black mud hut, standing near the ditches at the edge of the bare village, in the darkness and the dirt, underneath the low ceiling, underneath the low roof of sods, and yet cannot in anyway die, to her grief; while his buck-toothed thin wife feeds at her dark-yellow, hanging dry breast a bare-bellied, clear-eyed child, with its nose running, and its lips bitten into blood by the countless flies in the hut. The happy Pashka was sleeping his heavy, healthy sleep in the fresh wind, in his soldier's cap, heavy boots, and his new short coat. As for Khomut, the old man, who has not got even a short coat (he has only a long coat, frayed and with a large hole through the shoulder), whose drawers always hung so low upon his flabby thighs,—he was sitting with his back to the wind, bare-headed, stripped to the waist. He, senilely emaciated, yellow of body, with his shoulders elevated at a slant, with his twisted prominent backbone glistening in the light of the stars, was sitting with his big tousled head, ruffled by the fresh wind, bowed down, bending his neck which was already scrawny and all in coarse wrinkles. He was intently examining the shirt he had taken off, and, as he listened to Theodot, he would at times squeeze its collar band between his thumb-nails.

The student jumped down upon the hard and smooth

autumnal earth, and, stooping, quickly walked toward the dark, murmurous garden, toward home.

All three dogs also arose, and, showing dimly white, started running sideways after him, with their tails curled tightly.

1911.

A GOODLY LIFE

MY life has been a well-spent one; I got everything I went after. I even own real property,—my little old man right after the wedding signed the house over in my name; and I keep horses, and two cows, and we have a business all our own. Of course, not a regular shop, now, but just a little store, as they say,—but then, in our village, it will pass. I always was successful, but then I have a persistent character, at that.

As to all sorts of work, it was still my daddy that learned me. Though he was a widower, and took to drink, he wasn't far behind me in being awful smart, business-like, and heartless. When the serfs was freed, now, he up and says to me:

"Well, wench, I'm my own master now; let's save up some money. As soon as we save it up, we'll go to the city, buy a house all to our own selves; I'll marry you off to a fine gentleman, and live like a king. As for our masters, it's no use sticking here with them,—they ain't worth it."

Our masters, now,—although, to tell the truth, they were good and kind,—was the poorest of the poor; actual beggars, you might say. And so we went away from them to another settlement; as for the house, the cattle, and whatever household goods we had, we sold them. We moved right near to the city, and hired a cabbage

[209]

patch from a lady by the name of Meshcherina. She had been a *fräulein* in the Tsar's court; she was plain, freckled, and had grown gray as a maid,—nobody would take her to wife, so she lived in retirement. So, then, we hired the meadows from her, and settled down in our little hut, all peaceful and quiet. The weather's chill; fall is coming on,—but little we care! We sit and wait for good profits and never feel trouble coming along. But the trouble was right there,—and what trouble, at that! Our venture was drawing near the winding up, when suddenly something terrible happens. We had had our tea in the morning,—it was a holiday,—so I stood, just so, near the hut, watching the folks coming from church over the meadow. As for my daddy, he had gone to see about the cabbages. It was a sort of a bright day, even though it was windy, and so I was gaping and didn't notice that there was two men approaching me. One was the priest,—so tall, you know, in a gray cassock and carrying a stick; his face was dark, earthy; he's got a mane like any fine horse, just simply spreading out in the wind. The other was just a common peasant,—his farm hand. They walked right up to the hut; I got confused, made him a bow, and says:

"How do you do, Father? Thanks for thinking of us and calling."

But he, I see, is angry, sullen, doesn't even look at me; he just stands and breaks up clods with his stock.

"And where," says he, "is your father?"

"They've gone to the cabbage field," says I. "If you like, now, I can call them. But there he's coming, himself."

"Well, you just tell him to take away whatever goods

[210]

he's got, together with this dinky little samovar, and get away from here. My watchman is coming here to-day."

"What do you mean, a watchman? Why, we have already given the lady the money, ninety roubles it was. What do you mean, Father?" (Though I was young, I knew just what was what in such things.) "Are you joking, or something?" I says. "You ought to produce some proper paper," I says.

"No talk out of you!" he yells. "The owner is going to live in the city; I've bought the meadows from her, and now the land is my own property!"

But he, himself, waves his arms about, knocks his stick against the ground,—like as not to hit you in the snout any minute.

Father sees these goings-on, and starts running toward us,—he was awful hot-headed. He runs up and asks:

"What's all this noise about? What are you yelling at her for, Father, without knowing yourself what's what? You oughtn't to be shaking your stick, but ought to come right out and explain by what sort of right the cabbages have come to be yours? We are poor folks, now, we can go to court about it. You," he says, "are a person in holy orders; you can't hold no enmity against nobody; your kind can't touch the holy sacrament if you do."

Father, you understand, hadn't said as much as one saucy word to him; but the other, though he was a pastor, was as wicked as the most ordinary drab *moujik;* and so, when he heard that kind of talk, he just grew pale,—not a word could he say, but you could just see his legs quivering under his cassock. And then, don't he let out a squeal, and don't he go for father,—to hit

[211]

him over the head, you understand! But father got from under it, grabbed the stick, tore it out of the priest's hands, and then went smash! over his knee with it. The other tried to grapple with him, but father breaks it in halves, flings the pieces away as far as he can and calls out:

"Don't come near me, for God's sake, your reverence! You," he calls out, "are black and like a beetle, but I am still more of a beetle than you be."

And then he grabs him by the arms!

What with courts and law, father was sent to a convict colony for this here thing. I was left all alone in this world, and thinks I, what am I to do now? Plainly, you can't get through the world on righteousness alone; plainly, you must needs keep your eyes open. I figured it out a whole year, living with my aunt; then I saw there was nowhere for me to go,—I had to marry fast as I could. My dad had a good friend in town, a harness maker,—well, him it was that courted me. You couldn't say as how he made a striking bridegroom,— but still he was a good catch, at that. There was, to tell the truth, one man that I liked,—and liked right well; but then he was poor too, about as bad off as I was, also living with strangers, like me; but the other was his own master, after all. I didn't have a copper of dowry, and here, I see, he is taking me without anything,—how could I let a chance like that pass by? I thought, and I thought, and went and married him,—although, of course, I knew that he was an elderly man, and a drunkard, and always excitable; a cut-throat, to put it plainer. . . . I married him and became, you understand, not an ordinary wench any more, but Nastasiya Semenovna Zhokhova, a citizen's wife, living in a city. . . . Of course, it seemed flattering.

I suffered for nine years with this husband. That citizen business was just a name; we was so poor really that we was about as bad off as the *moujiks!* And then there was scrapping and rows every blessed day. Well, the Lord took pity on me, and took him away. The children I had by him all used to die on me; there was only two boys left,—one was Vanniya, going on nine; the other was an infant in arms. He was an awful lively and healthy boy; about ten months he started in to walk, to talk; all of my children, now, used to begin walking and talking about the eleventh month. He got to drinking tea all by his own self,—used to sink his little face in the saucer so's you couldn't pull it away, nohow. But this boy died, too, when he weren't a year yet. I come home one day from washing clothes in the river, and my sister-in-law,—we used to rent our rooms off her,—up and says:

"Your Kostiya was yelling and squirming all day today. I done all sorts of things to him already; I worked his arms and I patted him hard, and I gave him some sugar and water; but all he does is gag, and throw up the water through his nose. Either he's gone and caught a cold, or else he's ate something; for the children always put everything in their mouth,—how is a body to look after them?"

I was just scared stiff. I make a dash for the cradle and throw back the curtain, but he was already beginning to pass away then; couldn't even as much as cry out. My sister ran to get a doctor's assistant we knew; when he comes, he asks: "What did you feed him with?"

[213]

"He's eaten some manna porridge, now, and that was all."

"And wasn't he playing with something?"

"That's right, he was," says my sister. "There was a copper ring from a horse-collar knocking about all the time,—well, he was playing with that."

"Well," says the doctor's assistant, "he must have swallowed it, for sure. May your arms wither!" says he. "You've gone and done it now,—why, he's going to die on your hands!"

Of course, it turned out just like he said. Not even two hours had gone when he passed away. We took on and we took on, but there was nothing as could be done about it; for it's no use going against the will of God. So I buried him too; only Vanniya was left. Only he was left; but then, as they say, one is enough. A small creature, it's true, and yet he'll eat and drink as much as a grown-up. So I started scrubbing floors at the home of Nikulin,—a colonel in the army, he was. Him and his wife was rather well off; they paid thirty roubles a month for the rooms they had. They lived in the upper floor; the kitchen was below. The woman they had to get up their meals was a no-account little old woman; she wasn't responsible, and yet she was loose. Well, naturally, she got in the family way. Couldn't bend down to scrub the floors, couldn't pull a pot out the oven. . . . She went away when her time came, and I just grabbed her place: that's how I had gotten around the masters! To tell the truth, I've been clever and cunning from a girl up; no matter what I took a hold of, I'd do it neat, accurate, better nor any waiter. Again, I knew how to please them: no matter what the masters would say, I'd just say

[214]

"Yes, sir," or "Yes, ma'am," all the time, and "You are absolutely right. . . ." I used to get up when you could still see the moon. I'd mop up the floors, make the stove, polish up the samovar,—in the meanwhile the masters would wake up, but I had everything ready. And then, of course, I always kept myself clean, and was well-built, —I was spare, but still I was handsome. There was times when I'd even get to feeling sorry for myself: what were my beauty and my knowledge going to waste for, now, in such hard work?

Thinks I, I ought to take advantage of the opportunity. And the opportunity was, that the colonel was awful strong himself and couldn't bear to look at me calmly. His wife, now, was a German,—fat, ailing, and some ten years older than he. He weren't good-looking; heavy-bodied, short-legged, looking like a wild pig,—and she was still worse. Well, I see he's started to pay court to me, to sit in my kitchen, to teach me smoking. Soon as his wife went out, he was right there on the spot. He'd chase his orderly into town, as though on some errand, and be sitting there. He bored me to death, but, of course, I pretended otherwise: I'd laugh, and I'd sit and swing my leg,—getting him heated up in all sorts of ways, that is. . . . What can you do when there's poverty; and, as they say, this little was as good as a feast. Somehow one day, on the Tsar's birthday, he comes down to the kitchen in his uniform frock, in epaulettes, belted with that white belt of his like with a hoop, with kid gloves in his hands. He's buttoned his collar so tight that his neck is all swollen and he's all blue in the face; he's all perfumed,—his eyes shining, his moustache black and thick. . . . He comes down and says:

[215]

"I'm going to the cathedral with the missus right away; dust off my boots,—I've only gone through the yard and yet I managed to get all dusty."

He put his foot in its patent-leather boot upon a bench, —just like a big iron pillar, his leg was; I bent down, wanting to wipe it off, but he grabs me by the neck, even tearing my kerchief off; then he grabbed me tight about the bosom and was already dragging me behind the stove. I try this way and that,—can't get away from him nohow. And he is hot all over, just swelling up with blood,—trying to overpower me, that is; to get at my face and kiss me.

"What are you doing!" I says. "The mistress is coming,—go away, for the love of Christ!"

"If you will get to love me," he says, "I won't begrudge you anything!"

"Oh yes, now, we know all about those promises!"

"May I never leave this spot,—may I die without absolution!"

Well, of course, there was more of the same sort of thing. But, to tell the honest truth, what did I know at that time? I could have very easily been taken in by his words; but, glory be to God, things didn't turn out his way. Somehow he caught hold of me another time, at an unlucky moment. I broke away, all mussed up, and got mortal angry,—and there was the mistress, now; she was coming down, dressed up, all yellow, fat, like a dead person, groaning, her dress rustling on the stairs. I break away, and stand there without my kerchief,—and there she is, heading straight for us. He goes past her and shows his heels, but I stand there like a fool, not knowing what to do. She stood opposite me, and she stood some more, holding the silk skirt of her dress,—I remember like it was to-day: she was going out visiting, and had on a brown silk dress, and white mittens without fingers, and she carried a parasol, and wore a hat like a basket. She stood for a while, let out a groan, and went out. To tell the truth, though, she never said a word to him or to me. But when the colonel went away to Kiev, she just took and drove me out.

So I got all my little belongings together and went back to my sister,—Vanniya was living at her house, you understand. I went away from this place, and again I figure: my brains are just going for nothing; I can't save up anything, nor make a decent match and have a business of my own,—God has wronged me! I'll get in harness once again, thinks I, turn about somehow, and I *will* get what I'm after, and *will* have a capital of my own, or die trying! So I thought it all out, apprenticed Vanniya to a tailor, and then got a place for myself as maid with Samokhvalov the merchant. . . . And that was the beginning of my rise.

They gave me a wage of two and a quarter. There was two servants,—me, and a girl by the name of Vera. One day I wait at table, and she washes the dishes; the next day I wash the dishes, and she waits at table. You couldn't call it a large family: there was the master, Matvei Ivannich; the mistress, Liubov Ivanna; two grown-up daughters; and two sons. The master himself was a serious-minded man, not much given to talking,—he was never even at home on week-days, and whenever there was a holiday, he'd be sitting upstairs in his room, reading all sorts of newspapers and smoking a cigar. As for the mistress, she was a simple soul, kind, and, like myself,

[217]

from the middle classes. They wasn't long in marrying off their daughters, Anna and Klasha, and held two weddings in one year,—married them off to military men. Right there, to tell the truth, is where I begun to save up, —for the military men did give me a great deal in tips. If you just did anything, even a trifle,—like handing them the matches, say, or their overcoats and rubbers,—right off you'd have twenty kopecks, or thirty. . . . But then I used to go about awful neat, and I pleased the military. Vera, to tell the truth, was always putting on some airs, like some miss or something; she took short, mincing steps, was tender and awful easy hurt,—the minute anything would happen, she'd knit her downy eye-brows, her lips, like cherries, would start to quiver, and there was the tears in her eye-lashes. True, she did have pretty eye-lashes, great big ones, I never saw anybody else with anything like them. But then, I was wiser. I used to put on a smooth waist, cut on a bias, with open-work; I'd put a switch on my head with a black velvet bow, and I wore a starched white apron,—it would interest anybody just to look at me. Vera, she always used to lace herself tight in corsets; she'd lace herself so tight she couldn't stand it, and at once her head would start aching till she'd throw up,—but I never even had no use for a corset, and was all right as I was. . . . And when the military men were gone, the sons started in tipping me.

The elder had already reached twenty when I took the place, and the younger was going on fourteen. This boy had to sit all the while, poor fellow. He had broken all his legs and arms,—I seen that business many a time. When he'd break something, the doctor would come to him right away, bandage it up with cotton, lint, and all

[218]

that sort of thing; then he'd pour something over it like lime; this same lime would dry up together with the lint, would become like a splint; and when the hurt part was healed up, the doctor would just cut all that stuff, taking it all off,—and the arm, when you'd look at it, was all grown together. He couldn't walk by himself, but crawled around on his bottom. He used to simply dash upon sofas, and over thresholds, and up the stairs. He even used to crawl across the whole yard into the garden. He had a great big head, clumsy looking, like his father's; his temples coarse, red-haired, like a dog's wool; he had a broad, old-looking face. That was because he used to eat an awful lot,—he'd eat sausage, and chocolate bon-bons, and pretzels, and pastry made out of layers of dough,—whatsoever his heart might desire. But his little legs, his little arms, was like a sheep's, and all broken, all in scars. They used to keep him just so for a long time, making long shirts for him of different colours; sometimes blue, sometimes pink. They had a lady teacher from a parochial school coming over to our house to teach him. He was a great hand for learning, and had a good head on his shoulders! And the way he'd play on an accordeon—you couldn't find even a whole person to play like that! He'd play, and sing in time with the music. He had a strong, piercing voice. He used to go way, way up when he'd sing: "I'm a monk, and handsome too!" He used to sing that song often.

The elder son was in good health, but also a sort of innocent, not fit for any business. They gave him away for instruction into all sorts of schools,—and he was chased out of all of them; they couldn't learn him anything. Come night,—he'd get full some place or other, and be gone until dawn. Still, he really was afraid of his mother, and would not come in through the front door for anything. I'd get through with my work in the evening, and wait until the master and mistress would be asleep; then I'd steal through the rooms, open the window in his little den, and then go back to my place again. He'd take his boots off in the street, crawl through the window in only his stocking-feet, and never a squeak or a creak out of him. The next day he'd get up like he'd never been any place, and in some spot where we couldn't be seen he'd shove what was coming to me into my hand. It wasn't none of my worry, and I'd take it right gladly! If he was to break his neck, that would be his lookout. . . . And then I started in having an income from the younger, from Nicanor Matveich.

I was after what I wanted day and night, you might say. Once I took into my head that one idea, to absolutely provide for myself and to marry a decent party, I had taken a fresh hold on life. I used to save every little copper, now; money, you know, has little wings, once you let it out of your hands!

I got rid of this here Vera,—but she, to tell the truth, was there really without need; I just put it that way to the master and mistress: "I can get along all by my own self," I says; "you just add any trifle you like to my wage, and you'll do better nor now." So, then, I was left alone and managing everything myself. I wouldn't even take the wages in my hands,—soon as twenty or twenty-five roubles would gather, I'd beg the mistress to go to the bank and put it away in my name. Clothes, and shoes, and everything else went with the place,—what was I to spend money for? The only expenses I had was to put up a little stone at my husband's grave,—I paid two roubles seventy, so's people wouldn't talk. And right here, the Lord forgive us,—such was my luck and his misfortune,—this poor wretch had to go and fall in love with me. . . .

Of course, now I often think: maybe it was on account of him that God punished me through my son. Sometimes I can't get it out of my head,—I'll tell you right away what he went and done to himself. And besides, just consider that it really was very hard,—I used to look at this big-headed fellow, and what a vexation would take hold on me! "May this and that befall you," I'd think, "you was born, with a silver spoon in your mouth! Even though you be a cripple, yet how rich you live. . . . Whereas mine is all sound, and yet he don't eat or drink as much on a holiday as you do on a week-day, just so." Then I started in to notice,—it looked like he'd fallen in love with me; well, now, he just wouldn't take his eyes off my face. By that time he was already sixteen, and had taken to wearing wide trousers, and to belting his blouse; a red-haired moustache started cropping out. But he was homely, tow-haired, green-eyed—God deliver me! His face was broad, but he himself was as thin as a bone. At first, evidently, he got it into his head that he could be pleasing,—he began to dress up, to buy polly-seeds, and used to play on his accordeon so fine that you could listen to him for hours. He played well, to tell the truth. When he seen that his affair weren't coming along, he grew quiet and thoughtful-like. Once I was standing in the balcony, and I see him crawling through the yard with a new German accordeon. He had shaved and combed himself once more; had put on a three-buttoned blouse with a high collar, fastening at the side; his head was thrown back,—looking for me, that is. He looked and he looked; his eyes became longing-like and dim, and then he began a polka:

> "Let us go, let us go,
>   I would dance a polka through;
>   Dancing makes one braver; so
>   I can speak my love for you. . . ."

But, like as if I hadn't noticed him, I took and threw down a slop-bowl, with water! I threw it down, and then was scared myself. But he crawls, he struggles up the stairs, drying himself with one hand and dragging the accordeon by the other. His eyes were lowered, and he was all white, and he spoke meek-like, all acquiver:

"May your hands wither. What you've done is a sin, Nastiya."

And that was all. . . . True, he was a peaceful one.

He was losing flesh at that time, not by the day but by the hour; and the doctor had already said that he wasn't long for this world, that he was bound to die from a consumption. It made me shudder even as much as to touch him. But then a poor person ain't got no call to be particular,—money can do anything, and so he started in to bribe me. Just as soon as everybody used to fall asleep, right off he'd call me to him,—either into the garden or into his room. (He lived apart from everybody, living downstairs; his room was large, warm, and yet bleak; all the windows looked out into the yard, the ceiling was low, the wall paper was old and brown.)

"You just sit with me a while," he says, "and I'll give you some money for that. I don't want anything from

[222]

you,—I have simply fallen in love with you, and want to be with you; these walls have near drove me crazy."

Well, I'd take the money and sit for a while, and I got together about half a hundred in that way. And then I had about four hundred of wages and interest laid by. So, thinks I to myself, it's about time now for me to be crawling out of the harness, bit by bit. But, to tell the honest truth, it was a pity to do so,—I wanted to bide my time for another year or so, to save up a little more. But the main thing was,—he had let it slip once when he was talking with me,—he had a little toy saving bank that he was keeping most secret,—he had gotten over two hundred roubles in trifling sums from his mother. Naturally, with him lying sick, always abed, and all alone, his mother would thrust the money upon him to cheer him up. But no matter how I tried not to, I still would think once in a while: "The Lord forgive my transgression, but it would be best if he gave that money to me! It's of no use to him, anyway; he's like to die at any moment; whereas I'd be well-fixed for all time with it." I just waited to see how this business might be worked, as cleverly as possible. I became more kind to him, of course; began to sit with him more often. I used to come into his room, and then look over my shoulder on purpose, as though I had come in by stealth. I'd close the door and begin speaking in a low whisper:

"There now," I'd say, "I've got away; let's sit together like a lovin' couple."

Making believe, that is, like I had a meeting arranged with him, but that I was losing my courage, and yet at the same time was glad that I had got through with my work and could now be with him. Then I began to put on a weary air, to pretend I was in deep thought. And he was always trying to get the reason out of me:

"Nast, why have you grown so sad?"

"Oh, just so! I've got more than my share of trouble!"

And then I'd top that with a sigh, become quiet, and lean my cheek on my hand.

"But just what," he'd say, "is the matter?"

"Well," I says, "poor folks got a lot of things the matter with them, but who ever worries about them? I wouldn't even want to bore you with them."

Well, he guessed what was what pretty soon. He was clever, like I said,—he'd be a match even for a healthy person. One day I came into his room,—it was, as I remember even now, in mid-Lent; the weather was sort of gloomy, wet, with a fog outside; everybody in the house was sleeping after dinner. I come into his room with some needle-work in my hands,—I was sewing something or other for myself; I sat down near his bed and was just wanting to heave a sigh, and again make believe I was aweary, and then start leading him on to my idea easy-like, when he starts in talking about it himself. I can see him right now, lying in his pink blouse,—brand new, never yet washed; in blue wide trousers; in new small boots with patent-leather tops; his legs laid one acrost the other, and him looking out of the corner of his eye. His sleeves was wide, the trousers wider still, and his little legs and arms like match-sticks; his head was heavy, big, and he were all little himself,—it even made a body unwell to see him. To look at him, he seemed a boy, yet his face was that of an old man, although it was somehow youngish at the same time,—that was on account of him being clean-shaved,—and he had

[224]

a thick moustache. (Come to think of it, he shaved himself every day, that's how fast his beard would grow; his hands looked like they was covered with tow, and the hair upon them was all red, too.) Well, as I was saying, he's lying there, his hair parted on one side, his face turned toward the wall; he was picking at the wall-paper, and all of a sudden he says:

"Nast!"

I even shuddered all over.

"What is it, Nicanor Matveich?"

And meanwhile my own heart rolled up to my mouth.

"Do you know where my toy bank is lying?"

"No," I says, "how should I know that, Nicanor Matveich? I never had no evil designs in my mind upon you."

"Get up; draw out the bottom drawer in the ward-robe; take out the old accordeon,—that's where the toy bank is. Let me have it here."

"But what do you want it for?"

"Just so,—I want to count the money."

I got at the drawer, opened the cover of the accor-deon,—and there, stuffed into the bellows, was a tin elephant,—feeling pretty heavy. I take it out and hand it to him. He takes it, rattles it, lays it by him,—just like a baby, he was, honest to God,—and goes off into thought about something. He keeps silent, and he keeps silent; then he smiles, and says:

"To-day, Nast, I had a fine dream. I even woke up before daybreak on account of it, and it has made me feel very good all day, up to dinner. Just look,—I have even shaved myself, and have got all dressed up for you."

[225]

"But then, Nicanor Matveich, you always go about neat-dressed, anyway."

And I don't understand myself what I'm saying, I'm that excited.

"Well," says he, "I guess I will be able to go about in the other world. You can't even imagine what a good-looking fellow I'm going to be in the other world!"

I even got to feeling sorry for him.

"It's a sin to make fun of such things, Nicanor Matveich, and I can't even understand why you say such things. Perhaps," I says, "God will send you health yet. You'd do better to tell me what your dream was."

He started in beating about the bush again; started in to smile wryly,—"What good am I alive!" he says. Then he began, without rhyme or reason, to talk about a cow we had:

"For God's sake," says he, "tell mother to sell it; I can't stand it no more, that's how tired I am of it; I lie here in bed and look at the little barn where she's kept, and she always looks back at me through the bars,"—and all the while he's rattling the money, and keeps from looking me in the eyes. And I listen, and also can't understand half of what he's saying,—just like two persons out of their minds, we was, saying anything that came into our heads. Finally I couldn't stand it no more; for, thinks I, everybody will wake up at any second, and they'll be calling for a samovar, and then the whole business falls through! And so I interrupt him as soon as I can, going in for cunning:

"But no," I says, "you'd better tell me what dream you saw. . . . *Was it anything about us two?*"

Of course, I wanted to say something that would please him, and I struck it so right that he even changed colour entirely, and cast his eyes down. All of a sudden he takes the toy bank, gets a little key out of his trousers'-pocket, and wants to open it,—and can't, nohow; just, can't get at the key-hole, his hands are trembling so. At last he does manage to open it and pours out all it held onto his belly,—I remember it all like it was now: there was two paper bills and eight gold pieces; he scoops it all into his hand, and suddenly says in a whisper:

"Could you kiss me just once?"

My hands and feet just got numb from fright. But he's carrying on like he was going out of his mind, whispering, stretching upward to me:

"Nastechka, just once! God is my witness I will never say another word, never ask again!"

I looked over my shoulder,—well, thinks I, I might just as well be hanged for a sheep as for a lamb,—and I kissed him. So he was all just gasping; he grabbed me around the neck, caught my lips, and I guess he didn't let me go for a whole minute. Then he shoves all the money into my hand,—and turns his face to the wall.

"Go," he says.

I ran out and went straight into my room. I put the money away under lock and key, grabbed hold of a lemon, and started in to rub my lips. I rubbed them so hard that they simply turned all white. I was awful afraid, to tell the truth, that I might get a consumption from him. . . .

Well and good,—this business, then, turned out all right, glory be to God; so I begin to lay my plans for the next move, of more importance,—the one which I had the most struggles about. I felt that there was trouble brewing; I was afraid he wouldn't let me leave my place. "He'll start in," thinks I, "to pester me with his love, will want to become my husband on account of this money." But no; nothing happens, I see. He don't try to annoy me; he treats me rightly, the same like before, as though nothing had taken place between us,— even more modestly, it looks like,—and he don't call me into his room: that meant he was keeping his word. Then I bring the talk around to my going away, putting it up to my master and mistress: it's time for me to see about my son a little, now; to be free for a little while. They won't even hear of it. And as for him, you can understand how he felt, without my saying a word about it. I hinted about my going away to him at one time,— so he just got all white. He turns his face to the wall, and says with a sort of a bitter little smile:

"You have no right to do it," he says. "You have led me on, have got me used to you. You must wait,— I will die soon. But if you go away now, I will strangle myself."

A fine modest fellow he turned out to be, didn't he? "Ah," thinks I, "damn your shameless eyes! Here I have forced myself to do like you wanted, but you take to threatening me! Oh, no, you haven't come across one of that sort in me!" And I started looking for an excuse harder than ever. About that time, most luckily, the mistress gave birth to another girl, and a wet-nurse was hired for her; so I picked on that, saying that I couldn't get along with her. She was, to tell the truth, a wicked, daft old woman; even the mistress herself was afraid of her. And she used to drink, on top of that,—there was always a demijohn on duty under her bed,—and she couldn't bear anybody to be near her. So she began saying things about me, making trouble in all sorts of ways. Either I hadn't pressed the linen right, or else I didn't know how to wait at table at all. . . . But, if you was just to say one word to her, she'd get all in a trembling passion and run off to complain. She'd sob out loud, and, of course, not so much because she had been offended, but just dissembling. The further it went, the worse it got, so I up and says to the master and mistress:

"So and so," I says, "let me go; I can't bear to live on account of that old woman; I will lay hands on myself."

And in the meanwhile, I already had my eye on a house on Glukhaya Ulitza.[1] Well, hearing me speak like that, the mistress didn't even try to hold me any longer. True, when she was saying good-bye to me, she wanted me to come and live with them again, awful hard; or just to come on some holidays, or on birthdays:

"You must," she says, "always come to put things in order, to get everything ready. It's only when you're around," she says, "that I feel easy. I have grown used to you, like you was one of the family."

She saw me off with all honours,—which meant that she no longer held any grudge against me; she baked a great big white loaf, putting in a whole salt-cellar full of sugar. I thank her in all sorts of ways, but, of course, she wasn't anything much in my life,—so I thinks one thing, and I says another. I promised her all she wanted and more, scraping and bowing low before her,—

[1] Blind Alley would be the nearest English equivalent. *Trans.*

and went my ways. And at once, with the Lord's blessing, I got busy. I bought the house I had in mind, and opened a dram shop. The trade started off awful good,—in the evening, when I'd come to counting what I'd taken in during the day, there would be thirty, or forty, or sometimes all of forty-five roubles in the till,—and so I got the idea of opening up a store as well, so as, you understand, to get them coming and going. My husband's sister had long since married a watchman in the Red Cross; he was calling me gossip all the time, and was friendly with me,—so I went to him, got a trifling loan for all sorts of fixtures, permits, and started in doing business. And right then Vanniya had finished his apprenticeship. I took counsel with folks that knew a thing or two as to where I could place him, now.

"Why," says they, "where else would you place him, when there's no end of work in your own house?"

And they were right, at that. So I put Vanniya into the store, and stay in the dram shop myself. And then we were off! And, of course, I had even forgot to think of all this past nonsense,—although, to tell the honest truth, the poor cripple had just taken to his bed, at the time I was going away. Never a word out of him to anybody, but just lies down, just like he were dead, forgetting his accordeon even. Suddenly, lo, and behold ye, Polkanikha comes into my yard,—this same wet-nurse. (The little boys had nick-named her Polkanikha.[1]) She comes, and she says:

"A certain man has told me to give you his regards; says you should come and pay him a visit, without fail."

I went all hot and cold from vexation and shame!

[1] Wife-of-a-regiment. *Trans.*

[230]

"What a darling, to be sure!" thinks I to myself. "What an idea he has gotten into his head! What a mate he has found for himself!" I couldn't hold in and I says:

"I got no use for his regards; he ought to keep in mind the state he's in, and you, you old devil, ought to be ashamed to try and be a go-between. Do you hear me, or don't you?"

She just stopped short. She stands, all stooping, her swollen eyes glowing at me from under her brows, and just shaking her cabbage head; she'd grown daft, either from the heat or from vodka.

"Oh, you heartless creature!" says she. "He was even crying about you," she says. "All last evening he lay with his face to the wall, and sobbing out loud."

"Well," says I, "am I to start weeping bucketfuls? And wasn't he ashamed, the red-head, to be bawling before folks? Why, what a baby! Or was he weaned from the breast, or something?"

And so I put the old woman out as empty-handed as she had come, and didn't go myself. And right soon after that he took and really did strangle himself. Right then, of course, I felt great regret because I hadn't gone; but at that time I had other things to think about, besides him. I had one disgrace coming on top of another, right in my own house.

I had rented out two rooms in the house; one was taken by the policeman on our post,—a fine, serious-minded, respectable man, Chaikin by name; a young lady prostitute came into the other. Flaxen-fair she was, kind of young, and not at all bad to look at,—rather good-looking. She was called Phenia. Kholin the contractor used to come to see her,—he was keeping her;

well, I relied on that, and let her take the room. But right here some disagreement took place between them, and so he left her. What was to be done? She had nothing to pay with, but I couldn't chase her out,—she had run up a debt of eight roubles.

"Miss," says I, "you must earn off anybody; I don't keep no open house for strangers."

"I will try," she says.

"But then, somehow a body can't see you trying. Instead of trying, you always stick at home evening after evening. It's no use," I says, "to be placing your hopes on Chaikin."

"I will try. It makes me conscience-struck, just to hear you."

"A-ah!" I says, "what a conscience you must have, to be sure!"

She'll try and she'll try,—but there was no trying of any sort, if the truth be told. She did try to get around Chaikin but he wouldn't even as much as look at her. Then I see that she's going after my boy. No matter when I look, he's always hanging around her. All of a sudden, he gets a notion of getting a new jacket.

"Oh, no," I says, "you'll wait a while! As it is, I'm dressing you like any fine young gentleman; now it's boots, now it's a cap. I, now, used to deny myself everything, used to figure every copper as a gold piece, yet I'd supply you with everything."

"I'm not a bad-looker," says he.

"You daft loon," says I, "what am I to do, sell the house, or something, on account of your good looks?"

I notice that my business is getting poorer. I started having shortages, losses. I'd sit down to drink my tea,

[232]

—and even that had lost its taste for me. I started in to watch. I'd be sitting in the dram shop, and yet be listening all the time—I'd put my ear to the partition, without stirring, and listen. I'd hear them rumbling one day, I'd hear them rumbling the next. . . . I begun scolding him about it.

"And what business is that of yours?" he says. "Maybe I want to marry her."

"So that's how,—it's none of your own mother's business! I see your intention long since," I says, "only this is never going to be in this eternity."

"She's mad in love with me; you can't understand her; she is tender and shy."

"A fine love you can expect," I says, "from a deboshed slut like that! She's making fun of you, you fool," I says. "She's got the bad disease," I says, "all her legs is covered with sores."

He seemed turned to stone for a while; his eyes was all puckered up, like he was looking at the bridge of his nose, and he kept silent. "Well," thinks I, "glory be to the Lord, I got him in the right spot." But still, I was frightened to death: it was plain to be seen, you understand, that the poor fellow had fallen hard. "So that means," thinks I, "that I must finish her off as fast as I can." I take counsel with my gossip, and with Chaikin. "Tell me, now, what am I to do with them?" "Why," they say, "catch them on the spot, of course, and throw them out,—and there's the long and the short of it." And here is what they thought up. I made believe I was going out calling. I went away, walked for some time through the streets, and about six o'clock,—when Chaikin was relieved, that is,—I set out for home, soft

[233]

and easy. I run up and push the door,—just as I thought, it was locked. I knock,—no answer. And Chaikin was already standing around the corner. Then I started knocking on the windows, until the panes jarred. Suddenly the latch clicks,—and Vanniya comes out. He's as white as chalk. I hit him on the shoulder with all my might,—and go straight into the room. And there is was just like a feast had been laid out,—empty beer bottles; weak table wine; sardines; a large herring, all cleaned, as rosy as amber,—everything from the store. Phenka was sitting on a chair, with a blue ribbon in her braid. Soon as she saw me, she jumped up, staring at me with all her eyes; she was all white, and her very lips had turned blue from fear,—she thought I'd go for her, to beat her. But I just says, natural-like,—although I could scarcely breath; I was throwing my shawl open, and then muffling myself up again, by turns:

"What have you got here?" I says; "is it a bethrothal, or something? Or is it somebody's birthday? Well, why don't you welcome a body, why don't you treat me to something?"

They don't say a word.

"Well," I says, "why don't you say something? Why don't you speak, little son? Is that the kind of a host you are, my pet? So that's where my hard-earned money flies away, I see!"

He even got his dander up:

"I am of full age myself!"

"So-o," I says, "and what about me? That means that I'm to rent a hutch or something from your grace and this here little bitch? To get out of my own house? Is

[234]

that it, eh, So I've warmed a viper in my bosom, have I?"

And then he starts yelling at me!

"You have no right to insult her! You have been young yourself at one time,—you ought to understand what love is!"

And Chaikin, the minute he heard that uproar, was right there: he jumped in without a word, grabbed Vannka by the shoulders, and straight into a lumber room with him, under lock and key. (An awful strong man, he was,—like a bandit or something!) He turns the key on him, and says to Phenka:

"You are listed as a miss, but I can make a wolf out of you!"

(Meaning he'd make a note on her passport that would make her hounded like a wolf.)

"Do you want me to do that," he says, "or don't you? Vacate this room for us this very day, so's there won't be even a whiff of you left!"

She went into tears. But I added something on top of that.

"Let her first get the money what's coming to me!" I says. "Or else I won't even let her take away the least little lousy trunk of hers. Let her get my money ready, or I'll let the whole town know about her!"

Well, so we packed her off that same evening. When I was chasing her out, she took on something awful. She cried and she couldn't catch her breath for sobbing; she even tore her hair. Of course, her fix wasn't any too sweet. Where was she to go? All her goods, all her booty, was her own person. But never the less she went

[235]

off. Vanniya, too, quieted down for a while. He was let out from under lock and key in the morning,—and never a peep out of him; he was very much scared, and you could see by his face that he was conscience-stricken. He settled down to work. And so I even rejoiced and was set at rest,—but not for long. Again there were leaks from the till; and this here street-walker started sending a boy into the shop, and my son, now, would supply her with all sorts of delicacies! Now he'd give her all the sugar she wanted, now tea, now tobacco. . . . Or a handkerchief, or soap, again and again,—whatever came to his hand. . . . How was a body to watch him all the time? And then he started in to drink, harder and harder. At last he neglected the store entirely: he didn't even live at home, come to think of it,—he'd just come in and eat, and then he'd be off again without as much as a by-your-leave. Every day he'd go off to see her; he'd put a bottle under his coat, and away with him; and this same vodka, now, was already dear then. I run around like a chicken without its head,—from the dram-shop to the store, from the store to the dram-shop; and by that time I was afraid to tell him as much as a word,—he had become a downright tramp! He always was a good-looker,—he took after me entirely; his face was very fair and soft,—just like a young lady, he was; he had clear, intelligent eyes; was well-built, broad-shouldered, with chestnut curly hair. . . . But now his mug was all bloated; his hair got shaggy and came down over his collar; his eyes got bleary, and he got all tattered and had begun to stoop. He always kept silent now, looking at the bridge of his nose all the time,—in deep thought, like.

"Don't you bother me now," he'd say, "I'm liable to do something that will lead to prison."

And when he'd get tipsy, he'd start slobbering, laughing over nothing at all; he'd be playing *Time Fled Beyond Recall* on his accordeon, and his eyes would fill with tears. Well, I see my affairs are in a bad way,—time for me to get married, soon as I can. And right then they was trying to make a match betwixt me and a certain widower,—he had a store, too, and lived in a suburb. An elderly man, he was, but in good standing, with means. Just the very thing, you understand, that I was striving for. I find out as quickly as I can from trustworthy folks all about his life, down to the last stitch; I see there's nothing out of the way whatsoever. I got to decide about getting up an acquaintance as quick as possible,—the match-maker had only shown us to each other in church before that; I got to bring it about, you understand, so's we can visit each other,—sort of make an inspection, as it were. He comes to me first, and gives his credentials: "Lagutin, Nikolai Ivannich,—store-keeper." "Very pleased to meet you," I says. I see he's altogether a fine man,—not any too tall, of course, and all gray; but so agreeable, quiet, neat, diplomatic,—you could see he was a thrifty sort; he had never run up a copper of debt to anybody in all his life, he says. Then me and the match-maker went to see him, like it was on business. We get there. I see he's got a wine-cellar,—Rhine wines, mostly; and a store stocked with everything that goes with wines: cured lard, now, and ham, and sardines, and herrings. The house wasn't large, but neat as a pin. There was flowers and little curtains on the windows, the floor was swept clean,—even though he were a bachelor.

[237]

In the yard everything was in order, too. There was three cows and two horses. One was a three-year-old brood-mare,—he'd been offered five hundred for it already, he said, but he'd turned the offer down. Well, I just went into raptures watching that horse,—that's how handsome it was! But he only smiles quiet-like, walks with little steps before us, crackling his fingers, and telling us everything, like he was reading off some price-list: here's this and this, and there's that and that. . . . So, thinks I, it's no use trying to be too smart here; the business ought to be brought to an end quick. . . ."

Of course, it's only now that I'm telling all these things so briefly; but only my poor head knows what feelings I went through at that time! I couldn't feel my legs under me for joy,—I'd gotten what I was after, you see, I had found the party I was looking for! But I kept silent, I was afraid and shivering all over,—supposing all my hopes was to be dashed down? And that's almost what did happen; all my trouble almost went for nothing,— and I can't tell calmly the reason why, even now;—it was on account of this here poor cripple, and on account of my darling little son! We was managing this business so quietly, so genteel, that we thought never a soul would know. But no, I hear that the entire suburb already knows about my intentions and Nikolai Ivannich's; the rumour, of course, reached the Samokhvalovs as well,— never fear, it was nobody else but Polkanikha that whispered it to them. And he, the poor cripple, now, took and hung himself, like I'm telling you! "There now, you,—I threatened and you didn't believe me, so now, I'll do it just to spite you!" He hammered a nail into the wall above his head, fixed a cord from a sugar-loaf to it, drew it around his throat, and crawled off the bed. It wasn't no great trick; didn't take much brains! One day at twilight I was standing in the store, putting some things to rights,—when suddenly some one thunders again and again against a shutter in the house. My heart just went down into my shoes. I jump out on the threshold,—it's Polkanikha.

"What do you want?"

"Nicanor Matveich has passed away!"

She barked it out, turned on her heel, and went for home. But I, in the first excitement, didn't take anything into account,—it was just like I had been scalded with steam from fright. . . . I threw a shawl over my shoulders, and started after her. She runs, with her skirt caught up in front, stumbling, stooping,—and I keep on running too. . . . It was just a disgrace before the whole town! I run, and can't understand a thing. I had only one thought,—I'm ruined forever! Just think of what he'd gone and done,—may God not bear it against him! Just think what little conscience some people have! I run up to the house,—and there are as many people there as at a fire. The front entrance is ajar; whoever wants to pushes his way in,—everybody is curious, naturally. In my lightheadedness I tried to get in there too. But, glory be, something seemed to hit me over the head; I came to my senses and backed out. Maybe that was what saved me,—else I would have known what crow tastes like. If any one,—why, even this Polkanikha, say,—had remembered me! . . . "Here, now, your honour, is the one we think is to blame, who is the reason of it all; just you question her,"—and all would have been over with me. Try and wriggle out of it then.

A person may not have a blessed thing to do with it, but they grab you and put you away. . . . It wouldn't be the first time a thing like that has happened.

Well, soon as they buried him, my heart eased up a little. I'm getting ready for the wedding, hurrying to wind up my business, to sell what I could without loss,— when again there's grief and woe. I was knocked off my feet as it was, what with one worry and another, and was all roasted from the heat,—the heat that year was simply unbearable, with dust, with a hot wind, especially in our neighbourhood, in Glukhaya Ulitza, standing half way up on a hill,—when suddenly there was another bit of news: Nikolai Ivannich had taken offense. He sends over this same match-maker, now, that had brought us together, —a terrible slut, she was, and kept both her eyes peeled; never fear, it was she herself that put him, Nikolai Ivannich, up to it. Nikolai Ivannich lets me know through her as how he's putting off the wedding until the first of September,—he's got a lot of affairs to attend to, now,— and lets me know about my son, about Vanniya: to figure out what was best to be done with him; that he was to be placed anywhere at all,—"Because, now," he says, "I won't take him into my house, for no amount. Even though he be your own son," he says, "he's bound to clear ruin us, and he'll be upsetting me." (And really, just think of his position! Since he's never known any turmoil, had never raised any rows, of course he was afraid of any excitement: whenever he'd get excited, everything in his head would get muddled,—he wouldn't be able to say a word.) "Let her get rid of him," he says. And where was I to place him, how was I to get rid of him? The young fellow had gotten out of hand entirely; with

[240]

strangers he'd break his neck altogether. But there was no way of getting away from his riddance. As it was, I was all through with him ever since he'd come to know Phenka: she had just bewitched him, the bitch! He'd sleep all day and drink all night,—turning night into day. . . . I couldn't even begin to tell the trouble I went through with him that summer! He got me so that I began to melt away like a candle; I couldn't hold a spoon, my hands shook so. Soon as it got dark I'd sit down on the bench before the house and wait until he'd come in off the street,—I was afeared the boys in the city might do him up. . . .

Well, having gotten such a decision from Nikolai Ivannich, I call my son to me: "So and so, my little son," I says, "I've borne with you long enough, but you've turned out a weakling and have gone astray; you have disgraced me all over this neighbourhood. You've got used to having everything soft and nice, now, until at last you've become a tramp, a drunkard. You haven't got a gift like I have,—no matter how many times I fell, I always got up again; but you can't save up anything for yourself. Here am I,—I've come to be respected, and I own real estate, and I drink and eat no worse nor other folk; I don't deny my heart nothing,—and all along of being governed by common sense, always and above all things. But you, I see, want to stay a flutter-fly, like you'd always been. It's time you was getting off my neck. . . ."

He sits there and never a word out of him,—just picks the oilcloth on the table. I had just called him out to dinner, for he'd been sleeping all along, and his mug was all puffed up.

"Well, why don't you say something?" I asks. "Don't you be tearing that oilcloth,—get one of your own first; just you answer me."

Again he don't say a word; he bends his head and his lips quiver.

"You're going to marry?" he says.

"Well," I says, "it ain't known yet whether I am or whether I ain't; but, if I do marry, it will be a decent man, that ain't a-going to let you into his house. I ain't your Phenka, brother; I ain't no street-walker or something."

When all on a sudden he jumps up from his place and gets all in a passion:

"Why," he says, "you ain't worth one of her finger-nails!"

How was that? Good, eh? He jumped up, yelling till it didn't sound like his own voice, slammed the door like thunder,—and off with him. But I, even though I was no great hand at crying, just went off into tears. I cry one day, I cry another,—I had only to think of the words he could find the heart to say to me, and off I'd go. I cry, but I keep one thing in mind,—I would never forgive him such an insult till the end of time, and I would drive him off entirely. . . . But all this time he don't come home. I hear he's carrying on a feast at her house, dancing and prancing, drinking through the money he had stolen, and threatening me: "Never mind," he says, "I'll settle her; I'll lay in wait till she'll be going somewhere in the evening; and I'll kill her with a stone." He sends to the store to buy things,—to make fun of me, of course; now for ginger cookies, now for herrings. I just quiver all over from vexation, but I hold myself in and give what's wanted. One day I'm sitting in the store, when suddenly he comes in himself, drunk as a lord. He brings in some herrings,—a little wench had bought four of them that morning for his money, of course,—and slap with them down on the counter!

"How dare you," he yells, "send such abominable stuff to your customers? They smell; they're only fit for dogs to eat!"

He's yelling, with his nostrils all puffed out,—looking for an excuse.

"Don't you be raising no rumpus here," I says, "and don't be yelling; I don't make the herrings myself, but buy them by the barrel. If you don't like them, don't guzzle them,—here's your money back."

"But what if I had ate them and died?"

"Again," I says, "you're swine, and ain't got no call to be yelling at me,—who are you to be giving me orders? Guess you ain't such a much. You ought to speak decent-like, and not be crowding in with a row into somebody else's establishment."

But all on a sudden he grabbed hold of a steelyard off a bin and sort of hisses out:

"I'll swat you over the head," he says, "so's you'll stretch right out!"

And then he ran out of the shop with all his might. But I, the way I had sat down on the floor, that's the way I stayed,—I just couldn't get up. . . .

Then, I hear that they done for him,—the Lord had punished him on account of his mother! He was barely alive when they brought him in a cab,—unconscious drunk, his head bobbing, his hair caked with blood and covered with dust; his boots and watch had been stolen,

[243]

his new jacket was all in tatters,—there wasn't as much as a square inch of whole cloth left anywhere. . . . I figured and I figured,—take him in I did, and I even paid the cabby; but that very same day I sends my compliments to Nikolai Ivannich, and say that he be told for sure that he shouldn't be worried any more over anything; that I had decided about my son, now,—I would drive him out without any pity right off when he would wake up. He also sends back his compliments and bids them say: "Very wisely and well done, accept my thanks and sympathy . . ." and two weeks later he set the date for the wedding. Yes. . . .

Well, that's enough; that's where my story ends. Guess there's nothing more, to tell about. I've gotten along so well with my husband all my days, that it's just like a rarity nowadays. As I'm saying, what I went through whilst I was struggling to get into this heaven can't be told in words! But, truth to tell, the Lord hath rewarded me,—it is now the twenty-first year that I'm living with my little old man, fenced about as with a stone wall, and I know for sure that he wouldn't let nothing or nobody hurt me; it's only to look at him that he's so quiet! But, of course, no matter how I try, the heart *will* start yearning once in a while! Especially before Easter, in Lent, for some reason or other. I think I could die now,—it's fine, peaceful; they'll be after reading litanies in all the churches. . . . True, I've had enough of toiling and moiling in my time,—oh, but Nastasiya Semenovna was the persistent one! Ought I, with my mind, to be sitting on the outskirts of a town? My husband calls me Skobele,[1]

[1] A great Russian general and a universal military genius and strategist. *Trans.*

as it is. . . . Again, once in a while I get to longing for Vanniya. Never a bit of news about him in twenty years. Maybe he's died long since, but I don't know about it. I even felt sorry for him that time they brought him in. We dragged him in, and got him up into bed,—he slept like he was dead the livelong day. I'd climb up, and listen to his breathing,—to see if he was alive, now. . . . And in the room there was a sour stench of some sort; he's lying in bed, all tattered, chewed-up, snoring and gagging. . . . It was a shame and a pity to look at him, and yet it was my own flesh and blood! I'd look and I'd look, and I'd listen,—and then walk out. And what an anguish seized hold on me! I forced myself to sup, cleared away the table, put out the light. . . . Can't sleep, and that's all there is to it,—I just lie there and shiver. . . . And it was one moonlit night. Then I hear he's waked up. He's coughing all the time, all the time going out into the yard, banging the door.

"What you walking about for?" I ask.

"My stomach aches," he says.

I can hear by his voice that he's upset and grieving.

"Drink some of that mugwort and vodka that you'll find in a bottle standing in the image shrine."

I lay a little longer,—I may have dozed off a little,— when I felt through my slumber, that some one is stealing up over the flooring. I jumped up,—it was he.

"Mother, dear," he says, "don't be afraid of me, for the love of Christ!'

And then he went off into a flood of tears! He sat down on the bed, catching my hands, kissing them, raining tears on them,—and just unable to catch his breath,— that's how he was crying and sobbing. I couldn't bear

[245]

it—and went off on my own! It was a pity, of course, but there was no help for it,—all my future lot turned upon him. But then, I saw he understood all this very well himself.

"I can forgive you," I says, "but you see yourself, now, that there's nothing to be done about it. So you just go away as far as possible, so's I shouldn't even hear about you!"

"Mother, dear," he says, "why have you ruined me, just like you ruined that poor cripple Nicanor Matveich?"

Well, I see the man ain't in his right senses yet, so I didn't even start to argue with him. He cried and he cried, then he got up and went away. And in the morning, I look into the room where he'd slept, but he was already gone for a long while. That meant he had gone as early as possible for shame,—and then he just disappeared, like a stone in the water. There was a rumour, now, that he had lived for a while in a monastery at Zadorsk; that he had then travelled to Tsaritsin,—and there, never fear, he must have broken his neck. . . . But what's the use of talking about it—it only troubles the heart! No matter how much you cook water, it will still be water. . . .

But as to what he'd said about Nicanor Matveich,— why, I think it's even silly. It wasn't like I had been greedy after a great sum, or had pulled it out of his pocket. He knew his unfortunate condition himself, and was often taken with spells of sadness. He used to say to me at times:

"Nastiya, fate has made me a cripple, and my nature is an insane one: either I'm gay somehow, like just before some misfortune,—or else I have such a melancholy spell,

[246]

especially in summer, during the heat, with all this dust, that I could just lay hands on myself! I'll die; they'll bury me in the Chernoslobodskaya cemetery,—and this dust will swirl for all eternity on to my grave, from beyond the enclosing wall!"

"But, now, Nicanor Matveich, why take on so about that? We don't feel such things when we're dead."

"Why," he says, "what of it that we won't feel them,—the trouble is that one thinks about them while one is still alive. . . ."

And, to tell the truth, it was awful wearisome in the house, in the Samokhvalovs', when everybody would fall asleep after dinner, and the wind would be swirling this dust along! And he had laid hands on himself just at the time of the greatest heat, at the dullest time. Our whole town, to tell the truth, is wearisome. I was in Tula the other day, now,—why, you can't even compare them!

1911.

"I SAY NOTHING"

WHEN he had been a young man, everybody used to call Alexander Romanov Shasha; at that time he was living in the settlement of Limovo, in an iron-roofed house that stood facing the common, and his beatings were administered to him by his father, Roman.

Roman deemed himself the first man in all that district, —he used to shove his hand out to all the gentry and the squires whenever he would meet them. He had a store in the settlement, and a mill beyond it; but the way he got richer and richer was by buying up groves from the land-owners and then cutting them down. Makar, his own brother, had nothing to eat; all in tatters, he might be hobbling over the common, and, doffing his hat meekly, would say: "Greetings, brother." But Roman, well-fed, looking like a deacon, would answer him from his stoop: "Don't you brother me, you dolt. You've made your bow, so just keep on going on your way." What, then, must have been the feelings of the sole heir of such a man? He used to stroll through the village in a cap that had come from the city; in a sleeveless overcoat of the finest broadcloth, in boots with patent-leather tops. He was all the time cracking polly-seeds, and playing polkas on an expensive accordeon. Whenever he met any wenches or young lads,—all his relatives, all consanguine, everyone of them,—he would be followed by that sort of gaze from

[248]

which celebrities feel a chill run down their back. But he would meet such a gaze with a surly—even a ferocious —one; all his youth seemed to have passed in a preparation for that rôle in which he attained such perfection later on.

Roman, at the height of his prosperity, began to decline in strength, and to get muddled in his affairs. Grizzled, bearded, pot-bellied, clad in a sleeveless overcoat of casinette that resembled an under-cassock, it was only when he was in his cups that he plucked up heart; but when sober he was always despondent and deliberately churlish. He still retained his glory and his might. Out on the common, near the church, right opposite his windows, he had built a school; he was trustee over it, and could at any instant he liked make the teacher grovel at his feet. He was still able to give goods on credit to the landowners; to give bribes to the police inspector, without the least necessity; he could still regale one with smoked sprats, with a pickled lobster in a rusty can, with sherry and with wine from Tsimliyan, which is something like champagne,—and, even as he entertained, he would yell, if his guest were of the humbler sort: "Drink, you blockhead!" But it surely was high time to supplant him. But who could do it? That was just it,—there was no supplanting him. Shasha was withdrawing more and more into his rôle of a man upon whom had been inflicted an insult which could be wiped out only by blood, and his relations with Roman resolved themselves merely into Roman's dragging him around by his "temples." Shasha, to use Roman's words, could make an angel lose his patience,—it was impossible not to be dragging him around. And drag him around Roman did. But the

[249]

more he dragged him, the more unbearable did Shasha become.

Who but he should have taken pride in the house, the might, the ways of his father? His father would yell at him, in the presence of guests: "Go on, now, be a trifle more free and easy, you dolt!" But then, that was the way of those whom his father imitated, the way of the merchants; and was it not a matter for the highest pride to feel one's self a merchant's son? At times his father would even boast about him, self-complacently saying to the guest: "Wait, I'll show youse my son!"—and would shout all over the house: "Shash, c'mon over here,— Mikolai Mikhalich wants to have a look at ye!" But, oh, the way Shasha would enter the room where his father and the guest were sitting! He would enter with his face crimsoning, glowering from underneath his beetling and knit eye-brows, holding his arms stiffly akimbo, like a pretzel, and stepping still more stiffly, toeing in, and as elegantly as if he were dancing the fifth figure of the quadrille,—and, having made a scraping bow to the guest, he would instantly rush backward to the window, toward the lintel of the door; blowing out his nostrils, he would tear his hang-nails with his teeth, and, in the expectation of an affront from the visitor, answered all questions with the most ludicrous brevity and abruptness. . . . How, then, could one refrain from beating him? The guest would depart; Roman, having seen him off, would walk up to Shasha without a word, and, swinging back his arm, would grab Shasha fast by his hair. Without a word, Shasha would extricate his head out of his father's fingers, and, having run out into the ante-room, would smite his bosom with his fist:

"All r-r-right, father! I say nothing! I always say nothing!" he would hiss ominously.

"Why, she-animal that you are!" Roman would bawl at him. "Why, it's for this same silence and hoiti-toitiness that I'm a-beating you of! So, then, you're striving for the beating yourself? Why? Wherefore?"

"My ashes when I'm laid in my grave shall know it all!" Shasha would answer ferociously and enigmatically.

One could have wagered his head that he must have been in an excellent state of feelings. Had he not been born with a golden spoon in his mouth? He would order new boots two or three times in a year; he never ran short of money or of polly-seeds; he would promenade the main street with the teacher, and he played on the harmonica better and more spiritedly than everybody else; the wenches used to sing their "heart-breaking" songs without taking their languishing eyes off him. While in the fall, in the winter, he would pay court at evening parties to the coquettish daughters of the priest, to the daughters of the police inspector, dancing with them to the sounds of a talking machine; he was usher at weddings, donning a frock-coat, starched shirt, and new, tight shoes. But then, even his courting was somehow caustic, offhand. But what's the use! Even when all by himself, looking in the mirror as he whipped up his browny fleece with a metallic comb, he would squint at himself like some monster. His nose was squashed, his voice hoarse, his appearance that of a convict,—the *moujiks* used to call him a hangman. . . . No great honour, that, you would think. But no,—he took a delight even in that. "The low-down devil!" the *moujiks* would say. "Nothing ever pleases him; everything ain't his way, everything ain't right!"

And he, with all his might, tried to justify these by-names. "Who? Is it Shasha you mean by low-down?" Roman would ask with indignation. "Why, you can pave a pavement with blocks the likes of him! He's a fool, a play-actor, a born loafer,—and that's all there is to it! What's he putting on airs for? What the devil is he after?" But Shasha just looked on with a venomous smile, and never let a word out. "Well, now, just take a look at him,—do!" Roman was saying. "Just look what he's trying to make out of himself!" But Shasha only knit his eye-brows, making them turn up higher and higher; more and more rapidly did he bite his nails, and by now was convinced even himself that something dreadful was coming to a head within him. "Oh, father!" he would say, as though unable to hold out. "Oh, but I would like to tell you a certain thing!" Roman, despondent, with sagging pouches under his eyes, would smile like a martyr: "Well, what sort of a thing is it? Eh? Well, now, say it?" "Who, me?" Shasha would ask, throwing a glance at him from underneath his eye-brows. "Yes, you!" "My ashes when I'm laid in my grave shall know it all!" "But what is it that they'll know? Are you drunk, you good-for-nought?" "Drunk!" Shasha would answer. "Drunk? I say nothing. I al-ways say nothing!" And, almost weeping, Roman would again advance upon him, like a bear; would again catch him by the head, and, bending it down, would drag him by the hair in an excruciating transport.

From his twentieth year to his twenty-fifth, Shasha was almost never beaten,—unless it were sort of casually, of course. But he made up for this with something else.

He sought other occasions for self-torture,—and of occasions there were as many as he wanted.

He married—and it was a splendid match—the daughter of the manager of a great estate which belonged to a nobleman; his bride was a laughing, freckled girl, rather pretty. His marriage was celebrated magnificently. The owners of the estate resided abroad; therefore Shasha was able to go to the wedding ceremony in their carriage, and the priest, out of respect to this carriage, felicitated him upon his lawful marriage with especial eloquence and servility, although it did seem to Shasha that he was being made fun of. The wedding feast, too, was held in the owners' house. Wine flowed like a river. Roman, amid the general clamour of delight, started in to dance, shaking the parquetry, the mirrors and the chandeliers. The owners' flunky gave an excellent imitation of a railroad train: he began with a rumbling whistle through his fingers, then started in beating out, with his feet, the slow and heavy clatter of a train constantly increasing its momentum, and wound up with a riotous gallop. The sexton, having imbibed too much cognac at the feast, died on his way home. The deacon, having fallen down in his own yard into some half-liquid manure, was almost trampled to death by his sheep. The nastiest of autumn dawns, pallidly blue, looked in through the fog into the smoke-filled seigniorial halls,—but the lights were still burning there; the talking machine, now grown hoarse, was still gurgling out now the *Lezguinka*, now *The Lancers;* the ushers, all moist from the heat and their exertions, were still yelling as they supervised the dances; while the eyes of the young ladies grew glazed from fatigue, and

[253]

the soles of their white slippers flew off as they danced. . . . But Shasha did not spare even his own high celebration; having convinced himself that he was infernally jealous of his young wife and a certain rather young land-owner, he, feigning intoxication, suddenly stepped upon the long train of her dress during a waltz, and tore it off with a ripping sound. And after that he made a rush for a knife, trying to cut his own throat, and, upon being disarmed, he sobbed wildly, tearing off his starched collar and his white tie, calling upon the memory of his departed mother. . . . As for his behaviour after the wedding,—Shasha did everything that lay in his power to wreck his own domestic well-being, and to hasten the ruin of Roman.

Having attained the zenith, Roman was inevitably bound, as is always the case in Russia, to start rolling downward again, toward his former lowly lair. Soon after the wedding it turned out that he was entirely entangled, head and foot, in the toils of debt. He became awesome. His grizzled beard turned white. His face came to resemble a dirty-gray, milked-out udder. His eyes died out. His belly, grown flabby, hung down. But Shasha rejoiced malignantly: "I told you so! I told you so!"—and was finishing him off; he rioted, kicked up rows, demanded a winding up of Roman's affairs. And Roman, turning green from wrath, would rise up against him like a bear, thirsting to maim him,—but he no longer could; he no longer could! Crushed down by the thought of approaching disgrace, of approaching poverty, he took to drinking harder and harder. Having lost all shame, he got his mistress (a cook and a soldier's wife), into his own house. Shasha, not being contented with his wife, lived with her too, just to spite him. As for his wife, he used to exhaust her with his jealousy and his scares; he used to stay away from the house and to send *moujiks* with notes to her, upon which notes would be written: "Forgive me in death; I send my blessings to the children,"—and below there would be drawn a grave with a cross. His wife was for a long while deluged with tears. And then she got together with the teacher, and now gave Shasha every reason to be saying "All r-r-right! Only my ashes when I'm laid in my grave will know it all!" The upshot of it all was, that Roman was laid low by a stroke of paralysis; that only the wind-mill beyond the settlement was left out of all his wealth; that Shasha's wife, taking the children with her, fled to her father, who had gone to the city of Skopin. The while Shasha, drinking deep of the delicious draught of his misfortunes, treating everything and everybody with merciless criticism and opprobrium, was absenting himself in the village, drinking every bit as hard as his father, she pulled up stakes and disappeared.

Roman left the settlement for his mill beggared and barely alive. Beggared and widowed, gnashing his teeth with rage, Shasha followed him out of the village. What with toiling and moiling, even the mill would not have been a bad thing to live by. But how was Shasha to be bothered with it! How could you expect him to have the strength of getting up on his feet after the awful finishing stroke fate had dealt him! Even formerly he,— not understood, not appreciated, condemned to live in the midst of enemies and ill-wishers,—had had but one recourse left him: to say nothing, and again to say noth-

[255]

ing, and to say nothing without end. And now? Why, he could have piled up thousands from this mill alone; there would have been no getting into it for the carts full of grain surrounding it,—if he only had two or three hundred to get him a new shaft and new mill-stones. . . . Yes, but where was a body to get that money? It's only into the hands of fools that good luck plays; but you take an able, sensible man, and Fate will twist him into a ram's horn. Well, let it,—let it! "I say nothing," Shasha would say, malignantly rejoicing; "I al-ways say nothing!"

The broken trough,[1] familiar to him and appropriate to his former status of a *moujik*, again appeared before Roman in place of palatial chambers. Nor did the rub lie at all in the fact that, instead of smoked sprats and Tsimliyan wine, a big slice of black bread and a wooden vessel of water turned up on his table,—he would have eaten such food with his former relish; the rub was in the torments of his pride,—the most cruel of all human torments. In a big hut, leaning all to one side, with an earthen floor and with holes in its corners, atop the bare oven,—there did Roman sleep now. In the morning he would crawl out beyond the threshold, with a

---

[1] The reference here is to a famous folk-tale,—best known in Pushkin's version, *The Little Gold Fish*. A fisherman, having caught a little gold fish, is promised the fulfillment of all his wishes for its release. All his demands, instigated by his wife, are granted, beginning with a substitution of a new trough for a broken one, and up to the attainment of rank and wealth; but finally the wife insists upon the fulfillment of a wish so insolent that, upon his return from interviewing his benefactress, the fisherman finds his wife sitting at the same old broken trough, before his former humble hut. *Trans.*

tall staff in his hands. With pig-weeds and high rank grass was the outside of the hut overgrown; stinging nettles choked up the huge shell of the wide-open windmill. All this stood out on the bare ridge of the plains, nigh the highway. And Roman would go out to the edge of the road, and would place his trembling, cold paws upon his staff. He was without a hat; the wind tangled up his gray, shaggy locks, his gray beard,—the beard of a *moujik* Job. He was bare-footed, in short drawers of striped ticking, in a long blouse filthy from cinders and the rubbish of the oven. His legs were black and thin, his torso huge and emaciated. Those whom he had regaled and lectured at one time now rode past him. And Roman—it was not for nothing that Shasha had sprung from his loins—even rejoiced that folks saw him in poverty, in disgrace, and he bowed to the ground before them. And of evenings he would stand in the dark hut before a little painted board hung up in a corner, and with heavy sighs bowed before it still lower then he did before men, saying his prayers now in a whisper, now loudly—warmly and grievously thanking God for all that He had visited upon him, a miserable, stricken old man. . . . Shasha, now, enjoyed his humiliation in a gayer fashion, in low-down inns, in low-down pot-houses, drinking away the last scanty remnants of their former prosperity, and paying for his long tongue by being beaten. . . .

Then, from his twenty-fifth year on, his beatings became regular, administered to him upon a previously designated day; and no longer was he beaten the way his father used to beat him; he was beaten with heels now, until he would lose consciousness.

The soldier's wife remained faithful to the house of Roman. She also moved to the mill. And when Roman died—oh, how proud (with a malignantly joyous pride) Shasha was over this calamity,—she passed into Shasha's hands openly. But in the meanwhile her lawful husband had come home from service. She was as needful to him as snow in the summertime; but never the less he held it to be his most sacred duty and his inalienable right to avenge his sullied honour. And he ingeniously timed this revenge with the day of the folk-festival at Limovo.

Every year, on the fifteenth of July, on a great holiday popularly called the Kiriki, a fair is held in Limovo. Rain pours down in chill torrents; one is reminded of the summer only by the rooks in the fields, by the height and the density of the grains and the grasses, and also by the sky-larks, that sing above them in the rain and are blown aslant by the wind. But on the common at Limovo a little nomadic city of tents is already springing up. The traders from the city have arrived,—and it is an unaccustomed, strange sight to see in the settlement these city people, in their long-skirted coats. In building upon the common, and making it congested, they have changed the simple village picture with their thronging, their big, strong carts laden with goods; together with these goods they have brought the atmosphere of an Asiatic bazaar; their samovars smoke, and their braziers emit the fumes of frying mutton. . . . On the fifteenth, since the early morn, they are already standing behind their counters; while the *moujiks* with their women-folk and little ones keep on streaming in, flocking from all directions toward the village; they have

[258]

dammed up the common so that there isn't room for
a pin to fall. And above all this swarming, babel, hubbub, and creak of carts, booms the festal pealing of bells,
summoning to mass.

To the sound of these bells, in full view of all the
folks riding through the dirty by-lane that leads past
the wind-mill, Shasha is standing nigh his threshold; his
belt is loose, and, bending downward, he holds a wooden
vessel with water in one hand and with the other hand,
which is wet, he is rubbing his bearded, pock-marked face,
all puffy from sleep. How little does this thick-set *moujik*
in broken boots resemble the former Shasha! He ap-
pears calmer than before, yet still more morose. His
hair is fearfully thick even now, but it is already shaggy,
like a *moujik's*. Having washed himself, he tears his
hair apart with a wooden comb, combs out his tangled
round beard, clears his throat hoarsely, and eyes his little
mirror askance,—eyes his broad, porous face, with the
squashed nose. He hasn't forgotten that he looks like
a hangman. And really, he does look like one,—especially now. Having combed himself, he puts on a
blouse that he saves for gala occasions,—it is of red
calico, and its dye will come off on his body when
he will begin to perspire. On week days he becomes
stultified from ennui, from over-sleeping, from the fact
that no one any longer pays any attention to him, or
listens to him; his boasting about his former state, his
hints about that which was supposed to lurk within his
soul, and his foul tattling about his runaway wife, have
all long since palled upon everybody. But to-day is a
holiday; to-day people would look with curiosity upon
him, the erstwhile man of wealth now walking around on

his uppers; to-day he would be playing before an enormous crowd, to-day he would be fearfully beaten,—beaten until he would lose conscience,—right before the eyes of all this crowd. . . . And lo, he is already entering into his rôle; he is already excited; his jaws are tightly clenched; his eye-brows are distorted. . . . Having togged himself out, he puts on a rusty cap, and, with a constrained step, resolutely and steadily sets out for the village.

The strangest part of all is the piety with which he begins this day. He goes directly toward the church, and, without looking at anybody, but with all his being feeling upon him the eyes of everybody surrounding him, he bows and makes the sign of the cross with all his might. In the church he shoves his way to the very ambo, where at one time he had had his own rightful place, and at that moment he is filled to the marrow of his bones with contempt for the *moujiks*, reminding them briefly and sternly, like one having authority, that it wouldn't be a bad idea for them to wake up and stand aside. And the *moujiks* hastily comply. Glowering like a bull from underneath his eye-brows at the officiating priests and the icons, he prays frenziedly and austerely until the very end of the mass, haughtily demonstrating to everybody that he is the only one who knows just the right time to bow and to make the sign of the cross. Just as austerely does he walk through the fair after the mass, proud of the fact that he had already had a drink or two, that he could approach some trader in his tent as an equal, shaking his hand and leaning over the counter, scooping up a handful of polly-seeds and bothering the trader with his conversations about the

city, and about the state of trade. . . . He was also
proud of the fact that he could at times yell at the droves
of wenches, pressing one another against the counter, like
sheep; or at some *moujik* that, with a bag under his
arm,—there would be a young pig squirming around
in that bag,—has already tested all the penny whistles,
all the mouth organs, and could not, for the life of him,
decide which one to take. The people, pouring out of
the church, have flooded the common; the belfries are
pealing forth their chimes; the beggars are snufflingly
clamorous; the live-stock—which is also bought and sold
during the Kiriki—bleats and hee-haws; and in the dense
crowd, spitting out polly-seed shells and slipping up in
the mire between the tents, there are already many intoxicated men. Shasha has already managed to drink
some more, and feels that the right time has come. Having had his fill of talking with the traders, he goes with
resolute steps toward the carrousels. A countless multitude of people has gathered there, watching, until their
heads, too, begin to go 'round and 'round, the wooden
horses and their riders. Almost all of Limovo is there,
and, towering a head taller above everybody, is the
soldier's wife's husband. Shasha's hands grow cold; his
lips quiver; but he pretends not to notice his foe. He
approaches his acquaintances, pulls a bottle out of his
pocket, regales anybody who comes along, and drinks
himself. He talks a great deal, and loudly; he smokes,
and laughs unnaturally and malevolently; but all the
while he is on the alert, waiting. . . . And now, pretending to be hopelessly drunk, in a new cap with the store's
price tag still showing white upon it, clean shaven, well-
fed, with sleepy blue eyes, the soldier advances straight

[261]

upon Shasha, and with all his momentum, as though
without seeing him, strikes him in the chest with his
shoulder. Shasha, gritting his teeth, steps to one side
and continues his conversation. But the soldier comes
back, again passes him,—and once more hits him in the
chest with his shoulder! Whereupon, as though unable
to bear such insolence, Shasha distorts his face,—distorted enough without that,—and drawls out through his
teeth:

"E-eh, young fellow! Watch out that I don't shove
you in my own way!"

And the soldier, instantly checking his headlong progress, suddenly staggers backward and roars out furiously:

"What's 'at?"

Amid the hubbub and rumble of the fair, amid the
clanging of the carrousel bells and the delighted, hypo-
critically-sympathizing shouts of the oh'ing and parting
crowd, the soldier stuns Shasha and draws his blood
with the very first blow. Shasha, trying to get his fingers
into the soldier's mouth, true to an old usage of the
moujiks, in order to tear his lips, pounces upon him like
a beast,—and instantly falls down in the mire as if he
were dead, underneath the iron-shod heels that beat
heavily upon his chest, upon his shaggy head, upon his
nose, upon his eyes,—already glazed, as in a ram with
his throat cut. And all the folks "oh" and "ah" and wonder: "There's a queer, incomprehensible fellow for you!
Why, he knew, he knew beforehand how this matter
would end! Why did he go into it, then?" And truly,—
why did he? And toward what, in general, is he so insistently and undeviatingly heading, as he devastates his
ruined dwelling from day to day, endeavouring to erad-

icate even to the last atom the very traces of that which was created, in such an unprecedented manner, by the uncouth genius of Roman, and ceaselessly thirsts after humiliations, disgrace, and beatings?

Within the church enclosure, on the way to the door of the chapel, there were some horrible specimens of humanity, standing ranged in two files. In her yearning for self-torture; in her yearning-loathing of the curbing bit, of toil, of her mode of existence; in her infatuation with all sorts of hideous visages (both those of the tragedian and of the scaramouche), in her dark, criminal desires, in her lack of will power, her eternal disquiet, in her misfortunes, sorrows and poverty,—Russia breeds these people from of old, and without end. In Limovo alone some half-hundred of them gather. And what faces are these, what heads! Just as if they had come out of the crude wood-cuts made in Kiev, which depict both fiends and the striving anchorites of the Mother-Desert. There are ancients with such withered heads, with such scant locks of long gray hair, with such noses, as thin as thin can be, and with the slits of their unseeing eyes so deeply fallen in, that they seem to have lain for centuries in the caverns where they had been walled up still in the time of the Kiev princes. . . . And they had come out of there in half-rotted tatters; they had thrown upon their remains their beggars' wallets, fastening them cross-wise behind their shoulders with odd bits of rope, and had set off on their wanderings from one end of Russia to the other, through her forests, over her steppes, in the winds of her steppes. . . .

There are lantern-jawed blind men,—sturdy and squat *moujiks*, that look just like pilloried convicts who have

killed their scores of souls,—these have solid, square
heads, their faces seem to have been hacked out by an
axe, and their bare legs are swollen with livid blood and
are unnaturally short, even as their arms are. There are
common idiots, huge of shoulder and of leg. There are
malignant dwarfs with bird-like faces. There are wedge-
headed hunch-backs, who seem to be wearing pointed
caps made out of horse-hair. There are monstrous
marasmi, squatting back on their crooked legs like ter-
riers. There are foreheads squeezed in at the sides and
forming skulls that look like the cap of an acorn. There
are bony old women, without a vestige of a nose,—for
all the world like Death itself. . . . And all this mass,
prominently displaying its tatters, its sores and cankers,
vociferate in a Bulgarian, old-church sing-song, vocif-
erates in rough basses, and castrated altos, and indescrib-
ably depraved tenors, about Lazarus and his sores,
about Alexei the Man of God, who also, thirsting after
poverty and martyrdom, did forsake his father's roof,
"knowing not whither he went. . . ."

All these people, with their eye-brows writhing above
their dark eyes, with an intuition, an instinct, as keen
as that of certain primary sea creatures, instantly sense,
surmise, the approach of a generous hand; and by now
they have already grabbed up a not unconsiderable quantity of bread-crusts, of round cracknels, and of the
moujiks' coppers, grown green from contact with their
execrable tobacco. After mass, with a chanting still more
vigorous and importunate, they spread through the sea
of the people, through the fair. The cripples, too, move
after them,—legless creatures, crawling on their bottoms
and on all fours, or lying in their eternal beds, in little

carts. Here is one of these little carts. In it is a little bit of a man, about forty years of age, with his ears tied up in a woman's kerchief; his milky-blue eyes are calm, and he has stuck out of his old rags a thin little hand,— violet-coloured, six-fingered. He is pulled about by a bright-eyed little lad, with exceedingly pointed little ears, and with fox-like down upon his head. All around him is a multitude of the fraternity, all of them, for some reason or other, also tied up with kerchiefs. And out of all this fraternity one *moujik* with a large white face stands out he is all broken up, all maimed; there is no bottom to him at all, and he has on but one fusty bast shoe. Probably, he, too, had been beaten-up somewheres as thoroughly as Shasha: his entire kerchief, his ear, his neck and one shoulder are all in caked blood. In his long bag there are pieces of raw meat, cooked bits of mutton, bread crusts, and millet. His seat, now, is sewn up with a bit of leather,—and twisting himself all up, he squirms and starts off, on and on over the mire, extending in front of him his unshod foot, his leg half-bare, in lime-covered scabs that are oozing with matter and pasted over with strips of burdock.

"Look ye, ye faithful,—look and behold ye! This is reckoned, from of old, as the disease of leprosy!" a freckled tatterdemallion beside him is shouting in a rapid recitave, which is right rollicking. . . .

And it is toward these people that Shasha is heading. He lives for some two or three years more in his mill; he celebrates three or four fairs more; he again enters into battle with the soldier three or four times: kind-hearted folks bring him to by throwing water out of

[265]

wooden tubs upon him as he lies without breath or
speech; without opening his eyes, he drags his wet head
over the ground, back and forth, and moans out painfully through his clenched teeth.

"All r-r-right, good folks! I say nothing! I al-ways
say nothing!"

Then he is brought to the mill; he lies for two weeks
over the stove, little by little getting better, and soon he
is again traipsing around the low-down inns; he brags,
he lies, he curses out everybody and everything, he
smites his breast with his fists, threatening all his foes,—
but the soldier especially. But once the Kiriki turn out
to be unfortunate,—the soldier breaks Shasha's arm with
his heel, and shatters the bridge of his nose, and knocks
out his eyes. Lo, now Shasha is both blind and a cripple. The soldier's wife abandons him; his mill, his land,
is taken by good folks for his debts. And now Shasha
is safe in harbour; now he is a fully-privileged member
of the horde of beggars that stand in the church enclosure during the Kiriki,—bone of its bone, flesh of its
flesh. All in tatters, with a round and thick beard, with
his head clipped so closely that it looks like a hedge-hog,
he wildly distorts his eye-brows over his empty, drawn-
over sockets, and hoarsely bawls in time with the others the beggars' soul-wringing canticles. The chorus
sombrely rends the air, to the best of each member's
ability, and the voices of the leader stand out resonantly,
as they bawl out every syllable:

There once lived three sisters; there were once three Marys of
    Egypt,—
In three parts did they their wealth divide:
One part was set aside for the blind and the sick;

[266]

"I SAY NOTHING"

One part was set aside for prisons, for dark dungeons;
The third part was set aside for churches, for cathedrals. . . .

Shasha's harsh voice chimes in, soaring above that of the others:

> The time will come
> When the earth, the sky shall be shaken;
> The least stones shall crumble,
> The Lord's thrones shall tumble,
> The sun and the moon shall grow dim,—
> And the Lord shall cause a river of fire to flow. . . .

And blending, swelling, attaining a sinister and a triumphant force, the entire choir becomes throatily, sonorously clamorous:

> Mi-cha-el the Arch-angel,
> Shall make all earthly creatures perish;
> He shall blow his trumpets,
> He shall say to all mankind:
> Ye had your life and being,
> Having your own free will;
> Ye did shun church-going,—
> At matins ye were sleeping,
> At vespers ye were eating,—
> Your paradise stands ready:
> Fires never dying,
> Tortures past all bearing!

1913.

DEATH

IN the name of God, the Merciful, the Compassionate! . . .

This is a tale of the death of a prophet,—peace to his ashes!—told that the doubters may be convinced of the need for submission to The Leader.

"We have never beheld Him, nor do we behold Him now," say they. But the sun is not at fault in that vision has been denied to the eyes of a bat. The heart of man aye seeketh faith and protection. But who would seek protection from an owl? It is better to dream of the shadow of the phœnix, even though the phœnix may never have existed in this world. But the protecting shadow of the Creator exists since the start of time.

The black-eared jackal slinks in the steps of a lion: the lion knoweth where the prey is, and the black-eared one findeth sustenance in the remnants of the lion's repast. Thus did the Hebrews follow their prophet out of the land of Egypt. Through the favour of God did he fulfill the mighty deed he had set out to do.

In his infancy he had experienced the delight of slumber, of awakening, of endearment. The daughter of the king had rocked him in her arms, dark and rounded, smooth as a snake, but as warm as fruit in the sun. Joyously and intently did her dark eyes gaze upon him,

[268]

as they shone above him; and impulsively did she kiss him, pressing him to her cold breasts; she would pretend to strangle him, as is the wont of all maidens. When recalling the like, many a one exclaims within his heart: "Why was I not a youth then!" But there is a time for all things.

The Pharaoh did bestow upon him a ring with a seal of authority, and did clothe him in the garments of a courtier. When the freshness of the morning is supplanted by the warmth of the sun; when, in the marketplace, the fennel is sprinkled to draw the scent of the purchaser; when there is a smell of burning peat floating from the chimneys, and a smell of fog from the direction of the great river, upon which towering white sails slowly float by, two abreast, the while a thin-bearded buffalo, as dove-coloured and rough-skinned as a swine, dully contemplates them, as he arises from the slime near the bank,—at such a time the prophet, conscious of his powers and alertness, did ride about in his chariot, overlooking the labours in the fields, and had the right to lash the lazy ones over the head with his scourge, to yell at them until he became red in the face, so that he might afterwards, in the sweet consciousness of a duty fulfilled, repose in the light shade of the palms, upon a dry dike among the canals.

Having attained manhood, he spent ten years in wedlock. He shared his couch with a woman rich and wellborn; he took his pleasure of her in the night,—in the daytime his pleasure lay in his orders and his cares, in drink and food, in the buoyancy of his body, that liked equally well both the dry sultriness of an inner court, emanating from its heated slabs of stone, and the cool breath of a breeze throughout the house, blowing from the river and from the blossoming gardens of its island. He took pride in his children, in his household, in the respect shown to him of all men. And he was happy, even as many others are. But an unseen hand was making taut the bow of his life; it was testing the bow-string and the wood, preparing to loose the arrows of truth. And ten years more did he pass in the striving of his mind and his heart, in the silent acquirement of the wisdom of Egypt; for the wall is preceded by the foundation, and speech, by thought. And he hath said of the heathen priests: "Ye men of folly! Slaves, tormented by heat, may be forgiven for raising their arms toward the sun, and supplicating it as God. But the sun is not God. None may behold God. He is beyond our comprehension. He may only be sensed. There is but one God. He hath no offspring." Whereupon the Pharaoh was possessed by a fury, even as the *gour*, the wild-ass, is overtaken by his madness. "Who is he that dares to live and to believe without my sanction?" he exclaimed. "He hath no precious rings upon his fingers, nor is there a necklace about his neck. He is but my slave. Therefore shall I set up a persecution of him and of all his tribe. I shall flash like the lightning, I shall deafen like thunder." But the prophet gathered his strength together, even as a man that standeth before the steep ascent of a hill, and went upon his way, fearless and assured.

Musk is brayed, aloes are put in the fire, that they might give forth their perfume. A diver would never pluck a single pearl-bearing shell, were he to fear holding in his breath as he plunges into the sea. And when

[270]

the time had come to lift up the heaviest stone for the structure, to throw it up on the knee, to clasp it as firmly as possible and to carry it, the prophet did lift it, so strenuously that he felt a pain in his groin. And for forty years did he carry it in the desert, ever at a strain, ever enduring fatigue, and joyous in the consciousness that he was working the will of God, and not of the Pharaoh. And, having carried it to the required spot, to the spot indicated by the Builder, he did cast down the stone, so that it lay even and flush; and he did straighten up, and did wipe the sweat from his face, with a trembling arm that had grown weak and was aching to the very shoulder.

And the time came for him to die.

He had attained to a knowledge of the veritable God. He had become convinced that it was madness to represent Him in the form of idols made of stone, of clay, and of metal. God had put upon him the task of delivering the Hebrew nation out of bondage and from the temptation of idolatry,—and he had rent asunder the silken nets of this world, he had risen up and had conquered in the wrestling. God had put him to the proof,—for forty years to be a chieftain for the refractory and the weak, to command and instruct in a desert that held nothing but hunger and sultriness. And for forty years he had been as mighty as a king; as tireless as a day-labourer burthened with a multitude of children; as needy as a shepherd; brawny and tall as a wrestler, strong and tawny as a lion. His body, girt only about the loins with an animal pelt, had become black from the sun and the wind, while his feet had become rough and callous, like those of a camel. In his old age he had

[271]

become awesome to men, and none of them deemed him mortal. But his hour did approach at last.

O ye who hearken! In The Book it is written: "All are conceived in the lap of truth,—it is the parents that make Hebrews, Christians, Fire-Worshippers out of the children." But a sage is like a blind man: he feeleth every stone in his path, choosing the path that is the right one; he raiseth his face upward, yearning for the sole source of light and warmth. He considereth life, and he considereth death, lessening his fear before the latter. And there have been not a few of those who have received the chalice of the inevitable with equanimity; there have also been those who have said: "It is even as sweet as the chalice of life." However, it is but the fool that yearneth for the chalice of death during life,—such a one is loathsome to behold. But he also is a fool that giveth no thought to the inevitable, that forgetteth that all mortals ought to have but one Beloved, Who possesseth clemency and demandeth submission. O ye who hearken! Hearken attentively, as man ought always to hearken to man; and, as ye hearken, reflect. For, as we speak, we are but mixing the good words of others with the passable ones of our own, dealing with that which is foreign to none of us; and the purpose of our speech is consolation.

In The Book it is written: "I that am God am nearer to man than the artery that sendeth him slumber." God is compassionate. He knoweth what is good for us and what is bad. He did create us mortal, yet we think of resisting death. Vain striving! Have ye heard at what cost Iscander the Two-Horned attained the Land of Darkness? And yet, he did not succeed in quaffing of

[272]

the water of eternal life, of which he had been told: It is to be found in the Land of Darkness. The Angel of the Winds is not perturbed by the fact that his wings may extinguish the lamp of some poor widow. The Messenger of Death heeds neither the prayer of a shepherd nor the outcry of a sovereign. Bide a while: earth shall devour the brains within our skulls, that are now filled with projects. Death is no Mogul, and thou art no Atabek-Abou-Bekr: thou canst not ransom thyself with gold from Death. Therefore, seek ye consolation.

The prophet did oppose the will of God in the desert, and heavy as his punishment for his disobedience: God forbade him to enter the Promised Land. The prophet did wax wroth in spirit that he was mortal, and that death was already nigh him, for he was old. Spake he: "I shall do single combat with it." At noonday, passing through the camp of the Hebrews in the mountains of Moab, he did look, and beheld not his shadow upon the white stones nigh him. And he was seized with a fit of trembling from fear, and his head was confused, like that of a man that is fever-stricken. Thereupon he did go toward his tent, with the steps of a wounded beast advancing upon its adversary. And he girt a sword about him, and did command food to be brought to him. And he did eat much thereof, full greedily, till that he was sated. And he did feel aches and nausea, as though from poison, as though from the fruit plucked from the tree of hell; and he did wax green in the face, and was bathed in sweat, even as a woman in travail; and he did lie down upon the ground, crying out wildly: "Behold, I am dying,—bare your swords and arise in my defense!" Thus did he cry out upon the first day. On the second, his aches did wax greater, and he began to implore, moaning and wrathful: "Summon a physician for me!" But when the physician had revealed his impotence, and the third day had come, the prophet uttered low: "Oh, have mercy upon me! Death is unconquerable!" And he did grow weaker, and fell into a slumber, and did sleep through all the day, and his aches did depart from him. And, having come to, he beheld that it was already night and that he was alone, and again did he feel the delight of living, and the sorrow of parting with life. Whereupon two dark angels did enter in to him, that they might console and prepare him.

One sat down at the head of the couch; the other, at the feet of the prophet. "Speak!" said they. But he kept silent and made no reply to them, for he was in deep thought. He gazed out into the night, beyond the raised side of the tent, sensing their presence with dread, for truth had not yet entered within all his veins. And it was so quiet in the tent and the desert that all the three could hear the rustling of the hot wind as it swept by in the darkness. And the stars were flaming sombrely, as on all sultry nights.

"God is compassionate to all His creatures," spake the angel who was sitting at the head of the prophet's couch.

"Yet here is a man in torment; he was dying, and is dying now," spake the angel sitting at the prophet's feet.

They wanted to test the prophet, but he understood this. And he made answer, in his thoughts:

"This was not death, but an illness, a chastisement. Is it not better to think thus? For he that hath tasted of

[274]

death cannot speak about it. We know not what it is."

"The sun is the source of life," spake the angel sitting at the head of the couch.

"But then, it is also as deadly as the horned viper," spake the angel seated opposite him.

They wanted to test the prophet, but he understood this. And he made answer, in his thoughts:

"We do not know God's purpose. But He is benign, and His purpose also is benign. Is it not better to think thus? Man ought to dedicate his every moment to life, recalling death only that he may weigh all his deeds upon its scales, and that he may meet the inevitable hour without fear. How would he that trades know that he is dealing fairly with him that buys, how would he know that he is giving him that which is his due, if there were no scales? How would a man spend his day, if his heart were never to be forsaken by indignation over the thought that the sun would sink at its wonted hour, and if he were to be possessed with the desire of preventing it? He would be insane and futile."

"The slumber of the dead is sweet," spake the angel sitting at the head of the couch.

"But, just now, a man has died in the camp of the Hebrews,—happy, young, beloved," spake the angel seated opposite him. "Just hearken: there is the rustle of the hot wind; the stars flame sombrely; and the hyænas whine and whimper in their evil joy, hurriedly digging open the grave, sniffing its stench and anticipating the devouring of his entrails. But the sorrow of the dead man's near ones is more dreadful than the grave itelf."

They wanted to test the prophet, and they did succeed in wounding his heart with the last. But, in his thoughts, he spake to them:

"I am recalling every moment of my life; every moment of my sweet childhood, my joyous youth, my laborious manhood—and I lament them. Ye speak of the grave,—and my hands grow chill from fear. I beseech ye,—console me not, for consolation depriveth one of courage. I beseech ye,—remind me not of the flesh, for it will turn to corruption. Is it not better to think otherwise? Even his halting place, in a vale sheltered from the winds, where he may have passed but a day, a man will abandon with regret; but it is his duty to go on, if to go on be necessary. Speaking with dread of the grave, are we not speaking in the words of the ancients, that knew the flesh, but knew not God and the immortality of souls? Dreadful is the majesty of the deeds of God. Do we not mistake this dread for the dread of death? Say ye to yourselves more often: 'The hour of death is not as dreadful as we deem it. Else, neither the universe nor man could exist.'"

"He is a sage," spake the angel sitting at the head of the couch.

"He was refractory and arrogant," spake the angel seated opposite the first. "He dreamed of wrestling with God,—and now he shall be punished anew: never a mortal shall point to his grave in the mountains of Moab. And thereby shall his glory be diminished."

They wanted to test the prophet, but he understood, and answered them unwaveringly:

"Goodly is the glory of those that merit glory. But that which has earned diminution, must be diminished.

[276]

For even the most glorious of men would rejoice only in the true measure of glory."

Thereupon the angels, struck by the wisdom of the prophet, did exclaim, as they arose from their places:

"Truly, God Himself shall console thee! We can but bow down before thee."

They were dark, and they were standing in a dark tent. But their eyes shone, and the prophet beheld the starry radiance of their eyes. They retreated into the night, like shades, barely stooping at the doorway of the tent. As for the prophet, he remained alone in the midst of the night and the desert, lying upon the earth. And when the sun had arisen from behind the craggy mountains, and it grew light and hot within the tent, the prophet, feeling a great longing to rest amid coolness, did forsake his couch, and did bend his steps toward a vale in the mountains, seeking shade. But there was none even in the vale by now. However, in the inmost recesses of one mountain he came upon a cavern. And behold, two captives were hacking away with sharp picks at the entrance into this cavern. The stones at the entrance were as white as the snow upon mountain-tops, and were hot from the sun. And the black hair of the copper-faced captives, as well as the cloths about their loins, were wet with perspiration. But two fresh fruits, two apples, were lying upon a stone near the cavern, while in the cavern itself it was dark and cool. And the labourers, lowering their picks, spake, saying:

"We greet thee, lord and chieftain, in the name of God, the Merciful, the Compassionate. Lo, we have finished our labour."

And the prophet asked them:

[277]

"Who are ye, and what were ye doing?"

To which they did answer:

"We were preparing a treasure-chamber for the king. Enter, look about thee, and rest from thy journey and the heat. Refresh thy lips with the fruits, and tell us which is the sweeter and riper one."

And, having entered the cavern, the prophet did sit down upon a stone couch nigh one of its walls, and did feel the shade and the coolness. And, having bitten of the first fruit, he spake:

"Verily, this is life itself: I am drinking water from a spring, I scent the pleasant odours of the flowers of the fields, and I feel the taste of aspen honey. I am vigorous, and I am strong."

And, having bitten of the second, he exclaimed:

"Verily, there is nothing to compare with this: I am drinking the wines of paradise, sealed with a seal of musk, blended with the water of a well-spring that quencheth the thirst of those who draw nigh to The Eternal. I scent the fragrance of a celestial garden, and feel the taste of the honey of its flowers,—nor hath this honey any bitter tang. And lo, a blessed drowsiness befogs my head. Awake me not, O ye captives, till that my time be fulfilled."

And the captives,—they were angels, the captives of God,—quietly went on, as his speech died away:

"Till that the sun," uttered the first, reading the *Sura*, the Canticle, of the Great Tidings—"till that the sun be bent, till that the stars rain down from the sky, and the mountains remove from their place, and the she-camels be abandoned, and the seas do boil up. . . ."

"I am S'in," uttered the second, reading the *Sura* for

[278]

the Departing. "Glory be to Him that reigneth over all the universe! Ye all shall return to Him! . . ."

And, hearing their whispers, but without catching their words, the prophet did lie down upon the couch, and did repose in the sleep of death, knowing not thereof. And the angels did wall up the entrance to the sepulchral cavern, and did depart to the Master Who had sent them. And the prophet was joined to his people, having had his fill of days, and without perceiving the end thereof. Never a man, even to this day, has yet contemplated his tomb in the mountains of Moab. But his wisdom is imprinted in the memory of all peoples, and is recorded in Heaven in *Ghilliun*, the Book Eternal.

The Sheikh Saadi,—may his name be blessed!—the Sheikh Saadi,—many of his pearls have we strung side by side with our own, upon the string of a good style!—hath told us of a man who had tasted the bliss of drawing nigh The Beloved. This man had been lost in contemplation; but when he had come back to the everyday world, he was asked with a kindly mockery: "But where are the flowers from the garden of your reverie?" And the man made answer: "I desired to bring back the whole skirt of my coat full of roses for my friends; but, when I had drawn nigh the rose-bush, I was so intoxicated by its fragrance that I did release it out of my hands."

Let him that can connect the story of the poet with our own.

Peace and joy be the portion of all that dwell upon this earth!

1911.

THE GENTLEMAN FROM
SAN FRANCISCO

Alas, alas that great city Babylon,
that mighty city!
THE APOCALYPSE

THE gentleman from San Francisco—neither at Naples nor at Capri had any one remembered his name—was going to the Old World for two whole years, with wife and daughter, solely for the sake of pleasure.

He was firmly convinced that he was fully entitled to rest, to pleasure, to prolonged and comfortable travel, and to not a little else besides. For such a conviction he had his reasons,—that, in the first place, he was rich, and, in the second, that he was only now beginning to live, despite his eight and fifty years. Until now he had not lived, but had merely existed,—not at all badly, it is true, but, never the less, putting all his hopes on the future. He had laboured with never a pause for rest,—the coolies, whom he had imported by whole thousands, well knew what this meant!—and finally he saw that much had already been accomplished, that he had almost come abreast of those whom he had at one time set out to emulate, and he decided to enjoy breathing space. It was a custom among the class of people to which he belonged to commence their enjoyment of life with a journey to Europe, to India, to Egypt. He, too, proposed to do the same.

[280]

Of course he desired, first of all, to reward himself for his years of toil; however, he rejoiced on account of his wife and daughter as well. His wife had never been distinguished for any special sensitiveness to new impressions,—but then, all elderly American women are fervid travellers. As for his daughter,—a girl no longer in her first youth, and somewhat sickly,—travel was a downright necessity for her: to say nothing of the benefit to her health, were there no fortuitous encounters during travels? It is while travelling that one may at times sit at table with a *milliardaire,* or scrutinize frescoes by his side.

The itinerary worked out by the gentleman from San Francisco was an extensive one. In December and January he hoped to enjoy the sun of Southern Italy, the monuments of antiquity, the *tarantella,* the serenades of strolling singers, and that which men of his age relish with the utmost *finesse:* the love of little, youthful Neapolitaines, even though it be given not entirely without ulterior motives; he contemplated spending the Carnival in Nice, in Monte Carlo, whither the very pick of society gravitates at that time,—that very society upon which all the benefits of civilization depend: not merely the cut of tuxedos, but, as well, the stability of thrones, and the declaration of wars, and the prosperity of hotels,— Monte Carlo, where some give themselves up with passion to automobile and sail races; others to roulette; a third group to that which it is the custom to call flirting; a fourth, to trap-shooting, in which the pigeons, released from their cotes, soar up most gracefully above emerald-green swards, against the background of a sea that is the colour of forget-me-nots,—only, in the same minute, to strike against the ground as little, crumpled clods of white.

[281]

. . . The beginning of March he wanted to devote to Florence; about the time of the Passion of Our Lord to arrive at Rome, in order to hear the *Miserere* there; his plans also embraced Venice, and Paris, and bull-fighting in Seville, and sea-bathing in the British Islands, and Athens, and Constantinople, and Palestine, and Egypt, and even Japan,—of course, be it understood, already on the return trip. . . . And everything went very well at first.

It was the end of November; almost as far as Gibraltar it was necessary to navigate now through an icy murk, now amidst a blizzard of wet snow; but the ship sailed in all safety and even without rolling; the passengers the steamer was carrying proved to be many, and all of them people of note; the ship—the famous *Atlantida*—resembled the most expensive of European hotels, with all conveniences: an all-night bar, Turkish baths, a newspaper of its own,—and life upon it flowed in accordance with a most complicated system of regulations: people got up early, to the sounds of bugles, stridently resounding through the corridors at that dark hour when day was so slowly and inimically dawning over the grayish-green desert of waters, ponderously turbulent in the mist. Putting on their flannel pyjamas, the passengers drank coffee, chocolate, cocoa; then they got into marble baths, did their exercises, inducing an appetite and a sense of well-being, performed their toilet for the day, and went to breakfast. Until eleven one was supposed to promenade the decks vigorously, inhaling the fresh coolness of the ocean, or to play at shuffle-board and other games for the sake of arousing the appetite anew, and, at eleven, to seek sustenance in bouillon and sandwiches; having refreshed themselves, the passengers perused their newspaper with gusto and calmly awaited lunch, a meal still more nourishing and varied than the breakfast. The next two hours were sacred to repose,—the decks were then encumbered with *chaises longues,* upon which the travellers reclined, covered up with plaids, contemplating the cloud-flecked sky and the foaming hummocks flashing by over the side, or else pleasantly dozing off; at five o'clock, refreshed and put in good spirits, they were drenched with strong fragrant tea, served with cookies; at seven they were apprized by bugle signals of a dinner of nine courses. . . . And thereupon the gentleman from San Francisco, in an access of animal spirits, would hurry to his resplendent *cabine de luxe,* to dress.

In the evening the tiers of the *Atlantida* gaped through the dusk as though they were fiery, countless eyes, and a great multitude of servants worked with especial feverishness in the kitchens, sculleries, and wine vaults. The ocean, heaving on the other side of the walls, was awesome; but none gave it a thought, firmly believing it under the sway of the captain,—a red-haired man of monstrous bulk and ponderousness, always seeming sleepy, resembling, in his uniform frock-coat, with its golden chevrons, an enormous idol; it was only very rarely that he left his mysterious quarters to appear in public. A siren on the forecastle howled every minute in hellish sullenness and whined in frenzied malice, but not many of the diners heard the siren,—it was drowned by the strains of a splendid stringed orchestra, playing exquisitely and ceaselessly in the two-tiered hall, decorated with marble, its floors covered with velvet rugs; festively flooded with the lights of crystal lustres and gilded *girandoles,* filled

to overflowing with diamond-bedecked ladies in *décolleté*
and men in tuxedos, graceful waiters and deferent *maitres
d'hôtel*,—among whom one, who took orders for wines ex-
clusively, even walked about with a chain around his
neck, like a lord mayor. A tuxedo and perfect linen made
the gentleman from San Francisco appear very much
younger. Spare, not tall, clumsily but strongly built,
groomed until he shone and moderately animated, he
sat in the aureate-pearly refulgence of this palatial room,
at a table with a bottle of amber Johannesberg, with countless goblets, small and large, of the thinnest glass, with a
curly bouquet of curly hyacinths. There was something
of the Mongol about his yellowish face with clipped silvery moustache; his large teeth gleamed with gold fillings;
his stalwart, bald head glistened like old ivory. Rich,
yet in keeping with her years, was the dress of his wife,—
a big woman, expansive and calm; elaborate, yet light
and diaphanous, with an innocent frankness, was that of
his daughter,—tall, slender, with magnificent hair, exquisitely dressed, with breath aromatic from violet ca-
chous and with the tenderest of tiny, rosy pimples about
her lips and between her shoulder blades, just the least
bit powdered. . . . The dinner lasted for two whole hours,
while after dinner there was dancing in the ball room,
during which the men,—the gentleman from San Francisco among their number, of course,—with their feet
cocked up, determined, upon the basis of the latest po-
litical and stock-exchange news, the destinies of nations,
smoking Habana cigars and drinking *liqueurs* until they
were crimson in the face, seated in the bar, where the
waiters were negroes in red jackets, the whites of their
eyes resembling hard boiled eggs with the shell off. The

ocean, with a dull roar, was moiling in black mountains
on the other side of the wall; the snow-gale whistled
mightily through the sodden rigging; the whole steamer
quivered as it mastered both the gale and the mountains,
sundering to either side, as though with a plough, their
shifting masses, that again and again boiled up and reared
high, with tails of foam; the siren, stifled by the fog, was
moaning with a deathly anguish; the lookouts up in their
crow's-nest froze from the cold and grew dazed from
straining their attention beyond their strength. Like to
the grim and sultry depths of the infernal regions, like to
their ultimate, their ninth circle, was the womb of the
steamer, below the water line,—that womb where dully
gurgled the gigantic furnaces, devouring with their in-
candescent maws mountains of hard coal, cast into them
by men stripped to the waist, purple from the flames, and
with smarting, filthy sweat pouring over them; whereas
here, in the bar, men threw their legs over the arms of
their chairs with never a care, sipping cognac and *liqueurs*,
and were wafted among clouds of spicy smoke as they
indulged in well-turned conversation; in the ball room
everything was radiant with light and warmth and joy;
the dancing couples were now awhirl in waltzes, now
twisting in the tango,—and the music insistently, in some
delectably-shameless melancholy, was suppliant always of
the one, always of the same thing. . . . There was an am-
bassador among this brilliant throng,—a lean, modest
little old man; there was a great man of riches,—clean-
shaven, lanky, of indeterminate years, and with the appearance of a prelate, in his dress-coat of an old-fashioned
cut; there was a well-known Spanish writer; there was a
world-celebrated beauty, already just the very least trifle

[285]

faded and of an unenviable morality; there was an exquisite couple in love with each other, whom all watched with curiosity and whose happiness was unconcealed: *he* danced only with *her;* sang—and with great ability—only to *her* accompaniment; and everything they did was carried out so charmingly, that the captain was the only one who knew that this pair was hired by Lloyd's to play at love for a good figure, and that they had been sailing for a long time, now on one ship, now on another.

At Gibraltar everybody was gladdened by the sun,—it seemed to be early spring; a new passenger, whose person aroused the general interest, made his appearance on board the *Atlantida,*—he was the hereditary prince of a certain Asiatic kingdom, travelling incognito; a little man who somehow seemed to be all made of wood, even though he was alert in his movements; broad of face, with narrow eyes, in gold-rimmed spectacles; a trifle unpleasant through the fact that his skin showed through his coarse black moustache like that of a cadaver; on the whole, however, he was charming, unpretentious, and modest. On the Mediterranean Sea there was a whiff of winter again; the billows ran high, and were as multi-coloured as the tail of a peacock; they had snowy-white crests, lashed up—although the sun was sparkling brightly and the sky was perfectly clear—by a *tramontana,* a chill northern wind from beyond the mountains, that was joyously and madly rushing to meet the ship. . . . Then, on the second day, the sky began to pale, the horizon became covered with mist, land was nearing; Ischia, Capri appeared; through the binoculars Naples—lumps of sugar strewn at the foot of some dove-coloured mass—could be seen; while over it and this dove-coloured thing were visible

[286]

the ridges of distant mountains, vaguely glimmering with
the dead whiteness of snows. There was a great number
of people on deck; many of the ladies and gentlemen had
already put on short, light fur coats, with the fur outside;
Chinese boys, never contradictory and never speaking
above a whisper, bow-legged striplings with pitch-black
queues reaching to their heels and with eye-lashes as long
and thick as those of young girls, were already dragging,
little by little, sundry plaids, canes, and portmanteaux
and grips of alligator hide toward the companion-ways.
. . . The daughter of the gentleman from San Francisco
was standing beside the prince, who had been, through a
fortuitous circumstance, presented to her yesterday evening, and she pretended to be looking intently into the
distance, in a direction he was pointing out to her, telling, explaining something or other to her, hurriedly and
quietly. On account of his height he seemed a boy by
contrast with others,—he was queer and not at all pre-
possessing of person, with his spectacles, his derby, his
English great coat, while his scanty moustache looked
just as if it were of horse-hair, and the swarthy, thin skin
seemed to be drawn tightly over his face, and somehow
had the appearance of being lacquered,—but the young
girl was listening to him, without understanding, in her
agitation, what he was saying; her heart was thumping
from an incomprehensible rapture before his presence
and from pride that he was speaking with her, and not
some other; everything about him that was different from
others,—his lean hands, his clear skin, under which flowed
the ancient blood of kings, even his altogether unpretentious, yet somehow distinctively neat, European dress,—
everything held a secret, inexplicable charm, evoked a

[287]

feeling of amorousness. As for the gentleman from San Francisco himself,—he, in a high silk hat, in gray spats over patent-leather shoes, kept on glancing at the famous beauty, who was standing beside him,—a tall blonde of striking figure, her eyes were painted in the latest Parisian fashion; she was holding a diminutive, hunched-up, mangy lap dog on a silver chain and was chattering to it without cease. And the daughter, in some vague embarrassment, tried not to notice her father.

Like all Americans of means, he was very generous on his travels, and, like all of them, believed in the full sincerity and good-will of those who brought him food and drink with such solicitude, who served him from morn till night, forestalling his least wish; of those who guarded his cleanliness and rest, lugged his things around, summoned porters for him, delivered his trunks to hotels. Thus had it been everywhere, thus had it been on the ship, and thus was it to be in Naples as well. Naples grew, and drew nearer; the musicians, the brass of their instruments flashing, had already clustered upon the deck, and suddenly deafened everybody with the triumphant strains of a march; the gigantic captain, in his full dress uniform, appeared upon his stage, and, like a condescending heathen god, waved his hand amiably to the passengers,— and to the gentleman from San Francisco it seemed that it was for him alone that the march so beloved by proud America was thundering, that it was he whom the captain was felicitating upon a safe arrival. And every other passenger felt similarly about himself—or herself. And when the *Atlantida* did finally enter the harbour, had heaved to at the wharf with her many-tiered mass, black with people, and the gang-planks clattered down,—what a multitude of porters and their helpers in caps with gold braid, what a multitude of different *commissionaires,* whistling gamins, and strapping ragamuffins with packets of coloured postal cards in their hands, made a rush toward the gentleman from San Francisco, with offers of their services! And he smiled, with a kindly contemptuousness, at these ragamuffins, as he went toward the automobile of precisely that hotel where there was a possibility of the prince's stopping as well, and drawled through his teeth, now in English, now in Italian:

"Go away!* *Via!*"

Life at Naples at once assumed its wonted, ordered current: in the early morning, breakfast in the sombre dining room with its damp draught from windows opening on some sort of a stony little garden; the sky was usually overcast, holding out but little promise, and there was the usual crowd of guides at the door of the vestibule; then came the first smiles of a warm, rosy sun; there was, from the high hanging balcony, a view of Vesuvius, enveloped to its foot by radiant morning mists, and of silver-and-pearl eddies on the surface of the Bay, and of the delicate contour of Capri against the horizon; one could see tiny burros, harnessed in twos to little carts, running down below over the quay, sticky with mire, and detachments of diminutive soldiers, marching off to somewhere or other to lively and exhilarating music. Next came the procession to the waiting automobile and the slow progress through populous, narrow, and damp corridors of streets, between tall, many-windowed houses; the inspection of lifelessly-clean museums, evenly and

¹ English in the original. The same applies to the other phrases in this story marked with asterisks. *Trans.*

[289]

pleasantly, yet bleakly, lit, seemingly illuminated by snow; or of cool churches, smelling of wax, which everywhere and always contain the same things: a majestic portal, screened by a heavy curtain of leather, and inside,—silence, empty vastness, unobtrusive little flames of a seven-branched candle-stick glowing redly in the distant depths, on an altar bedecked with laces; a solitary old woman among the dark wooden pews; slippery tombstones underfoot; and somebody's *Descent from the Cross*, —inevitably a celebrated one. At one o'clock there was luncheon upon the mountain of San Martino, where, toward noon, gathered not a few people of the very first quality, and where the daughter of the gentleman from San Francisco had once almost fainted away for joy, because she thought she saw the prince sitting in the hall, although she already knew through the newspapers that he had left for a temporary stay at Rome. At five came tea at the hotel, in the showy salon, so cosy with its rugs and flaming fireplaces; and after that it was already time to get ready for dinner,—and once more came the mighty, compelling reverberation of the gong through all the stories; once more the processions in Indian file of ladies in *décolleté*, rustling in their silks upon the staircases and reflected in all the mirrors; once more the palatial dining room, widely and hospitably opened, and the red jackets of the musicians upon their platform, and the black cluster of waiters about the *maître d'hôtel*, who, with a skill out of the ordinary, was ladling some sort of a thick, roseate soup into plates. . . . The dinners, as everywhere else, were the crowning glory of each day; the guests dressed for them as for a rout, and these dinners were so abundant in edibles, and wines, and mineral

[290]

waters, and sweets, and fruits, that toward eleven o'clock at night the chambermaids were distributing through all the corridors rubber bags with hot water to warm sundry stomachs.

However, the December of that year proved to be not altogether a successful one for Naples; the porters grew confused when one talked with them of the weather, and merely shrugged their shoulders guiltily, muttering that they could not recall such another year,—although it was not the first year that they had been forced to mutter this, and to urge in extenuation that "something terrible is happening everywhere"; there were unheard of storms and torrents of rain on the Riviera; there was snow in Athens; Etna was also all snowed over and was aglow of nights; tourists were fleeing from Palermo in all directions, escaping from the cold. The morning sun deceived the Neapolitans every day that winter: toward noon the sky became gray and a fine rain began falling, but growing heavier and colder all the time; at such times the palms near the entrance of the hotel glistened as though they were of tin, the town seemed especially dirty and cramped, the museums exceedingly alike; the cigar stumps of the corpulent cabmen, whose rubber-coats flapped in the wind like wings, seemed to have an insufferable stench, while the energetic snapping of their whips over their scrawny-necked nags was patently false; the footgear of the *signori* sweeping the rails of the tramways seemed horrible; the women, splashing through the mud, their black-haired heads bared to the rain, appeared hideously short-legged; as for the dampness, and the stench of putrid fish from the sea foaming at the quay,— they were a matter of course. The gentleman and the

[291]

lady from San Francisco began quarreling in the morning; their daughter either walked about pale, with a headache, or, coming to life again, went into raptures over everything, and was, at such times both charming and beautiful: beautiful were those tender and complex emotions which had been awakened within her by meeting that homely man through whose veins flowed uncommon blood; for, after all is said and done, perhaps it is of no real importance just what it is, precisely, that awakens a maiden's soul,—whether it be money, or fame, or illustrious ancestry. . . .

Everybody affirmed that things were entirely different in Sorrento, in Capri,—there it was both warmer and sunnier, and the lemons were in blossom, and the customs were more honest, and the wine was more natural. And so the family from San Francisco determined to set out with all its trunks to Capri, and, after seeing it all, after treading the stones where the palace of Tiberius had once stood, after visiting the faery-like caverns of the Azure Grotto, and hearing the bag-pipers of Abruzzi, who for a whole month preceding Christmas wander over the island and sing the praises of the Virgin Mary, they meant to settle in Sorrento.

On the day of departure,—a most memorable one for the family from San Francisco!—there was no sun from the early morning. A heavy fog hid Vesuvius to the very base; this gray fog spread low over the leaden heaving of the sea that was lost to the eye at a distance of a half a mile. Capri was entirely invisible,—as though there had never been such a thing in the world. And the little steamer that set out for it was so tossed from side to side that the family from San Francisco was laid prostrate

[292]

upon the divans in the sorry general cabin of this tub, their feet wrapped up in plaids, and their eyes closed from nausea. Mrs. suffered,—so she thought,—more than anybody; she was overcome by sea-sickness several times; it seemed to her that she was dying, whereas the stewardess, who always ran up to her with a small basin,—she had been, for many years, day in and day out, rolling on these waves, in freezing weather and in torrid, and yet was still tireless and kind to everybody,—merely laughed. Miss was dreadfully pale and held a slice of lemon between her teeth; now she could not have been cheered even by the hope of a chance encounter with the prince at Sorrento, where he intended to be about Christmas. Mr., who was lying on his back, in roomy overcoat and large cap, never unlocked his jaws all the way over; his face had grown darker and his moustache whiter, and his head ached dreadfully: during the last days, thanks to the bad weather, he had been drinking too heavily of evenings, and had too much admired the "living pictures" in dives of *recherché* libertinage. But the rain kept on lashing against the jarring windows, the water from them running down on the divans; the wind, howling, bent the masts, and at times, aided by the onslaught of a wave, careened the little steamer entirely to one side, and then something in the hold would roll with a rumble. During the stops, at Castellamare, at Sorrento, things were a trifle more bearable, but even then the rocking was fearful,—the shore, with all its cliffs, gardens, *pigin* [1], its pink and white hotels and hazy mountains clad in curly greenery, swayed up and down as if on a swing; boats bumped up against the sides of the ship;

[1] Pino-groves. *Trans.*

[293]

sailors and steerage passengers were yelling vehemently; somewhere, as though it had been crushed, a baby was wailing and smothering; a raw wind was blowing in at the door; and, from a swaying boat with a flag of the Hotel Royal, a lisping gamin was screaming, luring travellers: "Kgoya-al! Hôtel Kgoya-al! . . ." And the gentleman from San Francisco, feeling that he was an old man,— which was but proper,—was already thinking with sadness and melancholy of all these Royals, Splendids, Excelsiors, and of these greedy, insignificant mannikins, reeking of garlic, that are called Italians. Once, having opened his eyes and raised himself from the divan, he saw, underneath the craggy steep of the shore, a cluster of stone hovels, mouldy through and through, stuck one on top of another near the very edge of the water, near boats, near all sorts of rags, tins, and brown nets,—hovels so miserable, that, at the recollection that this was that very Italy he had come hither to enjoy, he felt despair. . . . Finally, at twilight, the dark mass of the island began to draw near, seemingly bored through and through by little red lights near its base; the wind became softer, warmer, more fragrant; over the abating waves, as opalescent as black oil, golden pythons flowed from the lanterns on the wharf. . . . Then came the sudden rumble of the anchor, and it fell with a splash into the water; the ferocious yells of the boatmen, vying with one another, floated in from all quarters,—and at once the heart grew lighter, the lights in the general cabin shone more brightly, a desire arose to eat, to drink, to smoke, to be stirring. . . . Ten minutes later the family from San Francisco had descended into a large boat; within fifteen minutes it had set foot upon the stones of the wharf, and

[294]

had then got into a bright little railway car and to its
buzzing started the ascent of the slope, amid the stakes of
the vineyards, half-crumbled stone enclosures, and wet,
gnarled orange trees, some of them under coverings of
straw,—trees with thick, glossy foliage, and aglimmer
with the orange fruits; all these objects were sliding
downward, past the open windows of the little car, toward the base of the mountain. . . . Sweetly smells the
earth of Italy after rain, and her every island has its own,
its especial aroma!

The island of Capri was damp and dark on this evening. But now it came into life for an instant; lights
sprang up here and there, as always on the steamer's arrival. At the top of the mountain, where stood the station of the *funicular*, there was another throng of those
whose duty lay in receiving fittingly the gentleman from
San Francisco. There were other arrivals also, but they
merited no attention,—several Russians, who had taken
up their abode in Capri,—absent-minded because of their
bookish meditations, unkempt, bearded, spectacled, the
collars of their old drap overcoats turned up; and a group
of long-legged, long-necked, round-headed German youths
in Tyrolean costumes, with canvas knapsacks slung over
their shoulders,—these latter stood in need of nobody's
services, feeling themselves at home everywhere, and were
not at all generous in their expenditures. The gentleman
from San Francisco, on the other hand, who was calmly
keeping aloof from both the one group and the other, was
immediately noticed. He and his ladies were bustlingly
assisted to get out, some men running ahead of him to
show him the way: he was surrounded anew by urchins,
and by those robust Caprian wives who carry on their

heads the portmanteaux and trunks of respectable travellers. The wooden pattens of these women clattered over a *piazetta*, that seemed to belong to some opera, an electric globe swaying above it in the damp wind; the rabble of urchins burst into sharp, bird-like whistles,—and, as though on a stage, the gentleman from San Francisco proceeded in their midst toward some mediæval arch, underneath houses that had become welded into one mass, beyond which a little echoing street,—with the tuft of a palm above flat roofs on its left, and with blue stars in the black sky overhead,—led slopingly to the grand entrance of the hotel, glittering ahead. . . . And again it seemed that it was in honour of the guests from San Francisco that this damp little town of stone on a craggy little island of the Mediterranean Sea had come to life, that it was they who had made so happy and affable the proprietor of the hotel, that it was they only who had been waited for by the Chinese gong, that now began wailing the summons to dinner through all the stories of the hotel, the instant they had set foot in the vestibule.

The proprietor, a young man of haughty elegance, who had met them with a polite and exquisite bow, for a minute dumbfounded the gentleman from San Francisco: having glanced at him, the gentleman from San Francisco suddenly recalled that just the night before, among the rest of the confusion of images that had beset him in his sleep, he had seen precisely this gentleman,—just like him, down to the least detail: in the same sort of frock with rounded skirts, and with the same pomaded and painstakingly combed head. Startled, he was almost taken aback; but since, from long, long before, there was not even a mustard seed of any sort of so-called mystical emotions left in his soul, his astonishment was dimmed the same instant, passing through a corridor of the hotel, he spoke jestingly to his wife and daughter of this strange coincidence of dream and reality. And only his daughter glanced at him with alarm at that moment: her heart suddenly contracted from sadness, from a feeling of their loneliness upon this foreign, dark island,—a feeling so strong that she almost burst into tears. But still she said nothing of her feelings to her father,—as always.

An exalted personage—Rais XVII,—who had been visiting Capri, had just taken his departure, and the guests from San Francisco were given the same apartments that he had occupied. To them was assigned the handsomest and most expert chambermaid, a Belgian, whose waist was slenderly and firmly corseted, and who wore a little starched cap that looked like a pronged crown; also, the stateliest and most dignified of flunkies, a fiery-eyed Sicilian, swarthy as coal; and the nimblest of bell-boys, the short and stout Luigi,—a fellow who was very fond of a joke, and who had changed many places in his time. And a minute later there was a slight tap at the door of the room of the gentleman from San Francisco,—the French *maitre d'hôtel* had come to find out if the newly arrived guests would dine, and, in the event of an answer in the affirmative,—of which, however, there was no doubt,—to inform them that the *carte de jour* consisted of crawfish, roast beef, asparagus, pheasants, and so forth. The floor was still rocking under the gentleman from San Francisco, —so badly had the atrocious little Italian steamer tossed him about,—but, without hurrying, with his own hands, although somewhat clumsily from being unaccustomed to such things, he shut a window that had banged upon the

[297]

entrance of the *maitre d'hôtel* and had let in the odours of the distant kitchen and of the wet flowers in the garden, and with a leisurely precision replied that they would dine, that their table must be placed at a distance from the door, at the farthest end of the dining room, that they would drink local wine and champagne,—moderately dry and only slightly chilled. The *maitre d'hôtel concurred* in every word of his, in intonations most varied, having, however, but one significance,—that there was never a doubt, nor could there possibly be any, about the correctness of the wishes of the gentleman from San Francisco, and that everything would be carried out punctiliously. In conclusion he inclined his head, and asked deferentially:

"Will that be all, sir?"

And, having received a long-drawn-out "Yes" * in answer, he added that the *tarantella* would be danced in the vestibule to-day,—the dancers would be Carmella and Giuseppe, known to all Italy, and to "the entire world of tourists."

"I have seen her on post cards," said the gentleman from San Francisco in a voice devoid of all expression. "About this Giuseppe, now,—is he her husband?"

"Her cousin, sir," answered the *maitre d'hôtel*.

And, after a little wait, after considering something, the gentleman from San Francisco dismissed him with a nod.

And then he began his preparations anew, as though for a wedding ceremony: he turned on all the electric lights, filling all the mirrors with reflections of light and glitter, of furniture and opened trunks; he began shaving and

[298]

washing, ringing the bell every minute, while other impatient rings from his wife's and daughter's rooms floated through the entire corridor and interrupted his. And Luigi, in his red apron, was rushing headlong to answer the bell, with an ease peculiar to many stout men, the while he made grimaces of horror that made the chambermaids, running by with glazed porcelain pails in their hands, laugh till they cried. Having knocked on the door with his knuckles, he asked with an assumed timidity, with a respectfulness that verged on idiocy:

"*Ha sonato, signore?* (Did you ring, sir?)"

And from the other side of the door came an unhurried, grating voice, insultingly polite:

"Yes, come in. . . ." *

What were the thoughts, what were the emotions of the gentleman from San Francisco on this evening, that was of such portent to him? He felt nothing exceptional,— for the trouble in this world is just that everything is apparently all too simple! And even if he had sensed within his soul that something was impending, he would, never the less, have thought that this thing would not occur for some time to come,—in any case, not immediately. Besides that, like everyone who has gone through the rocking of a ship, he wanted very much to eat, was anticipating with enjoyment the first spoonful of soup, the first mouthful of wine, and performed the usual routine of dressing even with a certain degree of exhilaration that left no time for reflections.

Having shaved and washed himself, having inserted several artificial teeth properly, he, standing before a mirror, wetted the remnants of his thick, pearly-gray

[299]

hair and plastered it down around his swarthy-yellow skull, with brushes set in silver; drew a suit of cream-coloured silk underwear over his strong old body, beginning to be full at the waist from excesses in food, and put on silk socks and dancing slippers on his shrivelled, splayed feet; sitting down, he put in order his black trousers, drawn high by black silk braces, as well as his snowy-white shirt, with the bosom bulging out; put the links through the glossy cuffs, and began the torturous pursuit of the collar-button underneath the stiffly starched collar. The floor was still swaying beneath him, the tips of his fingers pained him greatly, the collar-button at times nipped hard the flabby skin in the hollow under his Adam's-apple, but he was persistent and finally, his eyes glittering from the exertion, his face all livid from the collar that was choking his throat,—a collar far too tight,—he did contrive to accomplish his task, and sat down in exhaustion in front of the pier glass, reflected in it from head to foot, a reflection that was repeated in all the other mirrors.

"Oh, this is dreadful!" he muttered, letting his strong bald head drop, and without trying to understand, without reflecting, just what, precisely, was dreadful; then, with an accustomed and attentive glance, he inspected his stubby fingers, with gouty hardenings at the joints, and his convex nails of an almond colour, repeating, with conviction: "This is dreadful. . . ."

But at this point the second gong, sonorously, as in some heathen temple, reverberated through the entire house. And, getting up quickly from his seat, the gentleman from San Francisco drew his collar still tighter with the necktie and his stomach by means of the low-cut vest, put on his

[300]

tuxedo, drew out his cuffs, scrutinized himself once more in the mirror. . . . This Carmella, swarthy, with eyes which she knew well how to use most effectively, resembling a mulatto woman, clad in a dress of many colours, with the colour of orange predominant, must dance exceptionally, he reflected. And, stepping briskly out of his room and walking over the carpet to the next one,— his wife's—he asked, loudly, if they would be ready soon?

"In five minutes, Dad!" a girl's voice, ringing and by now gay, responded from the other side of the door.

"Very well," said the gentleman from San Francisco.

And, leisurely, he walked down red-carpeted corridors and staircases, descending in search of the reading room. The servants he met stood aside and hugged the wall to let him pass, but he kept on his way as though he had never even noticed them. An old woman who was late for dinner, already stooping, with milky hair but *décolettée* in a light-gray gown of silk, was hurrying with all her might, but drolly, in a hen-like manner, and he easily outstripped her. Near the glass doors of the dining room, where all the guests had already assembled, and were beginning their dinner, he stopped before a little table piled with boxes of cigars and Egyptian cigarettes, took a large Manila cigar, and tossed three *lire* upon the little table; upon the closed veranda he glanced, in passing, through the open window: out of the darkness he felt a breath of the balmy air upon him, thought he saw the tip of an ancient palm, that had flung wide across the stars its fronds, which seemed gigantic, heard the distant, even noise of the sea floating in to him. . . . In the reading room,—snug, quiet, and illuminated only above the tables,

[301]

some gray-haired German was standing, rustling the news-papers,—unkempt, resembling Ibsen, in round silver spec-tacles and with the astonished eyes of a madman. Hav-ing scrutinized him coldly, the gentleman from San Fran-cisco sat down in a deep leather chair in a corner near a green-shaded lamp, put on his *pince nez*, twitching his head because his collar was choking him, and hid himself completely behind the newspaper sheet. He rapidly ran through the headlines of certain items, read a few lines about the never-ceasing Balkan war, with an accustomed gesture turned the newspaper over,—when suddenly the lines flared up before him with a glassy glare, his neck became taut, his eyes bulged out, the *pince nez* flew off his nose. . . . He lunged forward, tried to swallow some air,—and gasped wildly; his lower jaw sank, lighting up his entire mouth with the reflection of the gold fillings; his head dropped back on his shoulder and began to sway; the bosom of his shirt bulged out like a basket,—and his whole body, squirming, his heels catching the car-pet, slid downward to the floor, desperately struggling with someone.

Had the German not been in the reading room, the per-sonnel of the hotel would have managed, quickly and adroitly, to hush up this dreadful occurrence; instantly, through back passages, seizing him by the head and feet, they would have rushed off the gentleman from San Francisco as far away as possible,—and never a soul among the guests would have found out what he had been up to. But the German had dashed out of the reading room with a scream,—he had aroused the entire house, the entire dining room. And many jumped up from their meal, overturning their chairs; many, paling, ran toward the reading room. "What—what has happened?" was heard in all languages,—and no one gave a sensible answer, no one comprehended anything, since even up to now men are amazed most of all by death, and will not, under any circumstances, believe in it. The proprietor dashed from one guest to another, trying to detain those who were running away and to pacify them with hasty assurances that this was just a trifling occurrence, a slight fainting spell of a certain gentleman from San Francisco. . . . But no one listened to him; many had seen the waiters and bell-boys tearing off the necktie, the vest, and the rumpled tuxedo off this gentleman, and even, for some reason or other, the dancing slippers off his splayed feet, clad in black silk. But he was still struggling. He was still obdurately wrestling with death; he absolutely refused to yield to her, who had so unexpectedly and churlishly fallen upon him. His head was swaying, he rattled hoarsely, like one with his throat cut; his eyes had rolled up, like a drunkard's. . . . When he was hurriedly carried in and laid upon a bed in room number forty-three,—the smallest, the poorest, the dampest and the coldest, situated at the end of the bottom corridor,—his daughter ran in, with her hair down, in a little dressing gown that had flown open, her bosom, raised up by the corset, uncovered; then his wife, big and ponderous, already dressed for dinner,—her mouth rounded in terror. . . . But by now he had ceased even to bob his head.

A quarter of an hour later everything in the hotel had assumed some semblance of order. But the evening was irreparably spoiled. Some guests, returning to the dining room, finished their dinner, but in silence, with aggrieved countenances, while the proprietor would approach now one group, now another, shrugging his shoulders in polite yet impotent irritation, feeling himself guilty without guilt, assuring everybody that he understood very well "how unpleasant all this was," and pledging his word that he would take "all measures within his power" to remove this unpleasantness. It was necessary to call off the *tarantella*, all unnecessary electric lights were switched off, the majority of the guests withdrew into the bar, and it became so quiet that one heard distinctly the ticking of the clock in the vestibule, whose sole occupant was a parrot, dully muttering something, fussing in his cage before going to sleep, contriving to doze off at last with one claw ludicrously stretched up to the upper perch. . . . The gentleman from San Francisco was lying upon a cheap iron bed, under coarse woolen blankets, upon which the dull light of a single bulb beat down from the ceiling. An ice-bag hung down to his moist and cold forehead. The livid face, already dead, was gradually growing cold; the hoarse rattling, expelled from the open mouth, illuminated by the reflection of gold, was growing fainter. This was no longer the gentleman from San Francisco rattling,—he no longer existed,—but some other. His wife, his daughter, the doctor and the servants were standing, gazing at him dully. Suddenly, that which they awaited and feared was consummated,—the rattling ceased abruptly. And slowly, slowly, before the eyes of all, a pallor flowed over the face of the man who had died, and his features seemed to grow finer, to become irradiated, with a beauty which had been rightfully his in the long ago. . . .

The proprietor entered. *"Già è morto,"* said the doc-

[304]

tor to him in a whisper. The proprietor, his face dispassionate, shrugged his shoulders. The wife, down whose cheeks the tears were quietly coursing, walked up to him and timidly said that the deceased ought now to be carried to his own room.

"Oh, no, madam," hastily, correctly, but now without any amiability and not in English, but in French, retorted the proprietor, who was not at all interested now in such trifling sums as the arrivals from San Francisco might leave in his coffers. "That is absolutely impossible, madam," said he, and added in explanation that he valued the apartments occupied by them very much; that, were he to carry out her wishes, everybody in Capri would know it and the tourists would shun those apartments.

The young lady, who had been gazing at him strangely, sat down on a chair, and, stuffing her mouth with a handkerchief, burst into sobs. The wife dried her tears immediately, her face flaring up. She adopted a louder tone, making demands in her own language, and still incredulous of the fact that all respect for them had been completely lost. The proprietor, with a polite dignity, cut her short: if madam was not pleased with the customs of the hotel, he would not venture to detain her; and he firmly announced that the body must be gotten away this very day, at dawn, that the police had already been notified, and one of the police officers would be here very soon and would carry out all the necessary formalities. Was it possible to secure even a common coffin in Capri, madam asks? Regrettably, no,—it was beyond possibility, and no one would be able to make one in time. It would be necessary to have recourse to something else. . . . For instance,—English soda water came in large and long

[305]

boxes. . . . It was possible to knock the partitions out of such a box. . . .

At night the whole hotel slept. The window in room number forty-three was opened,—it gave out upon a corner of the garden where, near a high stone wall with broken glass upon its crest, a phthisic banana tree was growing; the electric light was switched off; the key was turned in the door, and everybody went away. The dead man remained in the darkness,—the blue stars looked down upon him from the sky, a cricket with a pensive insouciance began his song in the wall. . . . In the dimly lit corridor two chambermaids were seated on a window sill, at some darning. Luigi, in slippers, entered with a pile of clothing in his arms.

"*Pronto?* (All ready?)" he asked solicitously, in a ringing whisper, indicating with his eyes the fearsome door at the end of the corridor. And, he waved his hand airily in that direction. . . . "*Partenza!*" he called out in a whisper, as though he were speeding a train, the usual phrase used in Italian depots at the departure of trains,— and the chambermaids, choking with silent laughter, let their heads sink on each other's shoulder.

Thereupon, hopping softly, he ran up to the very door, gave it the merest tap, and, inclining his head to one side, in a low voice, asked with the utmost deference:

"*Ha sonato signore?*"

And, squeezing his throat, thrusting out his lower jaw, in a grating voice, slowly and sadly, he answered his own question, as though from the other side of the door:

"Yes, come in. . . ." *

And at dawn, when it had become light beyond the

[306]

window of room number forty-three, and a humid wind
had begun to rustle the tattered leaves of the banana tree;
when the blue sky of morning had lifted and spread out
over the Island of Capri, and the pure and clear-cut summit of Monte Solaro had grown aureate against the sun
that was rising beyond the distant blue mountains of
Italy; when the stone masons, who were repairing the
tourists' paths on the island, had set out to work,—a long
box that had formerly been used for soda water was
brought to room number forty-three. Soon it became
very heavy, and was pressing hard against the knees of
the junior porter, who bore it off briskly on a one horse
cab over the white paved highway that was sinuously
winding to and fro over the slopes of Capri, among the
stone walls and the vineyards, ever downwards, to the
very sea. The cabby, a puny little man with reddened
eyes, in an old, wretched jacket with short sleeves and in
trodden-down shoes, was undergoing the after effects of
drink,—he had diced the whole night through in a *trat-
toria*, and kept on lashing his sturdy little horse, tricked
out in the Sicilian fashion, with all sorts of little bells
livelily jingling upon the bridle with its tufts of coloured
wool, and upon the brass points of its high pad; with a
yard-long feather stuck in its cropped forelock,—a feather
that shook as the horse ran. The cabby kept silent; he
was oppressed by his shiftlessness, his vices,—by the fact
that he had, that night, lost to the last mite all those coppers with which his pockets had been filled. But the
morning was fresh; in air such as this, with the sea all
around, under the morning sky, the after effects of drink
quickly evaporate, and a man is soon restored to a care-

free mood, and the cabby was furthermore consoled by that unexpected sum, the opportunity to earn which had been granted him by some gentleman from San Francisco, whose lifeless head was bobbing from side to side in the box at his back. . . . The little steamer,—a beetle lying far down below, against the tender and vivid deep-blue with which the Bay of Naples is so densely and highly flooded,—was already blowing its final whistles, that reverberated loudly all over the island, whose every bend, every ridge, every stone, was as distinctly visible from every point as if there were absolutely no such thing as atmosphere. Near the wharf the junior porter was joined by the senior, who was speeding with the daughter and wife of the gentleman from San Francisco in his automobile,—they were pale, with eyes hollow from tears and a sleepless night. And ten minutes later the little steamer was again chugging through the water, again running toward Sorrento, toward Castellamare, carrying away from Capri, for all time, the family from San Francisco. . . . And again peace and quiet resumed their reign upon the island.

Upon this island, two thousand years ago, had lived a man who had become completely enmeshed in his cruel and foul deeds, who had for some reason seized the power over millions of people in his hands, and who, having himself lost his head at the senselessness of this power and from the fear of death by assassination, lurking in ambush behind every corner, had committed cruelties beyond all measure,—and humankind has remembered him for all time; and those who, in their collusion, just as incomprehensively and, in substance, just as cruelly as he, reign

[308]

at present in power over this world, gather from all over
the earth to gaze upon the ruins of that stone villa where
he had dwelt on one of the steepest ascents of the island.
On this splendid morning all those who had come to
Capri for just this purpose were still sleeping in the hotels,
although, toward their entrances, were already being led
little mouse-gray burros with red saddles, upon which,
after awaking and sating themselves with food, Americans
and Germans, men and women, young and old, would
again clamber up ponderously this day, and after whom
would again run the old Caprian beggar women, with
sticks in their gnarled hands,—would run over stony
paths, and always up-hill, up to the very summit of
Mount Tiberio. Set at rest by the fact that the dead
old man from San Francisco, who had likewise been plan-
ning to go with them but instead of that had only frightened them with a *memento mori,* had already been shipped
off to Naples, the travellers slept on heavily, and the quiet
of the island was still undisturbed, the shops in the city
were still shut. The market place on the *piazetta* alone
was carrying on traffic,—in fish and greens; and the people
there were all simple folk, among whom, without anything
to do, as always, was standing Lorenzo the boatman, famous all over Italy,—a tall old man, a care-free rake and a
handsome fellow, who had served more than once as a
model to many artists; he had brought, and had already
sold for a song, two lobsters that he had caught that night
and which were already rustling in the apron of the cook
of that very hotel where the family from San Francisco
had passed the night, and now he could afford to stand
in calm idleness even until the evening, looking about

him with a kingly bearing (a little trick of his), consciously picturesque with his tatters, clay pipe, and a red woolen *beretta* drooping over one ear.

And, along the precipices of Monte Solaro, upon the ancient Phœnician road, hewn out of the crags, down its stone steps, two mountaineers of Abruzzi were descending from Anacapri. One had bag-pipes under his leathern mantle,—a large bag made from the skin of a she-goat, with two pipes; the other had something in the nature of wooden Pan's-reeds. They went on,—and all the land, joyous, splendid, sun-flooded, spread out below them: the stony humps of the island, which was lying almost in its entirety at their feet; and that faery-like deep-blue in which it was aswim; and the radiant morning vapours over the sea, toward the east, under the blinding sun, that was now beating down hotly, rising ever higher and higher; and, still in their morning vagueness, the mistily azure massive outlines of Italy, of her mountains near and far, whose beauty human speech is impotent to express. . . . Half way down the pipers slackened their pace: over the path, within a grotto in the craggy side of Monte Solaro, all illumed by the sun, all bathed in its warmth and glow, in snowy-white raiment of gypsum, and in a royal crown, golden-rusty from inclement weathers, stood the Mother of God, meek and gracious, her orbs lifted up to heaven, to the eternal and happy abodes of Her thrice-blessed Son. The pipers bared their heads, put their reeds to their lips,—and there poured forth their naïve and humbly-jubilant praises to the sun, to the morning, to Her, the Immaculate Intercessor for all those who suffer in this evil and beautiful world, and to Him Who had been born of Her womb in a cavern at Bethlehem, in a poor shepherd's shelter in the distant land of Judæa. . . .

Meanwhile, the body of the dead old man from San Francisco was returning to its home, to a grave on the shores of the New World. Having gone through many humiliations, through much human neglect, having wandered for a week from one port warehouse to another, it had finally gotten once more on board that same famous ship upon which but so recently, with so much deference, he had been borne to the Old World. But now he was already being concealed from the quick,—he was lowered in his tarred coffin deep into the black hold. And once more the ship was sailing on and on upon its long sea voyage. In the night time it sailed past the Island of Capri, and, to one watching them from the island, there was something sad about the ship's lights, slowly disappearing over the dark sea. But, upon the ship itself, in its brilliant *salons* resplendent with lustres and marbles, there was a crowded ball that night, as usual.

There was a ball on the second night also, and on the third,—again in the midst of a raging snow storm, whirling over an ocean booming like a funeral mass, and heaving in mountains trapped out in mourning by the silver spindrift. The innumerable fiery eyes of the ship that was retreating into the night and the snow gale were barely visible for the snow to the Devil watching from the crags of Gibraltar, from the stony gateway of two worlds. The Devil was as enormous as a cliff, but the ship was still more enormous than he; many-tiered, many-funnelled, created by the pride of the New Man with an ancient heart. The snow gale smote upon its rigging and wide-throated funnels, hoary from the snow, but the

[311]

ship was steadfast, firm, majestic—and awesome. Upon
its topmost deck were reared, in their solitude among the
snowy whirlwinds, those snug, dimly-lit chambers where,
plunged in a light and uneasy slumber, was its ponderous
guide who resembled a heathen idol, reigning over the entire ship. He heard the pained howlings and the ferocious
squealings of the storm-stifled siren, but soothed himself
by the proximity of that which, in the final summing up,
was incomprehensible even to himself, that which was on
the other side of his wall: that large cabin, which had the
appearance of being armoured, and was being constantly
filled by the mysterious rumbling, quivering, and crisp
sputtering of blue flames, flaring up and exploding around
the pale-faced operator with a metal half-hoop upon his
head. In the very depths, in the under-water womb of
the *Atlantida*, were the thirty-thousand-pound masses of
boilers and of all sorts of other machinery—dully glittering with steel, hissing out stream and exuding oil and
boiling water,—of that kitchen, made red hot from infernal
furnaces underneath, wherein was brewing the motion of
the ship. Forces, fearful in their concentration, were bub-
bling, were being transmitted to its very keel, into an endlessly long catacomb, into a tunnel, illuminated by electricity, wherein slowly, with an inexorability that was
crushing to the human soul, was revolving within its
oily couch the gigantean shaft, exactly like a living monster that had stretched itself out in this tunnel. Meanwhile, amidship the *Atlantida*, its warm and luxurious
cabins, its dining halls and ball rooms, poured forth
radiance and joyousness, were humming with the voices
of a well-dressed gathering, were sweetly odorous with
fresh flowers, and the strains of the stringed orchestra

were their song. And again excruciatingly writhed and at intervals came together among this throng, among this glitter of lights, silks, diamonds and bared feminine shoulders, the supple pair of hired lovers: the sinfully-modest, very pretty young woman, with eye-lashes cast down, with a chaste coiffure, and the well-built young man, with black hair that seemed to be pasted on, with his face pale from powder, shod in the most elegant of patent-leather foot-gear, clad in a tight-fitting dress coat with long tails,—an Adonis who resembled a huge leech. And none knew that, already for a long time, this pair had grown wearied of languishing dissemblingly in their blissful torment to the sounds of the shamelessly-sad music,—nor that far, far below, at the bottom of the black hold, stood a tarred coffin, in close proximity to the sombre and sultry depths of the ship that was toilsomely overpowering the darkness, the ocean, the snow storm. . . .

1915.

THE END

[313]